THE LAST MONSTER

THE
Last
Monster

GINGER GARRETT

DELACORTE PRESS

To every reader who
still checks under the bed at night

• • •

Text copyright © 2016 by Ginger Garrett
Jacket art and interior illustrations copyright © 2016 by Dinara Mirtalipova

All rights reserved. Published in the United States by Delacorte Press,
an imprint of Random House Children's Books, a division of
Penguin Random House LLC, New York.

Delacorte Press is a registered trademark and the colophon
is a trademark of Penguin Random House LLC.

Visit us on the Web! randomhousekids.com

Educators and librarians, for a variety of teaching tools,
visit us at RHTeachersLibrarians.com

Library of Congress Cataloging-in-Publication Data
Garrett, Ginger.
The last monster / Ginger Garrett. — First edition.
pages cm
Summary: "Thirteen-year-old cancer survivor Sofia has been chosen as the next Guardian of
a book called The Bestiary, an ancient text. Drawn into violent and unpredictable mysteries,
Sofia learns that these misunderstood monsters from the book are in danger and she is the only
one who can save them" —Provided by publisher.
ISBN 978-0-553-53524-2 (hc) — ISBN 978-0-553-53525-9 (glb) —
ISBN 978-0-553-53526-6 (ebook)
[1. Monsters—Fiction. 2. Cancer—Fiction. 3. Amputees—Fiction. 4. People with disabilities—
Fiction.] I. Title.
PZ7.1.G375Las 2016
[Fic]—dc23
2015003381

The text of this book is set in 12.85-point MrsEaves.
Jacket design by Sarah Hokanson
Interior design by Heather Kelly

Printed in the United States of America
10 9 8 7 6 5 4 3 2 1
First Edition

ONE

Friday, February 21

I had to pick up a new leg after school.

Dark storm clouds hung low over the Children's Cancer Center of Atlanta. Mom took the last turn into the parking lot, and all the old familiar fears coiled around me. I groaned under their weight.

Mom glanced at me, worried.

"It won't stop people from staring," I mumbled.

"Is that really what's bothering you?" she asked softly.

I glanced at her and realized her knuckles were white. She was gripping the steering wheel as if it were a life preserver. Coming here was just as hard for her as it was for me.

"I'm fine," I lied. "The worst is over, isn't it?"

She slowed the car as we approached the entrance. "I'll let you off at the front door, in case it starts raining," she said. "But wait for me before you go back."

I nodded as I glanced out the car window. A hawk circled overhead, hunting some small, frightened thing that hid in the shrubs by the entrance. The bird screamed when it saw me, a shrill welcome.

Mom stopped in front of the double doors before leaning over to give me a quick peck on the cheek. Her lips were cold. This was our last big appointment for four weeks. We'd basically lived here for two months last year, from the end of October until just after New Year's; then we had switched to outpatient visits. After a month of rest to build my strength, I had started physical therapy. So this place had been my second home for almost four months. Now the idea of freedom felt surreal. "Free" was a strong word, though. It was more like I'd gotten extra length on my leash. I still needed to come back. Cancer was a part of my life that I would never escape.

The wind moaned as I opened the car door. I swallowed hard, my stomach in knots, as if this place were the nightmare I would never wake up from.

Inside, the TV in the waiting room was tuned to a twenty-four-hour health channel. I settled into a vinyl-cushioned chair that wheezed when I sat. The volume was so loud no one noticed. A special feature called *Meet Your Meat* was playing, a behind-the-scenes look at how meat products are manufactured. In the corner, a coffee machine sat undisturbed, its electric red eye watching us all.

"Sausage casings are made from the intestines of pigs, horses, or sheep. Machines remove the fat and mucus before extruding the final casing, which will give some lucky sausage that satisfying snap."

My eyebrows shot up in horror. Sausages were like babies; I had a general idea of how they were made, but I didn't want the clinical details. I glanced behind me, praying Mom would find a parking spot soon. We didn't do the "free" valet parking anymore. Tipping required cash, and we rarely had any now.

I noticed a boy about seven or eight years old, hunched over, holding a beach sand pail in front of his mouth in case he vomited. A little bit of drool clung to his chin. He still had his hair, though, so he was probably a new patient, trapped between terror and denial. He cringed as images of greasy pink sausages flashed above his head.

The TV was mounted on the wall. If there was a remote control, I had never found it. The only way to change the channel would be to reach way up and press the buttons, and somebody needed to do that fast before the poor little guy hurled again. He glanced at me and nodded weakly in the direction of his mother. She was standing by the windows, chatting furiously on a cell phone, her back to us. Fat drops of sleet began pelting the tinted lobby windows. A bright whip of lightning ripped across the sky and split in five directions, like a giant claw. Strange, even for a city known for its weird weather.

"And now we'll take a closer look at ground beef. The name itself is misleading, since it includes skin, connective tissue, fat, and even bone. . . ."

The kid put his head down and retched loudly into the bucket. I stood and walked to the TV, praying the other kids didn't notice how one of my legs moved differently from the other one. The prosthesis I wore was too big, and it made my gait clumpy. The new prosthesis would make my gait very natural, but of course everyone at school would stare anyway, trying to figure out which leg was real. They got them mixed up.

I pressed the channel button repeatedly, but every other station was running a special bulletin on the weather. A bad storm was coming. Lightning in the northern suburbs of Atlanta was especially dangerous; we had huge blocks of granite under the ground that attracted lightning. When a storm came, it didn't just give us a pretty show; someone usually got hurt.

Finally, I found the cartoon channel and released the button. I turned around to check on the boy and saw that his mom was still on the phone, unaware that he would never eat sausage again. The thunder boomed and a fragile-looking baby cradled in its mother's arms began to wail.

"Thanks," the boy said to me. "You're my hero."

I nodded and quickly looked away, my cheeks getting warm and probably red. My face had always been like a giant mood ring. "Hang in there," I said. "It's not always this bad, I promise."

If he could tell I was lying, he didn't show it. The boy rested his face on the side of the pail and sighed, eyes closed. I felt a little bit better too, which surprised me. All I had done was change a TV channel.

The baby's crying suddenly grew louder, as if it knew something we didn't.

Lightning flashed again, illuminating the room like a

sinister X-ray. Thunder chased it immediately, and the walls shook. It sounded like the hospital had been hit.

The TV blanked out with a hiss of static as all the lights shut off and the hum of the heater died away. There was nothing but darkness and cold silence. The baby whimpered; I could hear its breath coming in little stutters.

The lightning must have knocked out the lobby's power. The hospital's power grid was designed to protect patient rooms and equipment first, so it didn't surprise me that the power down here had gone out. Still, if lightning struck again, maybe the lights wouldn't come back at all. I got nervous about it. I knew a girl whose mom had parked their car under a bank's drive-through awning and lightning had struck their car, melting all their tires. Lightning ruled the skies here.

Everyone began talking loudly or crying, but all I could hear was the drumbeat of my own heart. What was taking Mom so long? The cancer center shared a parking lot with the children's emergency room and hospital, so maybe the lots were all full. Fridays weren't normally this busy, though.

Through the chaos, I noticed a little girl illuminated in the red glow from an overhead Exit sign on the other side of the waiting room. She had one hand wrapped around her IV pole; the other was dragging a pillowcase with something heavy inside.

Her face was gaunt and her long hair hung lifeless. Instead of a blue hospital gown, she wore a white nightgown that skimmed the floor. Bloodstains dotted the hem and there were rips in the fabric, as if she had been attacked. The *Walking Dead* television series filmed here in Atlanta; maybe she had wandered off the set and was lost.

A shadow rose from the floor beside the girl, like smoke from a fire. Goose bumps spread across my arms, as if my body recognized a change in the atmosphere, the warning of a lightning strike gathering energy before choosing its victim. In the blood-red glow of the exit light, the dark smoke blossomed, unfurling into the form of a woman dressed in flowing robes, her braided blond hair pinned under a crown of round gray stones, each with what looked like a blinking eye at its center. Every stone swiveled like an eyeball, each moving in a different direction, until they all came to rest on me.

She glared at me like I was her worst enemy, but I had never seen her before.

Dread surged through my body, an icy river of fear that burned down into my stomach, making me clutch it in pain. The woman sneered as she rested a paper-white hand with thin, spidery fingers on the girl's shoulder, making her flinch. The woman's fingers stretched down and around, covering the girl like the roots of a growing tree.

The girl shuddered as if the touch was cold, but her eyes never left mine. She needed to tell me something; I could feel her sense of urgency. She nodded once, slowly, willing me to come and help her.

I froze, panic overtaking my body. I didn't know her. I didn't *want* to know either of them. I pushed myself backward in my seat, sinking down. My heart pounded against my ribs, like it was trying to escape. Was this a nightmare? Or some sort of dream? I wasn't even asleep.

An emergency alarm blasted through the lobby. "Code Amber. Code Amber. All personnel report."

The power snapped back on, light exploding inside the room.

I turned to check on the vomiting boy to make sure he was safe. He was. When I looked back at the hallway, the girl and the woman were gone.

I exhaled in relief, then started breathing too fast, pushing the air out and sucking it back in until I felt lightheaded. Oh man, if I tried to tell someone about what I had just seen, they'd keep me overnight for tests, certain I was suffering a late side effect from chemo. It was possible. Chemo was just carefully measured poison, a Pandora's box of dreadful surprises.

A hand grabbed my shoulder and I lurched around, ready to scream, my hands balled into fists. It was Barnes, my prosthetic technician. He curled his hands into fists too. "You want to hit old Barnes? You want much of this?"

He broke into a huge grin and I could see all the metal bits that attached his dentures. I grinned back, more from relief than anything else. Barnes was probably about seventy or eighty years old, but he said he needed to keep up with his slang for all the young patients. I think he did it to make us laugh, and it worked on me every time. I felt the dread and fear of a moment ago melt away as I giggled. My nerves had made me slightly nuts. Everything was back to normal.

Mom walked in, waving to me before stopping at the

reception desk. I stood and took Barnes by the hand. He didn't notice mine was shaking. "You're supposed to say 'You want *some* of this?'"

"What-*ever*," he said, hitting the inflection just right. I had taught him well. His knuckles were red and swollen today, so I held his hand extra carefully, willing my own to soften into a steady grip.

"Code Amber is a missing kid, right?" I asked.

He didn't answer me, just took a few steps in the direction of his lab and turned back to wave to Mom. She nodded back, meaning she would follow in just a second. I knew she looked forward to talking to Barnes during our visits. He never used slang with her. They had had several disagreements and he was still endlessly sweet to her. A lot of men treated my mom that way.

"Maybe they should look down that hallway," I added, pointing to the right. I didn't want to sound too certain, but if the girl was real, that was where they'd find her.

An impatient wave was his way of saying my words were falling on deaf ears. And maybe they were; he had to tilt his head in my direction if I talked in a quiet voice. Plus, his hair was thinning at an alarming rate. He'd be as bald as me before long. I wondered if it bothered him to look in the mirror the way it bothered me.

"Let security do their jobs. You stay out of that."

"But, Barnes," I started to protest. "I just—"

He cut me off. "No arguing." Barnes had been in the navy a long time ago and still liked to bark a command now and then. He started down the hallway on the left and I followed, soft instrumental music greeting us through the speakers.

My hands started to shake again, but I couldn't shove them in my pockets; I needed loose arms for balance. I hadn't been here as an inpatient since January, but the silent terror I felt when I walked the halls of this hospital was hard to explain to anyone except another survivor.

When you leave the hospital for the last time, they call it being discharged. That's the same term the military uses when they release a soldier. Veterans say that once you've been in combat, you never completely forget it, or get over it. The pain stays embedded, like invisible shrapnel.

I think veterans of any war probably understand each other.

They would understand how all the scary, sad moments in here flooded my mind: the burnt smell of antiseptic, the quiet moans that echoed through the heating ducts at night, the dark stains in the bathrooms' white grout, the endless predawn hours I spent watching Animal Planet, witnessing predators take down the weak and frightened. The doctors had fought the cancer while I had clung to life. I didn't feel brave or strong, not here, not in this place where the enemy won so many battles and did not spare the weak.

My head throbbed. My awkward gait made one side of my neck muscles tight, which caused the headaches. It felt like my head was being squeezed in the grip of some angry god. I was grateful that my mom had insisted on the new prosthesis. We had tried to go the conventional route, using one that was too big so I could grow into it, but I hated the way I walked with it, and she didn't like it either. We shouldn't have been getting a new prosthesis just after picking the other one out, but Barnes had allies all over the hospital system. He was a veteran too, after all.

Pain, by the way, is the reason that hospitals don't play music that has voices and words. Words fail everyone in here. Every day when I was a patient, I had to point to a chart that showed happy and frowny faces. I had to point to the expression that represented how much pain I felt. With all the modern technology and medicine, we have to communicate through symbols about what we feel inside, like we're still drawing on cave walls.

Lightning flashed in the window behind us.

I realized Barnes had slowed down to wait for my mom. He was still at the end of the hall, near the lobby. No one else was in this corridor, so I raised my voice. "I thought maybe I saw a girl in the other hallway by the waiting room."

"Security is working on it," he called back. "Don't let it ruin your big day. You are one lucky kid. Wait till you see this leg."

I was thirteen, bald, and had one leg, and yet everyone told me how lucky I was. Life is a precious gift, people said. No one ever mentioned that it was a gift you didn't get to pick out. Apparently, God and I had very different tastes.

Mom finally caught up to Barnes and they walked together toward me. His lab was at the end of a very long passageway. He said he liked to work in solitude, but I wondered if his lab was so remote because other people freaked out when they saw what he had inside. He held the door for me and Mom.

"It looks so real," Mom gasped. "It's . . . beautiful."

My new leg rested on the table in front of us. The paperwork under it had a bar code and I could read my name printed in block letters. On the far end of the workbench was a bag with my name on it too, like a carrying case. Next to the case was a pair of crutches for when I didn't have the leg on.

Mom ran her fingers lightly over the leg.

"Mom," I groaned. "Don't pet it." She looked offended, so I shrugged. "It's weird."

"Oh, look, Sofia!" Mom giggled as she pointed. "He even got your cute little freckle just right." My real leg, the one they amputated, had had a heart-shaped freckle on the calf. Mom must have told Barnes about it, but I was hurt that she hadn't consulted me on something as personal as a freckle placement.

Barnes sat at his workbench, which was lit with two bright lights on either end, just like the adjustable kind we used in art class. He put on his jeweler's headlamp, which had a magnifying glass over one eye.

"Try it on, kid," he said. "Barnes has worked a minor miracle for his favorite patient." He looked like a grinning cyclops. "Feel how soft it is too. New material."

"Oh!" Mom said. "I left my phone in the car. I wanted to get a picture of you two. Do you mind?"

Barnes shook his head.

"I'll be back in a flash," Mom said as she bolted out of the room. I was jealous, and not just because she could move so fast.

It's hard to describe the sensation of staring at your leg on a table while you're standing at the other end of the room. This was probably why most patients weren't allowed in Barnes's lab at all but were ushered into a separate room with comfortable chairs. Maybe Barnes had decided he could trust me not to freak out in here because he knew I never tried to cheer people up. In a hospital setting, cheerful people are usually the most unstable.

I grabbed the carrying case and pretended to inspect it.

"What are you working on today?" I asked.

He didn't look up but motioned for me to hand him the tiny screwdriver that was just out of his reach. I did, glad to do anything but put that leg on. This one would be mine for a while. In January, Barnes had given me a temporary prosthesis that I had to practice walking on while he and Mom decided on a final model. It was like learning to ride a bike using training wheels. They wanted me to get the general idea before I graduated to the final leg.

After four weeks with that first clunker, I had another couple of weeks working with a newer design while Mom and Barnes argued about the final fit. This was the leg I'd have for at least a year, until I started growing again.

No one was sure when that would happen, because chemo can delay puberty. Cancer sucked on so many levels, and not just because of what it did to my hair. Since money was tight, we had agreed to do what everyone else did: get a bigger leg, put up with the gait issues for a year. Then we'd gone in to discuss my post-treatment plan of regular bloodwork and CT scans, and the doctor kept talking about the miracle of my cancer being caught early and entirely removed, because survival rates for bone cancer, especially once it spreads, haven't improved much in years. Mom and I realized then that maybe waiting a year to get a better leg wasn't a good idea.

Maybe I wouldn't have another year. No one was guaranteeing anything.

Anyway, most of the time, Barnes built the legs too big so the patients could grow into them over time, kind of like how a mom buys her kids shoes that are just a little too big so they don't outgrow them right away. Prostheses were incredibly expensive, and making them big helped them last longer, but Barnes knew I hated how the big one fit. He hadn't been all that surprised when I told him we wanted a new one.

What Barnes really wanted to build for me was a running blade, the kind of prosthesis that has no fake flesh and looks like a weapon instead of a leg. I hated them, but Barnes thought I would want to run again soon. I used to consider myself a major track star; as in, I'd been famous for majorly vomiting after every race, and sometimes beforehand too. I had run harder than anyone but never won a race. I got a lot of awards for participating, though. At least my best friend, Alexis, had thought I had potential.

"Barnes, you know what's sad? No one ever sees your best work," I said. "Your real talent, all that complicated stuff inside? The fake skin hides your genius."

He looked at me with his huge magnified eye. It blinked,

the fringed eyelid lowering and lifting like a garage door. "Your mother should be back any minute. She'll want to see how this looks."

I refused to take the hint. I knew he wasn't ashamed of his work, so which side was he on? Did he think prostheses should help patients blend in or stand out? Which one did he think was more important?

"People don't see how gifted you are," I continued. "Doesn't that bother you?"

He stood without turning back to me and opened the door. "I'm going to get you a soda pop," he called. "And then we're going to talk about the next genius prosthesis I'd like to create for you. No getting out of it today."

I couldn't risk following Barnes out, because he would talk about the blade. I didn't want a freaky prosthesis that everyone would stare at. Besides, right now it felt good to be alone in a quiet room at the end of a hallway where no one needed to be rescued from sausage documentaries. I looked at the leg again. When I put it on, it would look as if nothing had ever happened, as if the past had just performed a vanishing act.

"I want her to look completely natural, just like any other girl her age, and I will hold a thousand bake sales to pay for it, if that's what it takes," Mom had insisted during one of my last rehab sessions with the old leg. "My daughter deserves to look in the mirror and like what she sees."

It wasn't a good time to mention it, but I had *never* liked what I saw in the mirror, and I had certainly never felt just like any other girl my age. At school, it seemed like every other girl was pretty or popular. I was neither. I was timid and mousy, and had fallen through the rungs of the social ladder in elementary school. When I looked in the mirror, it wasn't to see what I looked like. It was to see what I could still fix. Truth was, there wasn't a lot left. On my best days, I had a vague resemblance to a snapping turtle: sharp pointed nose, squinty eyes, thin lips. That was what I saw, anyway.

Sighing, I slipped off my pants and then the stocking that went over my current prosthesis. I had zero energy after my first full day at school today, and it took me a couple of minutes to get the old prosthesis off.

A fast little squeaking sound caught my attention, but I ignored it. It was hard work wiggling around. At least I had remembered to wear boy shorts instead of underwear.

The noise grew louder, closer. I finally looked over. The girl from before stood framed in the doorway, breathing hard, one hand on her IV pole, one hand dragging the sack. Why hadn't security found her already? She was attached to a pole; how hard could it be?

I spotted a tear in the fabric of the pillowcase; inside was a big book, like the kind they made ages ago, with an engraved leather cover and tons of thick ivory-colored pages. She had been dragging around an old book? Most kids carried a teddy bear. What was wrong with this girl? I craned my neck to try to get a view of the hall, but I couldn't see anyone—or anything—else out there.

I pushed against the floor with my one foot, scooting

myself back in the chair. Barnes or my mother would be here any minute, but for now I was stuck in my boy shorts and only one leg.

"Everyone is looking for you," I said.

She stared at me, her face impassive, not a muscle moving. Only her eyes danced with happiness and relief, as if she had just finished a long race.

"Now I know why you were chosen," she whispered. "I saw you take care of that boy. You are a kind person and you'll be brave for them."

I had no idea what she meant, but she was starting to scare me. "We need to call security," I said. "We have to let someone know you're safe."

Tears formed in her eyes. They rose, spilling down her cheeks as her chin quivered. "I will be. He promised."

The girl glanced down the hall fearfully and licked her upper lip, catching a tear. I immediately grabbed the pair of crutches and forced myself up. "Please don't cry," I said softly. "Let's just call someone, okay?"

One more big, fat tear fell from her cheek onto her nightgown. She stared at the spreading wet spot, as if mystified. Her gaze moved to the bottom of her hem and then to the bloodstains.

"I'm not like you," she sighed. "I tried to be brave and kind, but they scared me." She paused, and looked at the ground as if ashamed. "Plus it's hard to keep secrets. It's lonely."

A gray mist snaked around her feet. The girl's eyes widened in terror, and she slung the pillowcase forward, hitting me in the shin.

Thrown off balance, I stumbled back, landing on my butt, hard.

She reached for the tape that held the IV line inside her other arm. "She doesn't want me to give it to you. She's going to be very angry."

I scrambled to grab the crutches again and stand back up, but the floor was too slippery. The mist was growing thicker and rising. I vowed to write a strongly worded letter to the hospital about the decision to wax the floor of a prosthetics lab.

"Don't!" I yelled, shoving the pillowcase behind me to get it out of the way before I tried to stand again. "You have to leave your IV in until a nurse takes it out."

"Tell them all I'm sorry, especially the Golem." With that, she ripped the IV line out as the mist rose over her head and the outline of the same woman began to form. Blood bubbled up from the place where the IV had punctured her skin.

"Mom! Barnes!" I yelled. "Somebody!"

She took off running, her IV pole crashing to the floor. Her bare feet padded hard against the blue floors as blood dripped from the IV line and trailed behind her.

"Help!" I screamed. "Stop her!" I crawled into the hallway.

Barnes was rounding the corner carrying two soda cans when she crashed into him and fell. The cans flew out of his hands and burst against the walls. A shower of dark cola erupted, and Barnes shielded himself. The girl scrambled back to her feet and ran into the waiting room, then directly out into the storm.

I caught one last glimpse of her through the window at the end of the hall. Her white nightgown blew in the wind as she ran. Above her, lightning split, and in that brief flash, the terrifying shadow woman was illuminated across the sky. She pointed one long finger at me, her eyes blazing until her face dissolved into the night rain.

I took a deep breath, forcing myself to slow my racing heart. The drops of blood and the girl's tears and the evil shadow flashing through a dark sky shredded by lightning . . . Black dots gathered in the edges of my vision. My thoughts were a blur and so was the hallway, the floor tiles swimming in shifting shapes.

My mom's high heels clacked rapidly toward me. I couldn't breathe or speak as she began calling my name more loudly. Security guards in blue uniforms swarmed the entrance; flashing blue and red police lights danced outside.

The black dots in my vision got thicker, my own dark storm.

Suddenly, I knew why they called it blacking out.

TWO

"Your test scores on evolution were disappointing," Ms. Kerry said with a clap of her hands, waking up a kid in the front row. "And contrary to what several of you implied, our principal, Mr. Reeves, is *not* proof of the missing link."

Two boys from class who wore eyeliner and dyed their hair black laughed quietly.

"However, one student in particular had a fascinating answer to the extra-credit question on the next stage of human evolution. Sofia, would you care to read your answer?" Ms. Kerry spoke slowly whenever she addressed me, as if losing a leg had affected my hearing. People were nice to me in the most extraordinarily stupid ways.

I shook my head. "No." Then, to be polite, I added, "I would not care to do that." I said it fast, hoping she'd get the point. I had come back to school last week for half days from

Monday to Thursday so I could build stamina and rest in the afternoons if I needed to. Friday had been my first full day of seventh-grade reality. When you have a prosthetic leg, you burn more calories than other people, even just doing ordinary stuff. The body looks whole, but invisibly, it's always working to make up for the loss. If my doctors thought it was my body that needed to adjust, they were wrong.

I was suddenly receiving a ton of attention. People who didn't know my name last year had signed a Welcome Back, Sofia banner, as if my absence had left a big hole at the school. We all knew it hadn't, but everyone pretended it was a big deal that I was back. I knew people were reacting to the cancer, not me. They were terrified of it, so they celebrated that it hadn't killed me, because everyone's worst fear is that it could kill them.

The banner wasn't really for me, even if it had my name all over it. No one would understand that, and I didn't try to explain. But it felt wrong, even dishonest, to be called brave or have anyone want to be friends with me now.

I felt more invisible than ever, yet overwhelmed with attention. How weird was that?

Right now everyone was staring anyway, including my former best friend, Alexis, who was sitting two rows up, wearing her track team jersey. Before class started, she had motioned for me to take the seat next to her, but I had pretended not to see her. We had said hi to each other a couple of times, but there hadn't been a chance to say anything else, and I was grateful for that. I had no idea what to say yet. We hadn't really talked since my life fell apart, just a few quick, awkward phone calls, but with the winter break and all the excitement of January's huge snowstorms, maybe she didn't miss me that much anymore. I hoped she didn't hurt inside like I did.

Alexis's long, curly brown hair was pulled up in a high pony. She must have run with the team that morning. I envied her for that, and for all that hair. I wondered if you could envy someone so much you actually hated them. I wished we could be friends again, but that wasn't fair to her. We had spent most of our time together at track or cross-country practice. Now I couldn't run. Was she supposed to rearrange her whole life just to spend time with me? A real friend would let her go. She needed to run because it made her happy, and she needed some happy in her life. There was too much drama at home for Alexis; running was her only refuge.

"Oh, I don't mind, then." Ms. Kerry pulled my paper from the stack on her desk. "I'll read it for you."

I lowered my face into my hands. This was going to be painful, and I knew pain.

Ms. Kerry began. "The extra-credit question was, 'Pretend that you have discovered the next step in human evolution. How will humans change, and why?' Here's Sofia's answer:

"Humans will lose their eyesight, because most of what everyone sees now is fake. Like the people on TV. They look real, like they're really there, but they're not. When people want to know the weather? We look at a screen instead of the sky. People don't even see what's real about the ones they love. Instead, they see what they wish we were, or what they wanted to be themselves.

And it hurts if you know that the image will never be real. So humans were made to see real things, but no one does. So we'll all go blind soon. Or maybe we already are."

Everyone snuck glances at me while she read my answer. I was the weird, quiet girl who used to hide behind stringy brown hair that fell into my eyes and covered my face as I worked, the girl who always had a book in her hand instead of a phone. They didn't know much about me except that I stayed off the social radar, but they forgot that I had been pushed off a long time ago. Besides, teachers never embarrassed kids in class for reading, not like they did for passing notes and texting. No teacher had ever grabbed my book and read a passage to the class just to teach me a lesson. So my personal thoughts and interests were kind of a curiosity to everyone, especially since my name was now on a banner near the front office. I was the bald mystery girl with a fake leg ("Is it the left?" "No, it's the right."), and now I had just accused all of them of being blind. (It actually was my left.)

Alexis turned and stared at me, probably wondering if my answer was a cry for help, a sign that I was finally reaching out. My face grew hot from frustration and embarrassment. Honestly, I was just trying to score some extra points, because Mom would do her happy dance when my next report card had all As.

At least I hadn't written about my latest theory on global warming: that global warming was really caused by the Earth getting bigger every year, and therefore closer to the sun. Millions of people die annually and get buried in the ground. Millions and millions, year after year, decade after decade . . . shouldn't the Earth be getting bigger all the time?

Ms. Kerry was passing out the tests, instructing us to correct any wrong answers before the end of the period. Above me, a thin black spider slipped down from its web, floating on an unseen current. No one else noticed it. My pencil kept slipping from my hands as I worked on my test. I hunched over my paper so no one would see. I had finished my chemo three months ago, but it had a lot of side effects that took months longer to go away, if they ever did, including how my muscles felt like rubber bands. Even holding a pencil was challenging at times. I dropped it repeatedly while I corrected my answer on natural selection. "The weak get weeded out" took me two whole minutes to write. Finished with that sentence, I shook out my hand and let it rest.

I squinted up at the spider, trying to decide what species it was. I had seen a documentary on them on Animal Planet. Spiders looked horrifying, but they were delicate and even beautiful in a strange way. Plus they had eight legs. If they lost one, it probably wasn't a big deal.

The spider slipped farther down and I leaned back in my chair and cupped my hands, hoping it would land in them so I could get a closer look.

I accidentally locked eyes with the new guy, who was staring at the spider too. Technically, he wasn't new anymore, since he had transferred here over the winter break, but I'd overheard girls gossiping about him nonstop since I'd been back. Apparently he was wild and unpredictable, but the stories they told sounded far-fetched. I doubted he had really meant to superglue a sixth grader to the bench in the cafeteria. Plus, no one had seen him put the plastic roaches in the teachers' lunch bags, so it wasn't fair to assume he had done that either.

He grinned at me and nodded. This was my second full day back, so to him, *I* was the new kid. I looked away immediately, but my cheeks fired up again. My face felt like a kiln. He was incredibly cute.

"Don't forget to turn in your permission slips for the field trip," Ms. Kerry said.

Natalie giggled from the back row. Ms. Kerry walked over and lifted Natalie's cell phone from underneath her paper. The screen was lit up with an incoming text. Candy and Natalie both glanced over at the new guy and blushed.

"Billy, the girls in class are wondering if you have a girlfriend yet," Ms. Kerry said.

The class froze, waiting for his response. I tried not to stare. Hot guys were an alien species to me.

"I'm currently accepting applications," he said, and the rest of the class started laughing. He looked right at me when he said it. I buried myself back in my test while Ms. Kerry got everyone under control.

A few minutes later, I stole a quick peek to check on the spider, but it was gone.

Suddenly, Candy squealed. Jumping out of her seat, she pointed at the floor. Everyone saw the spider. Matt, a football player who was shaped like a giant meat loaf with ankles, stood up and used his sneaker to grind it into a smudge.

I made a sad noise, a little choking sound, but no one noticed.

"I hate spiders," he said, and sat back down. "And I'm not afraid to smash things." He glared at Billy. Billy probably didn't know yet that Matt had had a crush on Candy since the fifth grade. Candy enjoyed the attention but not him, if that makes sense. Attention was like money to her. She wanted all that she could get.

The bell rang, and everyone shuffled their papers and books into their bags for the next class.

"Oh, Sofia, I am so sorry," Ms. Kerry called over the commotion. The halls were now swarming with kids. Last week she had insisted on giving me a five-minute head start, but I didn't want or need the special treatment. I had tried to tell her I didn't need it, but she'd just given me a big smile and promised me that it wasn't a problem at all, really. She was glad to do it for me. Ugh. "This is not about you" was what I wanted to say, but I couldn't, because she was only trying to help. The harder everyone tried to make my life easier, the worse I felt.

Everything was supposed to get back to normal, although I did have a couple of new teachers this term. I'd always been in advanced classes, but when I got my diagnosis in October, I had dropped back to on-level classes, which made keeping up with my classwork easier. *School* should have been easier too, if school was only about learning facts and figures. But it's not. Middle school is about learning your label, locating your pack, and avoiding humiliation. Why didn't teachers acknowledge that? School was like the Eagle Cam that had run a live camera feed of an eagle's nest last summer. One of the little babies had been in danger of falling out of the nest, and everyone saw it but none of the scientists helped it. The baby bird fell and died and people watching over the Internet were furious. It's not okay to just let it fall, they said, and the scientists argued that it was wrong to interfere. Nature had to run her course, like Mother Nature was a sweet old lady who could be trusted.

For the record, Mother Nature is a total thug. Teachers should at least admit that school is a dangerous social experiment, not a serene learning environment.

I braced myself to face the hormonal hive out there, wishing I had time to write a goodbye note to Mom. Even if I made it through the crush of humanity, the toxic cloud of body spray might disorient me, and I'd wander the school for days. I'd be like the class hamster they found two years after it escaped from the science lab, living off a forgotten bag of Skittles in the school library with a crazed look in its eyes.

Alexis was waiting for me in the hall. I tried to move past and pretend I didn't see her.

"Hey," she said. "Want me to walk with you?"

To avoid her, I walked right into the path of a sixth grader zigzagging through the crowd. The sixth graders had a separate hall, but there was a shortcut through the seventh-grade hall that led straight to the gym. He was probably racing to dress for gym before any bullies walked into the locker room.

The collision knocked my book bag off my shoulder, sending my papers flying out all over the hall.

People trampled over them, dragging papers underfoot in every direction. "Oh, come on!" I snapped.

Alexis froze, as if she knew it was her fault. And it was. She assumed we could be best friends again just because my mom finally let me come back. She wasn't seeing the situation clearly.

Then Billy appeared, rescuing my papers one by one. I was so surprised that I didn't speak or move. My Language Arts essay fluttered through the air and landed in front of Matt's locker. Matt sauntered over to it, unaware that he was now standing on my essay. Billy grabbed him by the shoulder and nudged him off the paper. "Watch where you're standing," Billy said.

Matt lowered his head like he was going to headbutt Billy. "Touch me again and you'll be dead meat!" Matt replied.

Billy grabbed the paper, then stood up and placed his hand back on Matt's shoulder with a sad look on his face. "All meat is dead. I thought you knew."

Matt shoved Billy's hand off, then stomped away.

"Come back!" Billy called after him. "You shouldn't be alone right now!"

He walked over to me and held out my paper. I hesitated before reaching to take it. Then Billy changed his mind and held the paper up to look for something.

"Sofia," he said. "With an 'f,' not a 'ph.'" He lowered the paper and grinned at me. "I like that name. And I liked your answer on that science test. I wish I had written it."

I was rendered mute by the sheer force of his hotness plus this bizarre circumstance. I mean, he was talking to *me*.

Willingly. It wasn't like a teacher had assigned us to be lab partners.

My hand fluttered up to touch the bandana on my head. He took a breath like he was about to ask me something.

"Sofia, hi." The voice calling out behind us was like a needle snapping off in my vein. I turned to see Candy walk up to us, her eyes never leaving Billy's face. She didn't really want to talk to me, of course. I was a human placeholder, taking up space until others had something interesting to say.

"Hello, Candy," I sighed.

Candy was an unfortunate name for such a sour girl. Maybe her parents had been confused when they'd first seen her as a baby, pink and soft. But all babies look like that, including rats and vultures.

She gave Billy her brightest smile, the one reserved for when she was running for class office. "You know each other?" she gushed. "That's great. I've been so busy organizing the school dance I haven't had a chance to catch up with Sofia." She didn't even look at me when she said my name.

Candy's friends circled around us. Predators hunted in packs.

"I'm the student council president," she said to Billy, "but I'm sure you knew that already."

Billy extended his hand and shook hers. "It's an honor to know an elected official."

The Winter Gala was the Saturday after next, but how much work could it be to hang crepe paper in the gym and ask the PTA to donate snacks? Stale cookies do not a gala make.

Besides, the dance was already doomed. It had originally been scheduled for January 29, the day the infamous Snowpocalypse hit the city, trapping kids taking school buses on the road and stranding people overnight at stores and offices. The teachers weren't happy at all about giving up a Saturday evening to chaperone us, even if the dance would end at eight p.m., but I guess Mr. Reeves wasn't willing to schedule it any sooner and this was the only good date. Anyway, lots of people were complaining about the change. School functions were usually held during the week, but this had been an unusual year. For all of us.

Change makes people hostile. I don't know why.

The bell was going to ring any minute. I mentally mapped out the quickest route to my next class. I hated being late and walking in alone. Moving with the herd offered protection from people who stared.

Candy's manicured talons grasped her perfect midnight-black hair and swept it into place. Billy's eyes darted side to side. He was looking for an exit route too. He caught my eye and I nodded slightly to the left, indicating where I was going. My stomach rumbled. I had just accomplished something extraordinary. I had made contact with the hot guy, tuned in to his wavelength. We were *communicating*. It made me a little dizzy.

Candy's smile stayed plastered on. I could tell she was trying to decide if he was mocking her. But that wouldn't make sense, because Candy was, to be fair, completely gorgeous. No one humiliated the pretty people.

"So, Sofia," Candy said, turning to me with teeth bared in a full-wattage smile, "I was planning my wardrobe for the week and a crazy idea popped into my head. I couldn't believe I hadn't thought of it before."

I raised my eyebrows. Candy had never said hello to me in the halls before today, and suddenly she was acting like we were friends.

"We need to talk this week, Sofia. I think you're going to love this."

Her best friend, Natalie, interrupted. "A group of us are going to get pedicures after school. Want to come?"

Candy glared at Natalie. "Sorry about that," she said.

My prosthesis had toenails that could be painted, but there was no way I was going to say that in front of Billy. He could see that something was wrong with me, but I didn't want to give him the whole picture yet. We had only just met. It would be like trying to hang a tire swing from a sapling. Too much too soon. Besides, I'm sure he had seen the Welcome Back, Sofia banner and someone would connect the dots for him.

Natalie huffed in her own defense. "Why is that a bad thing to say? Plus, Sofia, yours would be half off!" She grinned at me, thrilled to have just thought of this.

Mother Nature should let us submit names for natural selection.

Billy frowned, obviously confused, and stared at me.

It made sense. No one had talked to him about me while

I was gone, because no one talked to me when I was here. Alexis was probably the only person who missed me, and she wasn't the type to gossip.

"Wait. Why would yours be half off?" Billy asked. No one moved. Candy had picked the worst possible moment to start being nice to me. "Nice" was going to ruin my life.

Mr. Reeves walked around the corner. He frowned when he saw our group standing there. "Save it for after school."

Candy and her friends scattered, but Billy stayed where he was. Did he think I would stick around and explain? Not a chance. I walked away without a word.

"Wait!" he called, but that only made me walk faster. "You never answered the question! I'm so confused. Why would yours be half off?"

All around me, people were rushing to class, and the sounds of the lockers slamming made my head throb. The doors swung and snapped shut like rows of hungry metal jaws. The bell rang, a shrill and piercing alarm, but there was no waking up from this nightmare. When would I learn that?

On Tuesday, October 8, of last year, a month into seventh grade, I fell during a cross-country training run. Which wasn't unusual, but the pain afterward was. My left leg had been bothering me for weeks, but I assumed it was from training so much. I loved the long training runs because there was no pressure to win. Alexis and I could run side by side, our feet finding the same steady rhythm, and then our breathing too, until I was certain that even our hearts were beating in time. We plodded through the wooded trails behind the school, the world becoming ours in a way no one but a runner could understand. School drifted from our thoughts as we sailed through waving branches and down the winding path.

Autumn in the South is a long, gorgeous goodbye, so I didn't want to miss any of it. Instead, I popped ibuprofen every night, willing the pain to go away. I loved how the birds and butterflies swooped carelessly close as we ran, distracted by their preparations. Most of them migrated in the fall as the flowers wilted and curled brown and then the leaves above burst into orange and red flames, like Mother Nature was cremating what remained of the year. The colors, the noise, the rush of wings overhead . . . all leading to the long gray silence of winter.

I wanted to see every moment, and a stupid bum leg was not going to stop me.

So I popped some painkillers and ignored it . . . until that run.

After I fell, I couldn't stand back up. The pain was unbearable, "disproportionate," the paramedic said, as if my problem were mathematical. In a way it was, because tumors are caused by cells that have a fatal error and spend all their energy multiplying the mistake. Their miscalculation wove its way through my bone with ferocious enthusiasm. A simple X-ray at the ER clinic showed the presence of a shadowy mass. Nearly two weeks later, we had the results of the biopsy: primary bone cancer. The good news was that the doctors didn't think it had spread. The bad news was that the tumor had my nerves and blood vessels in a bear hug. Removing it would be tricky, even if everything went well.

It didn't.

I was supposed to have three rounds of chemo before surgery to shrink the tumor, but I kept getting all kinds of infections. The biopsy might have caused one of them, but no one really knew. Every round of chemo took nearly three weeks. Finally, the doctors canceled the last round because they worried I wouldn't survive it. Everything that happened after that came so quickly it was like hitting the fast-forward button.

On December 7, I turned thirteen.

I celebrated my thirteenth birthday by having my leg amputated.

There was a certain irony to that.

Germs were a constant threat. It was cold and flu season, and the news was full of stories about strange and lethal viruses floating around. Alexis tried to visit me in the hospital at first, but she had a cough and the nurses sent her home. Mom was freaked out and didn't want me to have any more visitors until I was absolutely safe. She assumed that after my surgery, I'd be healthy enough to see Alexis.

But I didn't want Alexis to see me like that, ghostly pale with tubes sticking out of me. I was always dozing off in the middle of a sentence. I was also incredibly skinny, and I wanted to put on weight before Alexis saw me. People think recovery is a simple process that moves in a straight line, but it's more like trying to build a house of cards with a deck that is bent and torn in weird places. It's frustrating and complicated, and I didn't want Alexis to see how weak I was. Just staying awake to watch a whole episode of something on TV took effort.

I had always wanted to be just like Alexis, strong and brave. I was in awe of her. I didn't know why she had chosen me as her best friend last year at the beginning of sixth grade. She just ran with me one day at practice, before she even knew my name. We were getting to know each other. And then, before our first official race, I heard her crying in a bathroom stall in the locker room, so I crawled under the door because she refused to open it. "My sister is sick again" was all she would say. We were only track buddies, not best friends yet, so I wasn't sure how hard to push her to talk.

She shook her head, like her sister disgusted her, and then she stared at me for a long time. "You have toilet paper on your forehead," she finally said.

I pulled it off and felt my cheeks get hot from embarrassment, but then Alexis doubled over in laughter. I laughed too, and she stood up and hugged me. From that point on, I knew we were best friends and not just running buddies, because if you crawl under a bathroom stall to talk to someone and they hug you for it, that's pretty special.

After that we ran together every chance we got, because we didn't have any classes together that year and I could never come over after school to hang out because our moms worked and we rode different buses. Alexis liked that I wasn't on social media very much, because she said that meant I wasn't a drama queen, constantly comparing myself to everyone. It actually meant we couldn't afford a computer or smartphone, but that was just one way that Alexis could take something bad about me and decide it was one of my best features.

Then summer came.

We both signed up for summer cross-country practice with the high school girls. The program was free, and the older girls got community service credit. We ran twice a week. After practice, usually around lunchtime, Alexis and I would get a ride back to one or the other's house and hang out until our moms got home from work. But those hours together were sometimes harder than running.

It was just us, and we weren't running side by side. We had to face each other when we talked, and that was suddenly weird. We started to talk about the serious things, like why I didn't have a dad and how much I wished I could cry at night about it but I couldn't find the tears and so what was wrong with me? Then one day we talked about Alexis's frustration at being so thin. Formless, she called it, as if she were more raw material than finished work.

"I wish I was as skinny as you." That's what I actually said. We were sitting on the couch eating popcorn. Movie credits were rolling on the TV screen. Alexis's face turned dark with anger.

"Don't you ever say that again!"

I swallowed, too shocked to say anything else. Alexis's chin trembled and she cleared her throat a couple of times.

"Remember when I told you my sister was sick?" She wasn't looking at me, but I nodded anyway.

"That's why she's not here this summer. She's spending it at a treatment facility for anorexics. All she ever wanted to be was skinny. It's like she wants to evaporate. She thinks that if her body doesn't take up any space, people will like her more." Alexis kicked the carpet with her foot in disgust. "I hate being skinny, and you know what? I think she hates me for it too. Maybe my whole family does."

We talked about it a few more times over the summer. Alexis was terrified she would lose her sister, and her whole family, to an enemy she couldn't see, one that had its own peculiar laws and punishments. Alexis didn't want to be thin. She was terrified that somehow she would fall prey to the same disease. But she didn't want to give up running, because it made her feel so good, and she rarely ate junk food, except ice cream. Even then, she just liked it . . . she didn't love it. She couldn't help being skinny. It wasn't her choice. She was just made that way. She had the body her sister wanted, and she was worried that her sister hated her for it.

Alexis wasn't motivated by food or looks or even popularity. She lived more in her head, which I thought was cool, even if she said she wanted to live more from her heart. She sighed that afternoon when we first talked about her sister, and then put her head on my shoulder. "I just want to be able to run and eat and live, without feeling like everything I do depresses someone else. I'm tired of feeling like I only remind my sister of everything she'll never be."

Our conversations scared me at those moments, like we

were testing a patch of ice, unsure how strong it was. And by the start of seventh grade, when we had said pretty much everything we had ever wanted to say to a best friend, there were little invisible cracks all around us. There was nowhere to hide. I knew she saw them, because she hesitated before we talked about the deep stuff. I hesitated too, not wanting to go forward until I knew for sure what those cracks meant, because cracks can mean different things. Like, before a baby chick is born, a crack appears in the egg, and that's a good thing. But before glass shatters, a crack runs across it. So which was it? Had we destroyed our friendship by sharing too much, or was something beautiful about to be born?

When school started, her sister came home and I started to shy away a little. I wanted to give Alexis space to spend time with her family, and we were both so busy with homework and running that having some distance between us felt inevitable. I began to move a little too fast between classes, not sure of the right things to say. I was trying to make it easy on Alexis, to give her plenty of room to heal and be certain, so she would know that being best friends had been her choice. That I was here for her when she was ready to catch up, but I wasn't a burden.

Turns out the tumor caught up to me before she did.

So how could we be friends now? I couldn't run with her, and I didn't want to hold her back from the only thing that made her happy. What if she stopped running to hang out with me and she started to hate me for forcing her to make that choice? Maybe she didn't want to be around another person who was sick. What if I was that last straw people talk about, and she stopped fighting this plague of perfection that had already claimed her sister? If she had to choose between running and me, I wanted her to choose what made her happy.

The tumor had been in *my* leg, but it affected everyone. I saw what it was doing to my mom. Cancer didn't make victims; it took hostages. So I decided. It couldn't have Alexis.

She had to be free, because I wasn't.

THREE

Tuesday, February 25

I hit the snooze button and snuggled deeper into my warm bed. Downstairs, the dryer beeped softly three times as the furnace hummed its one long, low note. I loved waking up alone, listening to the sounds of our home, without strangers with coffee breath standing over me reading a chart or adjusting a tube.

I heard Mom in the kitchen. She fixed breakfast only on school days, like a consolation prize. The microwave door slammed closed, and she turned up the volume on the television's traffic report.

I swung my leg off the side of the bed and leaned forward to grab the nightstand. Grunting, I hoisted myself up and hopped over to part the curtains, inspecting the neighborhood. Our house was just two doors down from the elementary school bus stop, and the kids got picked up super early.

Caitlyn, a kindergartner with long blond pigtails, waved furiously up at me and lost her balance, tipping over backward. Her backpack was larger than her body, making her look like a turtle in its shell. I waved back as she stood and then ran to the bus stop. We'd been friends ever since I had first seen her trying to teach her cat, Newman, to walk on a leash. Caitlyn was an optimist.

It was time to get my prosthesis on, and that took forever. I groaned just thinking about it.

The light from the hallway made the cracks around my bedroom door glow and cast an outline of my head on the window. I had a pencil-thin neck and a big round head with short, stiff bristles of new hair. My shadow looked like the outline of a toilet scrubber. My eyes followed the shadow down to the pajama pant leg hanging limp below my left hip, like a balloon with no air, the kind you find behind your dresser six months after the party. Shadows could lie and distort what was real, but this one was all true. My body was strange and frightening, even to me. Especially to me.

I grabbed a bandana for my head, watching my outline move with me.

Mom knocked before she swung my door open. "You're still not dressed?" she gasped.

I adjusted the knot at the back of the bandana without turning around. She always wanted to check the progress of my hair growth, but I wouldn't let her. If you've ever heard of shocking a pool with chlorine, that's sort of like what the drugs did to my body. My hair had thinned and fallen out in wispy handfuls, until a nurse helped me shave what was left one night when Mom went downstairs to the hospital cafeteria for a soda. I thought it would be easier for us both that way.

Mom got really upset when she came back. I didn't know shaving my head was something we were supposed to do together, like shopping for a dress or getting a manicure. Even now, it's hard to explain why I did it that way, except that I wanted to face my new reality, and it wasn't entirely about my hair.

When a brief surge of courage hit—which may have actually been a fresh dose of morphine, I can't be sure—I decided to accept the inevitable and go bald. Whether that was an example of optimism or fatalism would be a great subject for a Language Arts essay. Either way, I knew my hair wasn't my best feature.

So why not get it over with?

Now my once-brown hair was growing back as ghost-white bristles. If you think something can't get any worse, you don't have all the facts.

"I don't feel so good," I said, not turning around.

Mom ignored me and reached for the new leg. She carefully set it next to me on the bed, handling it like fine china. I shuddered when I thought about how much it cost.

The price wasn't just money; it was Mom's dream of going to night school to finish her degree. We had serious debt now, and she couldn't afford the classes. My dad had left before I was born and didn't pay child support, so we didn't have any help with the medical bills that insurance wouldn't cover. Drive-throughs, department stores, and cancer centers: they all take Visa and MasterCard. But we weren't entirely on our own; her coworkers loved her. They had taken up a collection and bought me some gift cards when I was in the hospital. I got to pick out some new clothes and a soft blue chenille bedspread that I adored.

Mom lightly ran her fingers over different outfits in my closet. "Well, this one will draw the eye up," she said, holding a tunic out to me. I held my nose, pretending I was trying not to retch. Mom bit her lip and turned back around.

Mom spied another outfit to show me, and slid the clothes down the bar to get it. In the far corner, on the floor, sat the pillowcase from the girl at the hospital. It was tucked inside a bigger plastic bag with the hospital's logo on the side. Mom didn't even notice it.

I blinked in confusion. That pillowcase shouldn't be here; it wasn't mine. I didn't want it.

We hadn't talked much about the incident at the hospital. It made Mom uneasy. The news made a brief mention of a girl brought into the emergency room with wounds from a suspected animal attack. Police were investigating, but the girl had used a fake name and they didn't have any leads. They didn't even know what had attacked her. The nurse had begun to clean the wounds and hook up an IV, but when she stepped out of the room for a moment, the girl slipped off the gurney and ran. It was all very peculiar.

When I had revived from passing out, my prosthesis, the carrying case, and the paperwork had already been loaded into the car by hospital staff. The pillowcase had been with me in the room, so someone must have assumed it was mine and packed it. Mom never realized it wasn't part of my personal stuff.

I sucked the inside of my cheek, thinking. I doubted the news story. If a dangerous animal really was on the loose, someone would know. A homeless man had reported seeing a freakishly large dog that night, but no one else had seen it. The Atlanta area had quite a few Bigfoot sightings every year, plus a persistent rumor of a pterodactyl-like bird hiding in the woodlands, so police didn't usually investigate reports of bizarre animals.

Mom was holding up a long sweater and cargo pants, wiggling her eyebrows at me.

"Yeah, whatever," I said, my chest tight. I cleared my throat.

"You loved it when you saw it online," Mom said.

"I was on drugs," I reminded her. I forced myself to breathe and look right at her, not at the pillowcase. Why had that girl shoved it at me like she wanted to get away from it? I tried to remember what she had said, something about me being brave and kind and . . . *chosen.*

The girl had been completely crazy. Crazy enough to—

"Put it on," Mom said, laying the outfit on the bed beside me. "And hurry up. I've got your favorite breakfast ready."

"I didn't know McDonald's delivered," I murmured.

Mom paused at the door and gave me a bright smile. "See? We *are* back to normal." Her voice cracked a tiny bit on the word "normal."

I stared at the pillowcase and then, without moving, examined the entire floor of my closet for any sign that the girl was there too. I braced myself to see tiny blood-splattered feet. A pair of pants had fallen off the hanger when Mom had shuffled my closet around, but she hadn't noticed. I stared at the lump on the floor, expecting it to move.

It didn't.

Mom must have been waiting for me to reply, because I heard her finally shut the door softly. I hadn't meant to be rude. I'd make up for it later.

Besides, before last year, she never shut my door. I had complained about that all the time. But now she shut it, and I knew why. It was hard to see that some things would never be like they were. We had each lost our hopes for the future, and neither of us knew where to find new ones.

I didn't have my prosthesis on yet, so no matter what happened next, I wouldn't be able to run away. I slid my body to the floor, sitting on my butt, preparing myself to scoot closer to the closet to inspect the pile of clothes. I'd be able to nudge the pile with my leg, and if it moved, I'd scream.

Pushing both palms flat against the carpet, I scooted a few inches, eyes focused on the lumpy pile in the right corner.

In the left corner, the pillowcase shifted.

I stopped, my hands frozen in midair.

It sat in the center of the closet floor now, not the corner. It had to be a trick of the morning light moving across my carpet. Or maybe Mom had moved it and I hadn't seen her. The book inside was clearly visible.

Slowly, I reached for my prosthesis, grateful to feel how heavy it was. I could swing it like a club if I had to.

I pretended to be wiping imaginary lint from the hollowed cup area of the leg, but from the corner of my eye, I continued to spy on the book. I had the strangest feeling it was spying on me too.

"Get moving up there!" Mom yelled.

Adrenaline shocked me at the sound of her voice, and I jabbed my prosthesis into the pile of clothes.

Nothing was there.

The book didn't move either.

I was an idiot.

Pulling the leg back, I used it to whack the closet door. The door slammed shut, sending a burst of air back at me. It had a strange but familiar smell, like the air after a storm. But this storm had brought something with it. It smelled like an animal. And leather. And old churches where candles burned all night.

The latch on the closet door popped and the door swung open.

Slowly.

The book was out of the pillowcase, against the door. As the door opened farther, the book fell forward, its cover facing me.

I climbed onto the bed, my heart hammering in my ears. This book was moving itself, which was impossible.

Books were lifeless.

The thick, cracked cover bore embossed swirls and something written in a strange language—the title, probably. The book was about a foot wide, and thick like two dictionaries stacked together. Deep cracks ran up and down the spine. There were two badly scratched brass buckles across the sides, and leather belt straps with black grimy edges ran through them.

A shiver shot down my back and into my belly.

Mom pounded on my bedroom door and I flung my hand over my mouth to keep from screaming. "Let's go!" she called. I heard her footsteps as she kept moving down the hall.

"Coming!" I yelled. I didn't stir.

Outside my window, tiny snowflakes began to drift down. I sensed that the earth had suddenly tipped, and its axis, so deep and hidden from all our eyes, was shifting. It rarely snowed in Atlanta, and we had already survived two bad winter storms. Snow in late February, even a light dusting like this, was rare. It made me feel like anything was possible, and I wasn't sure that was good.

I moved to one side of the bed and quickly put on my prosthesis and then my clothes, my eyes never leaving the book. It didn't move again.

My bedroom felt warmer, like I wasn't alone. Standing up, I took a deep breath, kicked the book back into the closet, and shut the door, fast.

Something nagged at me, like a name you can't remember. Maybe it wasn't a storm that had crept up on us on the way to the hospital.

Maybe it was something much, much bigger.

FOUR

My stomach still churned like a rock tumbler every time I opened the front doors to the school. I was glad I hadn't eaten much this morning. Forcing my shoulders back, I made myself take a deep breath. If I took small steps, my gait was perfect. The new prosthesis felt smooth. Barnes was brilliant.

I maneuvered close to the lockers, my left shoulder grazing the metal. This way it was less likely that anyone would run into me and knock me down. It was too awkward trying to get back up, and then everyone went nuts with the apologies. But being careful meant being slow, and I hated being slow.

In the wild, a predator would already have me by the throat.

I didn't want to think about that right now. I didn't want to think at all, especially about what I was going to do with a possessed book in my room. I would have thrown it in the trash, except I was afraid to even touch it.

Mr. Reeves stood in the doorway to his office. Everyone on staff knew about my treatment schedule, including the new leg. He caught my eye and grinned, giving me a thumbs-up. I smiled politely, resisting the urge to roll my eyes.

The point of a prosthesis is to lead a normal life. Normal people don't get a thumbs-up for having all four limbs, do they? And having a prosthesis didn't automatically make me brave or a hero either. Heroes choose their paths. I hadn't chosen anything, not even where to put that stupid freckle.

I passed the counselor's office and noticed that the lights were on. Mr. Reeves had informed my mom and me that our counselor had retired this past Christmas because his wife was ill, so I was surprised that anyone was in there. Maybe they had hired someone over the winter break. A woman with long blond hair swept into a messy chignon sat at the desk. I loved that hairstyle. I had tried a chignon once, back when I had hair, but the only thing I got right was the messy part.

"Sofia," she called. Her voice was low and raspy, like a movie star's.

I stopped and ducked my head in. "Uh, yes?"

She smiled and stood, extending her hand to me. I entered, adjusted my backpack, and shook her hand. It was ice cold.

"Do you have a minute?"

"Uh . . ." I glanced down the hall.

"I'm sure your teachers won't mind if you're a little late." She didn't ask if I minded.

I shrugged and sat in the empty chair she gestured to. She

hadn't put anything in her office yet: no posters or framed photos, not even a pencil cup on her desk. The office was lifeless. I shivered; it was freezing cold in here.

"Your backpack looks heavy," she said, a smile spreading again across her face.

"It is," I replied. "Lost of books."

She leaned forward. "And what are you reading, Sofia?" She placed her elbows on the desk and wove her long fingers together, making a steeple. Her nails were clipped short and painted black. She rested her chin on her hands as she stared at me. I shifted in the chair, suddenly uncomfortable. Her eyes were light gray, almost blue, like a thin frost covered the irises. I swallowed nervously.

"Are you reading anything *interesting*?"

The bell rang and I jumped without meaning to. She stared but didn't say anything else. Something about this conversation didn't feel right.

"I really should get to class," I said, and stood.

"They say only two things can change the course of your life," she said. "The books you read and the people you meet. Don't throw your life away, Sofia. Not for a book. And not for the fool who wrote it."

I stepped back into the hallway and noise flooded my ears. Kids brushed past me from all directions and I was swept back into the morning hallway rush, revived by the heat of all the bodies in motion.

When I glanced back, the office was dark and completely empty.

I got to homeroom with Ms. Forester. Her son was a

marine serving overseas. She had raised a soldier, so she frowned on us acting like weenies. Sitting in my chair, I stuck my hands under my thighs until they stopped shaking. A few minutes later, I walked up to her desk while everyone was doing their work.

"Do we have a new counselor?" I asked.

Ms. Forester glanced up from grading papers. "Not yet." She looked back down at her papers, then paused, like she realized who was asking. "Do you need to talk to someone? I can ask Mr. Reeves about finding someone for you."

"No!" I smiled like that was a silly suggestion. "I was just curious."

She stared at me with a confused smile.

"Because I noticed the counselor's office is empty. . . . It is empty, right? No one is in there?"

She frowned, her head cocked to one side.

I couldn't tell anyone about the book and I couldn't tell anyone about the disappearing woman, so I decided to keep my head down and my mouth shut for the rest of the day. I managed to avoid Alexis and Billy in science, although Billy made that easy by getting called to the principal's office at the beginning of class. Apparently he'd had detention yesterday and something bad had happened.

After class, I summoned the old power of blending in, hiding in plain sight, fading away, which is also known as sitting in a bathroom stall for as long as possible between classes.

Mom's car inched through traffic all the way home while she stole glances at me every few minutes. I counted six churches as she drove. One had a cross that stood taller than all the other roofs, like a stern reminder to be on our best behavior.

"This city is God-struck," a neighbor once said when I had asked why we needed so many churches. I wasn't sure what that meant, but it sounded right. They all seemed to have the same basic beliefs, about being kind and honest, but some also thought you should get baptized by being dunked underwater, while others thought the water ought to be sprinkled, while some thought the real secret was to go door to door and interrupt people's dinners.

"Did your leg hurt today?" Mom asked, veering around a slower-moving car. She honked the horn, frowning. Speed limits in Atlanta were more like baseline readings. They gave you a general idea where you were starting from. I counted one more church.

"Not much." Sometimes I had phantom pains, sharp flashes that came and went for no obvious reason. Part of my brain didn't believe my leg was gone and misinterpreted nerve impulses. In the hospital, when chatty doctors lowered themselves to sit on the side of the bed during my daily checks, I'd instinctively try to make room for them and move my left leg out of the way.

Then I'd remember it already was.

So phantom sensations sounded crazy but felt real, just like everything else right now: a strange girl who told me I'd been chosen, a book that moved by itself, and disappearing school counselors. I had an impulse to stop at one of those churches and ask someone inside how they knew for sure what to believe. How did they know what was real?

I was making this too complicated. Mom would believe me without any proof. She believed in crazy-sounding things like phantom sensations. She might also believe in books that moved or counselors that disappeared. It was okay to doubt what had happened, but I shouldn't doubt her. Even if this was all a strange side effect from treatment, I could tell her.

I drummed my fingers on my knee, trying to think of the best way to start the conversation.

Her hand rested on my arm. "I'm so proud of you," she said softly. "You've done an incredible job holding it all together."

I then realized how exhausted she looked. Her eyeliner was smudged, leaving dark circles under her eyes, and her face was pale and thin.

"Thanks, Mom." I tried to smile. "My leg didn't hurt that much. I promise. It was a pretty good day, overall. I forgot to tell you: I even got an A on my science test. I rocked the extra credit."

"That's my girl," she said.

Once we got home, Mom lugged her black leather briefcase to the kitchen table. The other customer service reps just used totes or grocery bags, but Mom said it was important to look the part of a successful businesswoman. Mom was stuck in a job that didn't pay much, and she was hoping to break out of it.

"Dinner in twenty," she said. She went to a peg by the back door and grabbed her apron. I heard her sigh with exhaustion.

Upstairs, I opened the door to my quiet bedroom. The closet door was still shut. Tomorrow I would definitely tell Mom about the strange things I had seen, and she would tell me it was a side effect. We might even laugh. I would show her the book and she'd take it to the trash, shaking her head and laughing.

Sitting on the edge of the bed, I began the long process of removing my leg. Even considering my hair, I really had been lucky. After the amputation, my oncologist told us that the margins around the tumor were clear and all tests were negative for cancer, which meant I didn't have to do more chemo. The only time Mom and I had let go and cried together was when the doctor told us the news. Most of the time, Mom tried to cry in the bathroom so she wouldn't upset me, as if I didn't already know that trick. Everyone knows that trick. It made me feel worse, actually, when she did that. I cried under my blanket at night. I hoped she didn't know that one.

I wiggled the leg off and then bent down to peel away the stocking that protected my stump. "Stump" was an ugly word but better than "residual limb." That made it sound like a hygiene problem. Anyway, I was done with all of that . . . at least until my next appointment with Barnes. Before that, I had another round of blood work, but the lab techs never talked about the leg. I'm not even sure if they knew I had a prosthesis.

Outside, the sun was setting. Shadows shifted on my walls, illuminating dozens of little jagged holes where I had ripped off my track and cross-country ribbons. Only my *Doctor Who* poster remained. I had hidden the ribbons and team jersey in a box under the bed. Someday, I'd be strong enough to throw them out. For now, it was like that wistful feeling you get when you hang up your Christmas stocking. Some part of you still wants to believe in Santa, and some part of me still wanted to believe that none of this was real.

The crack under my closet door glowed. The light was green, like someone had just turned on a string of Christmas lights.

My closet didn't have a light inside.

I stared at the light, my heart beating rabbit-fast in my chest.

Something thunked against my bedroom door and I gasped.

"You left your crutches in the bathroom," Mom called. "Dinner in ten!"

Resting my head on my hands, I tried to tell myself to get a grip. It wasn't fair to my mom to freak out over an unexpected side effect like this hallucination. She'd have to put me back in the hospital, and she had been through so much already.

I didn't need her help to ignore this. I gritted my teeth, ready to get this over with. Once I knew it was all in my mind, I'd feel so much better.

The closet doorknob twisted, first to the left, just slightly. I exhaled once, then sucked in a breath and held it, counting to ten. The knob returned to center.

I let my breath out slowly. My shoulders contracted like someone had punched me, slow motion, in the chest.

It twisted again, right.

The door swung open, sending goose bumps across my skin.

The book stood upright, like it was staring at me.

Green light rolled from the book like fog, making a faint hissing sound as it crossed the carpet. The fog felt warm as it touched my ankle, probing it. Then it wrapped itself around me, as if it was making sure I was real. I couldn't breathe; my eyes watered from holding my breath, this time by accident. Hallucinations weren't supposed to touch you, were they?

As the book moved across the floor toward me, the cracked leather corners caught on the carpet. I tried to raise a hand to warn it to stop, but my arm was deadweight. I managed to exhale, a little shrill wheeze of panic.

The book's cover opened slightly, revealing a strange gold and green and blue etching inside. It might have been of an animal; I wouldn't get closer to check.

It seemed to be waiting for me. I was so polite even my hallucinations had manners.

There was one way to know for sure if I was imagining this. If I couldn't grab it, it wasn't real.

With a fast shallow breath, I flung my hands down and grabbed the book's spine. It wriggled against my grip, like a big fat animal that had to be dragged from its den.

The book was real.

My physical therapist said I had weak core muscles. She was right. I had to adjust my grip twice before I could lift the book up next to me on the bed, and I was panting from the effort. Or maybe from anxiety.

I edged one finger under the cover and paused.

Nothing happened.

Biting my lip, I flipped the cover open. Green light flooded my room, but it wasn't a scary, venomous green light. No, this was the green of spring, of grass and leaves and iridescent hummingbirds, a green I had almost forgotten, one I desperately needed to see again. When they released me from the hospital, it had been a shock to find that it was winter and the whole world was dead and gray. Now I longed to see life, and spring, return to the cold world.

The next page was made of leather. It was thick, with ragged edges and stitching on the sides.

In the center were words in fancy black script.

The Bestiary of Xeno,
The Last Living Student of Aristotle,
Master of Them That Know

Beneath this was a beautiful image of a great winged bull. I had no idea what a bestiary or Xeno was, but I had heard of Aristotle. I had once thought they named a clothing line after him, but that, Ms. Kerry had told me gruffly, was a company called Aeropostale. Aristotle, she said, was a famous ancient philosopher who loved to document every animal he could find. He wrote endless descriptions of all the lives he found in nature, and many scientists consider him the first biologist. He founded his own school and loved teaching.

I turned the page again. The next one felt thinner. It wasn't made of leather, but it wasn't exactly paper either. It was like a thin fabric. Every page seemed to be different, as if added at different times.

I didn't recognize the language, but thankfully someone had scribbled a translation beneath the original wording.

Year 436, Ab urbe condita

"To Aristotle's disciples, to the healers, and to all who love Truth,
Though our Master, Aristotle, is now dead, murdered at the hand of our enemy, I carry on.
Herein are the secrets about the oddities of this world, the forgotten, the misused, and the feared. You and I are called as witnesses to their Truth, which is our Truth, and the Truth of the human condition. For we know ourselves best only when we see through the eyes of the strangers among us.
Do not misunderstand. These are not playthings, pets, or wild animals that may be tamed.
These are monsters.

Xeno

Outside my window, a mournful howl rose from the belly of some awful beast. I shivered and snapped the book shut. The room went dark.

FIVE

I huddled on the school steps in the morning cold, my teeth clacking. Mom had dropped me off early at my request. She was shocked that I'd asked, of course. And since I'd never gone at that time before, neither of us realized the school wouldn't actually be open.

Last night she'd popped into my room unexpectedly and practically dragged me down the stairs for dinner. She thought I was sitting on my bed with the lights out because I was depressed. She hadn't noticed the book next to me, maybe because my room was dark. The book had stopped glowing when I shut it.

When I finally climbed into bed at nine-thirty, the book was nowhere to be seen. Mom tucked me in and I lay there, eyes wide open. Nothing moved in the darkness, and I fell asleep working through the details of a plan.

Thankfully, my school had a good library. If I was hallucinating, it meant my subconscious wanted to tell me something. Or I was crazy. Either way, I needed to know if there was any truth in the book. I didn't believe in monsters, but this was Atlanta, and it was a city with very old secrets.

People forget that Georgia was one of the original thirteen colonies, and when the English arrived, they discovered that the Native Americans believed this area to be a hive of supernatural activity. To the northeast of Atlanta, there is a canyon with a name that translates as "terrible," because tribes believed evil spirits lived there. It isn't far from Blood Mountain, which the tribes fought a horrible war for control of. It was believed to be the home of powerful and good spirits called the Immortals.

Plus, compared with other American cities, especially the ones we studied in school, like Boston and Philadelphia, all the buildings around Atlanta appear new. You have to look hard for a glimpse of the past. That's because General Sherman and his men burned the city during the Civil War. The city's history is in the ashes buried under our feet. When you're in Atlanta, you're always walking on the dead.

So Atlanta is a mysterious city with weird weather.

This winter especially had been unexpectedly brutal. The morning cold snuck in between the tiny stitches of my sweater. My skin stung all over, even on my head. If I had worn a wig instead of my favorite bandana, my head wouldn't feel like an ice cube. Mom had bought me a wig, but apparently she thought hairstyles were like wingspans, and that a larger size offered an evolutionary advantage. I refused to wear it. I didn't like hats either, because when you pulled a hat off, the bandana came off with it.

Now, with nothing to do but wait, I remembered the last time I had been this cold and alone. Instinctively I reached down and touched my left hip. The only place that was colder and lonelier than an operating room was the hallway just outside it. I had been left there while they prepped the room, drowsy from the pre-op drugs, when I heard a child wailing in pain somewhere in the hospital. My blanket had slipped from the bed and I had shivered in fear, drifting in and out of consciousness.

Suddenly, the track team burst around the corner of the school, moving in a pack. They always left the track and ran one last lap around the school before hitting the showers. Alexis was easy to spot, with her ponytail swinging side to side as she ran. I ducked my head and pretended I didn't see her.

The metal bolt slid back behind me and I turned to see Mr. Reeves opening the door. "Sofia! Come in! It's freezing out there!"

"Thank you," I mumbled, wondering if my lips were blue.

Mr. Reeves wanted to say something more. I saw his mouth open and heard him take a long breath. People did that around me, like they were about to dive into another world where they couldn't breathe the air.

"I have to get to the media center," I said before he could find his voice.

I hustled through the foyer and turned down the hall to

my left. A basketball whizzed past my head. I ducked to avoid it and lost my balance, stumbling right into the path of two girls from the basketball team who were chasing the ball. The girls fell and I got slammed back into the lockers.

The team was using the long, empty hallway for passing and dribbling practice. The coach blew on her whistle, hard, screeching at the girls to get back up and continue the drill. The girls went right back to practicing, leaving me standing there, stunned. They were so focused on the ball that they hadn't even noticed me. That was exactly what I wanted, so even if my back was bruised and stinging, I should have been happy. The tear rolling down my cheek was just misinformed.

Thankfully, the media center doors were unlocked. Ms. Hochness, our librarian, was already at work sorting returned books. She was a really curvy woman the boys had secretly nicknamed Ms. Hotness. Her wispy blond hair swirled around her head like a personal cloud.

"Good to see you, Sofia. What do you need today?" She didn't hyperventilate when she saw me, which I appreciated. She glanced up to make sure I had heard her, smiled, and went back to work sorting a stack of books about sweet girls who loved shy ponies.

"I need to know everything about Aristotle," I said. He was my starting point, since I had already heard of him. The rest I would Google.

"He's dead," she said flatly. "I hope you can account for your whereabouts."

I blinked, not really getting the joke.

"Just a little librarian humor," she sighed. Then she nodded and crooked her finger at me, motioning for me to follow, and walked toward the nonfiction bookshelves.

"How's your mother?" she asked, not looking back, just walking and expecting me to keep up.

I took my first deep breath of the morning.

"She's good."

"Still nervous about you being back at school?" Ms. Hochness asked. "With all these germy kids?"

"Completely," I laughed. Ms. Hochness made it okay. I didn't know how. She just had that odd magic some adults have. "Thanks again for those books you sent me at the hospital. They were great."

I wondered if she knew I was lying. I had stopped reading right after my diagnosis. No one here knew.

I used to love books, and carried one everywhere. I enjoyed anything except the kind written especially for girls. That was weird, I know, but those books seemed to be softer and sweeter, and I couldn't be soft, not when I was in middle school, where bullies might try to slam your fingers in your locker or snap pictures with their cell phones when you changed for gym class. That hadn't happened to me yet, but I had to be ready since I wasn't even remotely popular.

After the diagnosis, when Mom and I spent every day together, she finally noticed that I had stopped reading but blamed the meds and the nausea and exhaustion. It wasn't cancer's fault, though. I stopped reading because I had never felt so alone, and books weren't helping. Books are like messages in a bottle washing up on a deserted island. It horrified me to know how many people were struggling to be heard, like they were stranded and calling out for help.

The realization had started back in September, in science class. Nothing ruins your life like the facts.

Let's start with color. What I call the color blue—that may not be what other people see. If you're color-blind, you don't see the same colors. You literally don't see the same world. And some people have extra color receptors in their retinas; they see about ninety million additional colors. The colors really do exist, but *no one else can see them.*

I remember sitting in class and wondering, do I see what no one else sees or do they see what I can't? We'll never know.

And then there's taste. When Alexis and I split a bag of chips, were we tasting the same thing? No one knows, because no one has the same number of taste buds. Some people have a ton, so they can taste flavors other people can't. Some people don't have many, so they can't taste much; oatmeal tastes about the same as a chocolate chip cookie, which I find deeply disturbing. Alexis likes broccoli because it tastes good to her, but to me it tastes like a dirty diaper left in a hot car. So when Alexis and I split a bag of chips, we thought we were sharing the experience but we weren't.

I will never know what anyone else tastes, or sees or hears or feels. No one will. Everyone is alone in the way they experience the world. My reality isn't your reality, because we're different in a basic, cellular way. That's frightening. I didn't want to be alone. And books, I realized, were just one way people tried to communicate their reality. But it felt hopeless.

The social workers warned Mom that depression was common after cancer, especially once the intense treatments were over. They warned her to look for the telltale signs. But the depression doesn't come from having cancer; it comes from knowing how alone you really are. There are no words, and even hospitals know that. All my life I've loved words and reading, and then I realized there was no book written in my native language. No book could heal the sadness of being so alone, because *everyone was alone*. That's why I had stopped reading. Books depressed me. What good did it do me to know that everyone else was alone too? No book could save me from that truth.

Ms. Hochness gestured to a long metal shelf. "Histories are in the middle, essays about him to the left, and his personal notes are to the right."

"Can I take them all?" I asked. "And I need to look something up online." The media center had the best computers in the building.

She nodded and started pulling books off the shelf. "Help yourself to the computers. I'll grab these for you and put them on a table."

Sitting in a cubicle, I pulled up an Internet search engine and typed in "bestiary." I learned that it meant a book of mythical animals. I typed in the other name in the book: "Xeno." Google told me it was an ancient Greek male name meaning "strange voice." Nothing else was recorded about him and monsters, of course.

Finally I typed in "the year 436 Ab urbe condita." I

learned that it meant Xeno wrote his letter 436 years from the founding of the city of Rome, also known as 318 BCE.

I chewed my lower lip, staring at the screen. There was no way that book was so old. But if it wasn't a hallucination, what was it? A joke, or a prop that got lost from one of those dragon and wizard games or some TV series that filmed in Atlanta?

Maybe the books on Aristotle would have some answers.

I made my way back to the table and could barely see Ms. Hochness over the growing pile of books she had pulled. "Aristotle wrote dozens of books. Maybe hundreds," she said.

I was going to have to read hundreds of books? My eyes widened.

Ms. Hochness raised one finger as if to warn me. "But they were destroyed after his death." She lowered her voice like she was telling me a juicy secret. "Consider this: He was the greatest natural scientist the world has ever known. Yet no one really knows how he died; some blame a mysterious stomach ailment, but others say Aristotle had powerful enemies. I've always wondered if there's more to his story than we know."

"Yeah, apparently there's a lot more," I said. "I mean . . ."

Ms. Hochness cocked her head to one side.

I shrugged, the universal body language of thirteen-year-old girls.

She led me to a table closest to the one good heating vent in the room, past a shapeless form slumped over a desk.

"A new kid. Transferred in from a fancy private school in the city," she whispered. "He was already asleep there when I arrived this morning. I don't even know how he got in."

"Serious student," I whispered back.

Something about the look she gave me—one eyebrow arched up and a wry smile—told me I was wrong. His records must have told a different story.

A glittering pool was spreading out from his mouth across the table. A badge that read "I Love Hot Chicks," with a chicken nugget roasting over a flame, was displayed on his jean jacket. And he smelled bad, like the-last-day-of-the-state-fair bad, when they're loading the animals from the petting zoo and trashing the old corn dogs that didn't sell.

An open book rested under his arms, and Ms. Hochness gently pulled it from under the drool-hole.

The guy woke up with a start, then looked around, dazed. He and I both did a double take.

It was Billy.

She turned the book around. "What have you been drawing, Billy?"

He wiped his eyes with the back of his hands and winced at the harsh overhead lights.

"I was making the cats anatomically correct," he said. "I'd think that would be important to a school deeply committed to academic excellence."

"You want the picture to be more realistic?" she asked.

He nodded.

"Then this poor cat needs a support garment," Ms. Hochness said. "Because she's going to have back trouble later."

Billy cringed.

"Here's another dose of reality." Ms. Hochness smiled sweetly. "Defacing school property carries an automatic penalty of detention."

"I'd love detention in the library," Billy countered. "Detention in the computer lab is so boring. Books are where the real action is."

The corners of Ms. Hochness's mouth twitched. She was trying not to smile.

"Anyway," Billy said, "it's my dad's book. He's a vet. I draw the pictures to let him know I have a keen interest in the family business."

I had never heard anyone my age use the word "keen" in a sentence before. I liked it. It was undeniably polite, with a sneaky touch of snark.

He glanced up at the clock before stuffing everything into his backpack and walking toward me. Something fluttered out from all his stuff. I buried myself in my work and prayed he would keep walking.

Instead, he sat down at my table. "Tornado season is coming."

I cleared my throat and kept reading.

"You watch TV during storms?" he asked.

I didn't answer. I wished I had put on lip gloss this morning, even though I never wore it. I was so pale. Plus this baggy sweater made me look like a cat trapped inside a parachute. Maybe I should have worn that wig instead of the bandana. He wouldn't have recognized me.

He sat back and sighed. "Why won't you talk to me?"

Ironic, because the chatter in my head was deafening.

He sighed and continued. "So, when you watch TV during a storm, the station sometimes stops the show and you hear this random male voice say, 'We interrupt this program to bring you an emergency weather report. . . .' And you're mad at first, really mad, and you have to change channels to find something else to watch while a reporter blathers on and on about some stupid storm, right?"

I nodded even though I never did that. Secretly, I always worried it would hurt the reporter's feelings somehow.

"But then you really like the new show. You're glad you got interrupted. 'Cause you would have missed out. And maybe now it will become your favorite show. You can't wait to see what happens next."

Was he still talking about TV? I had a feeling the subject had changed.

He picked up one of my books. "Aristotle!" he yelled.

Ms. Hochness gave us an arched-eyebrow stare.

Billy scooted lower in his seat and looked at me like I had passed another secret test. "You are the most interesting girl I've ever met. You're not afraid of spiders, you read Aristotle, and you don't want to hang out with the popular girls, even though they want to hang out with you. Plus your extra-credit answer put into words everything I've been thinking for the last year."

I wished he had said I was pretty, not interesting. Scabs were interesting . . . and so were turtles and mildew on bread. Ugh.

He kept talking. "And I'm sorry about Natalie embarrassing you. Somebody filled me in during detention. I want you to know, I don't care. I mean, I care. But not enough to talk about it. Unless you need to. And I hope you don't." He turned red and cleared his throat. "What I'm trying to say is, don't be embarrassed around me."

But it clearly embarrassed him to say that. He was strange . . . and maybe wonderful. But he was definitely too much for me. I had gone from lowly outcast to class pet on a pedestal so fast that it was a wonder I didn't have a nosebleed. Hot guys would only add to the social chaos.

"I really need to read now," I said. His sea-green eyes made it hard to concentrate.

He ignored my hint, pushing the book out of my reach.

"At one of my other schools, we saw a documentary on the ancient philosophers." Billy scooted closer to the table. "Back then, parents worried that the truth would corrupt young minds. Some people were even put to death for seeking the truth." He lowered his voice and leaned even farther toward me. I pulled back, worried about my breath. "Ask too many hard questions and . . ."

He made a slicing motion across his neck with one finger.

I glanced at Ms. Hochness, who was refilling the candy jar on her desk. "I think we're safe in here," I said.

He sat back suddenly and folded his arms behind his head. Little white hairs clung all over his shirt. "I better stick around while you read," he said. "For your own good."

A shrill, rattling noise, like one made by an animal, came from the hallway, and we both jumped in our seats.

Then Billy stood. "Almost forgot," he said, and it sounded

like an apology. "Look, if I don't see you again, Sofia, know this: you've restored my faith in humanity."

He left so fast I didn't even have a chance to point out the paper he had dropped. He was definitely a rare combination of strange and sweet, like a popcorn-flavored jelly bean.

When I was sure he was gone, I walked over and picked up the paper. It was a picture of his family, his mom and dad and him as a little kid. The photo had been torn and then taped back together. It seemed private, like it was more than just a picture.

"Something wrong?" Ms. Hochness asked. She stood in her office doorway.

I didn't want to show her the picture for some reason. "Nope," I replied. I tucked the picture in my bag. Later I would find his locker and slip it in through the crack.

"Need more time?" Ms. Hochness asked.

"Yeah, thanks," I replied.

Ms. Hochness ducked back into her office to call Ms. Forester and let her know that I was staying a few more minutes after the bell. They'd probably agree it was a good idea to let the hallways clear out. So occasionally, I admit, having a prosthesis worked in my favor.

I went back to the books, eager to find answers. There wouldn't be any about a student called Xeno, because he didn't exist, at least according to the Internet.

But plenty had been written about his "master," Aristotle. "Master" was an ancient title for teachers, which was a disturbing discovery I vowed to keep to myself.

Aristotle, I learned, began his career as a medical doctor

but wanted to document everything in nature, so he looked for truth under every leaf and in every eye.

He believed we were two things at once: what the world saw on the outside and the thing hidden inside that we would become. He tutored Alexander the Great, the warlord with fabulous hair who conquered most of the ancient world, including the Persian empire. The Persians were the first people to decide that men should wear pants instead of flowing skirts.

I groaned and looked up from the pile of books. This was not the information I needed, but the last piece of my plan was the most embarrassing.

"I need books on monsters," I told Ms. Hochness.

"Novels?" she asked.

"Nonfiction." My cheeks got really hot. I might as well have asked about the Tooth Fairy and Santa.

She brought me a few books on folklore and urban legends. Each of them featured a ghoul on the cover. One creature was dripping with blood; the other had a severed arm in its mouth. I nodded and she scanned them; then I threw them in my book bag, not wanting to see the covers. Was that what monsters really looked like? I was hoping more for the Muppets.

Then I heard the first scream.

SIX

Outside the library, teachers were yelling for help. I hustled to the door, right behind Ms. Hochness, to the sounds of pounding footsteps and shouting. People were slipping on the floors because they were running too fast, or else they were pressed flat against the lockers in horror. A terrified goat raced past and nailed Ms. Hochness on the foot. She cried out, bending down to grab her toes, which gave me a good view of the hall.

The hit-and-run goat had a huge number three painted on its side. His beady eyes were wide with fear. Mr. Bronson, our beefy gym teacher, sprinted after it, his sneakers giving him traction. The goat bleated in panic and went down in a whirlwind of hooves and biceps. Mr. Bronson grabbed it in a wrestling hold, and its thick pink tongue stuck out and waved like a flag of surrender as dark pebbles shot from its rear end in every direction. This made some of the sixth graders scream even louder before the goat broke free and ran off.

Another goat had cornered Mr. Reeves by the boys' restroom. This one had a big number one painted on its side. Number One lowered its head and rammed Mr. Reeves right in the no-no zone. The principal fell to his knees, his mouth open in a silent scream. Number One charged down the hall toward the administration offices just as a math teacher pulled the fire alarm.

Once the fire department arrived, Number Three was caught within thirty minutes. We got updates from firefighters whenever they walked back to the truck. The older guys had to clear their throats a lot to keep from laughing.

Number One was found standing on a table in the room for in-school suspensions. He had braced his front hooves against the wall and was eating the posters.

We stood in the cold, waiting an hour more for them to catch Number Two, but Number Two was never found, despite a thorough search. The decision was made to let us back inside, but we were instructed to travel in pairs for the remainder of the day. The teachers rushed us from class to class and made us eat lunch at our desks so we could all get back on schedule.

When the final bell rang, I knew Mom would be waiting in the carpool line. I hoped she hadn't heard about the goats. She didn't need anything else to worry about.

Billy brushed past me, heading toward a silver pickup. Mr. Reeves was watching him from a distance, a notepad open and pen in hand.

"Hey!" I called.

Billy stopped and turned back. When he saw me, he grinned like he had waited all day to talk to me.

Mr. Reeves made a note. I had never been in his notes before.

Billy sauntered over. "I guess I'm still here."

"Where else would you be?" I asked.

He cast a glance at Mr. Reeves, but didn't answer me.

"You dropped something in the library," I said, and passed the picture to Billy facedown, like it was a secret.

Billy looked at the picture, then back at me.

My stomach flipped. I liked his eyes. I liked his *whole face.*

He ran a hand through his thick brown hair and nodded thoughtfully. I had passed yet another test I didn't even know about. He leaned in but I pulled back, terrified that he might try to kiss me. I didn't know how those things worked. He stepped closer and tried again.

"Can you keep a secret?" he whispered, his breath tickling my ear.

"Yes," I said. I sounded like a dork, and not just because of my one-syllable answer.

He took a breath, then whispered again. "There was no Number Two." He pulled back to watch my reaction as I figured out what that meant.

My mouth fell open.

"Mr. Reeves made me clean the bathrooms yesterday during detention, even though I told him I wasn't the one who sent the email, but he said—"

I was frowning, so Billy backtracked. "Apparently, after my detention in the computer lab, the sixth graders all received emails from the school that said they had to dissect a human head in science class. If they refused, they'd be held back a year. Parents were furious. Mr. Reeves said cleaning someone else's mess would teach me not to make my own. But I'm glad I didn't get caught today."

"Because you would have been expelled," I said, trying not to laugh with Mr. Reeves watching.

"Because I wouldn't get to see what happens next."

Mom tore the grocery list in half. I took the bottom portion and she took the top before we both checked our watches. It was our usual grocery store challenge: We each had to get an equal number of items, at the best price, and then meet back at the registers. Whoever got there first and scored the best deal controlled the TV remote after dinner.

Tonight's grocery challenge was a spaghetti dinner. I had to find pasta, sauce, and bread. Mom was going to hit the produce department and get everything to create an epic salad. Frankly, I think she decided to lose the contest just to cheer me up. Pasta was shelved next to the sauce, so I had a clear advantage. Plus, I was kind of squeamish about the produce department. You had to touch everything and sometimes even smell it. It always felt inappropriate to do that in public.

Six minutes later, I was waiting at the registers. The produce department was to the left, around the corner from the pharmacy. Mom didn't emerge. I shifted my weight and worked out my plan. Since I was going to control the remote, we would watch a short show, and then I'd make an excuse to head to bed early and read.

I had a very particular book in mind. I was pretty sure it was safe to explore it, and I wanted to know what else was in there.

When Mom still didn't come around the corner, I groaned and went to find her. She was spoiling my victory, but at least we wouldn't watch any boring British dramas tonight. Turning the corner, I spied her talking to a woman wearing yoga pants and a pullover, as if she had just left the gym. She had long blond hair swept into a perfect ponytail, like a model on a magazine cover.

"Mom!" I called, and took a step toward them.

The woman standing next to my mom turned around, and a dark smile slowly spread across her face. It was the woman from the counselor's office. My breath caught in my throat.

"Sofia, be there in a sec," Mom called. "I'm just talking to someone."

I moved closer. The woman stood between us.

"Your mother and I were just talking about all the difficult struggles that girls your age must face. It's so important for us moms to know how to support our girls."

She placed an odd emphasis on the word "our." I nodded but said nothing. Mom put a red onion in her basket and stuck out her hand to the woman.

"Again, it was lovely to meet you. Thank you for your advice."

"Well, I hope I didn't overstep my bounds," the woman

replied in her rich, soothing voice. "I guess I just know from experience that once the wrong door gets opened, it can take forever to shut."

At the registers, when I was sure the woman wasn't following us, I grabbed Mom's arm.

"What advice did that woman give you?"

Mom shrugged slightly. "Just how important it is that girls your age feel like they fit in. Being the odd girl out is a sign of trouble, she said. She's right about one thing: this is a hard age."

I focused on emptying my basket for the cashier. The advice didn't sound sinister. But then, I didn't get the sense that woman was a fairy godmother.

"Yeah, but, Mom," I said, carefully placing my last item, the jar of spaghetti sauce, on the belt. "I just don't fit in. I've tried. Does that mean I'm headed for trouble?"

"Not unless you count my cooking as trouble." Mom shook her head and set her bag of lettuce on the belt. "And you fit in just fine."

I shrugged like I was debating that, and she smiled at me.

"You know what's weird?" Mom asked a minute later. "She said she just got out of a spin class, but she wasn't sweaty at all."

I glanced behind me with a frown.

"Some women are just perfect," Mom sighed. The cashier handed her the receipt and Mom tucked it neatly into her wallet. She had more receipts than money.

The television switched on downstairs. Mom was watching the news while she did the dishes. The loud clanks and clinks were accented by a man's deep, authoritative voice. The only man's voice we ever heard inside these walls came from the TV. I wished Mom would get married. But she had survived two broken hearts, so even though I wanted a dad, I never pressured her to risk a third heartbreak. Sometimes hiding what I felt seemed like the only way to show that I loved her.

Mom didn't like to talk about my dad. He left when he found out she was pregnant with me. Mom said it was a complicated situation and he wasn't ready to be a dad, so she offered him a deal: he never had to pay child support if he relinquished all parental rights in the divorce. He took it.

Then, when I was in third grade, my mom was engaged to the man of her dreams. He was going to be my first real father. But four weeks before the wedding, he was killed in a motorcycle accident. Mom's wedding dress hung in her closet for a year before she finally gave it away. I wish there were a ribbon for people who survived broken hearts. I'd wear one for my mom. I was thirteen now, and maybe she thought it was too late for us both to have a happily-ever-after as a family, but I still wanted her to have one.

I opened my closet door and didn't see the book. Panicking, I looked in each corner, then around the room. I knew Mom hadn't moved it when she hung my laundry up. She would have asked me about it. Finally, I bent down and peeked under my bed. The book sat in the shadows. It looked like it had hidden itself.

I pulled back, surprised. But if that was what it had done,

that was a good thing. Keeping the book hidden was one thing I didn't have to worry about. If it was real, which it wasn't, exactly.

Definitely.

Maybe.

I sat on the edge of the bed, reached for the book, and tried to pull it out, but my body had the muscle tone of a wet noodle. I grunted and tried two more times before I was able to get the thing into my lap.

I opened the book and flipped past the dedication. On the left side of the next page was a picture of a young girl with long white hair wearing a golden yellow dress. The girl stood in a room with a wooden floor and a window with bars on it, like a prison. In her hands she clutched a bottle. I couldn't tell if it was supposed to be poison or medicine. At her feet crouched a strange creature with long white teeth, red eyes, and floppy dog ears. It had lizard feet and a dragon's sharp, pointed tail. I didn't understand what the picture meant. The lines were delicate and exact. Someone must have spent hours making it.

Around the edges of the picture were gold and blue swirls, with tiny scrolls of leaves and ocean waves. I ran a finger over the picture. It had a slight texture—not bumpy, like an oil painting, but wavy and just a little warped, like paper that's been wet, then dried. And it was definitely paper of some kind, not leather.

On the opposite page was a similar frame of blue and gold, but it had a giant eye staring right at me, front and center. I didn't like that.

I turned the page.

The next one was blank except for two words in an old, fancy script, each letter fat and thick, with blurs of ink around the edges.

Leaning down to look more closely, I read:

Welcome, Sofia.

I slammed the book closed. The freaky girl from the hospital must have written that before she gave it to me.

No, that was impossible. She didn't know my name.

Then it had to be the creepy counselor who had warned me not to throw my life away for a book, because she *did* know my name. But how? She wasn't a real counselor. And how would she have gotten access to the book or know I would open it?

I started to feel that irresistible temptation to do what I knew I shouldn't, like digging a fingernail under the edge of a scab.

I opened the book and flipped right back to the same page. It was blank.

As I continued to stare in confusion, tiny scratches appeared, like someone was trapped inside an Etch A Sketch. I covered my mouth with one hand and watched.

Whoever or whatever it was scratched out one letter at a time. It was torture, guessing what the letter would be, waiting for each letter to be complete, guessing at the word it would make. A question formed.

Shall we begin?

I jerked back and blinked to clear my vision. When I opened my eyes again, the four words were still there. This was really happening.

The newscaster's voice floated up the stairs. *"Tonight, we look into the threat of meningitis in schools: what you can do to keep your child safe."*

Mom would be glued to the television.

I stared at the book. Who was talking to me? And how were they doing it? Was I supposed to write my answer? And what were we going to begin?

"I don't exactly know . . . ," I said. "I mean, I've never talked through a book. I'm not exactly sure how this works."

Immediately the words were rubbed away, one by one, fast. Someone was magically erasing them. Tiny scratches appeared in their place, faster now, like someone on the other side was excited. I watched, half frozen with disbelief.

Neither am I.

I am trapped, alone, between the realms of life and afterlife. This book is my window between our worlds.

I can only speak through these pages.

I am human, even now, and am bound by human limitations.

I can hear what you say and watch what you do, wherever you are. But I cannot read your mind, and I do not know the future. However, I do—

"Seriously? You can hear me?" I gasped, leaning forward. "I'm talking to a *person*?"

You interrupted me.

"Sorry," I murmured. It was probably an adult.

There are many believers but only one Guardian. Though the truth speaks to everyone who listens, I myself can only speak to the one who holds this book. The Guardian has almost always been a child, because children are not often suspected of wielding great power. But know this: The power is not in the book. The power is in you, and in your choices.

Please understand: this is life and death. Do everything I say, exactly as I say. No Guardian who obeyed me has died of her injuries. No matter what happens, trust me. I have walked countless roads and seen the rise and fall of many empires.

When no more words appeared, I cleared my throat. "May I ask a question now?" I said. The page remained blank. I assumed the answer was yes.

"The girl who gave me the book—is she okay? What happened to her?"

Her name is Claire, and she is well. Claire did not want this life. She is not strong like we are.

"Who are you?" I whispered.

The last student of the Master of Them That Know, Aristotle. My name is Xeno.

"Xeno, if that were really true, you'd be dead by now," I said.

NOT DEAD

"Okay, trapped," I answered. "Between two worlds. And you're talking to me through a book, a book about monsters and someone called a Guardian. Xeno, if that's even your real name, I don't believe you."

I did not ask you to believe. I asked you to trust. Will you do that and help me protect this last, great secret?

Xeno thought I could guard a last, great secret? My mom couldn't even leave me alone with an open bag of potato chips. Stalling for time before I answered, I glanced around my room, at the pockmarked walls, at the closet full of clothes to hide what made me different, and I felt that aching hole in my heart from missing my best friend even though I had to act like I didn't. I was pretty good at keeping secrets, but mine all sucked.

Maybe I needed a new secret. I was so tired of being me. Reading and answering this book was like playing a game of dress-up. Xeno and I were pretending. He was offering me the chance to be someone else. None of this was real.

And I hated real.

"I'd love to," I said.

Excellent.

The book was lost for generations and has only recently returned to the light. I am anxious to begin. Many friends have wandered and been lost.

If you are ready, press your hand to the page.

So far, this was interesting. A little scary, maybe, but a definite improvement over staring at my blank walls.

I pressed my palm flat against the page. It was soft and warm, like an animal's belly. The black letters beneath my palm pressed back against my hand. I could feel their ridges and sharp lines tickling me. Then the letters turned a warm and deep gold color, seeping together in one puddle that stretched itself into a long thin line and surrounded my hand with the outline of a much bigger hand. It was a man's hand holding mine, and it radiated heat.

In the distance, a shrill scream split through the night air. Animals all over the neighborhood reacted, dogs barking madly and cats screeching as if they'd seen an enemy. But softer, farther away still, a different creature sang. It was not a song with notes of growls or cries, but a song in a language of long ago, like something brought up from the ocean floor.

My heart seemed to expand and open. Something in my bones remembered this song, as if this were music I had made when I took my first breath as a newborn. For the very first time, I heard the world as I was meant to.

The television went quiet downstairs. Mom would be coming up for bed. I shut the book with a sharp snap. Musty air swirled up at my face from between the pages. Something familiar was in that smell again. Something warm and salty and . . . It reminded me of the way Alexis's dad smelled when he hugged me after a track meet. Comforting and loving. What was happening to me?

I heard Mom's footsteps on the stairs. I only had a split second left before I needed to hide the book. I flipped it back open.

"But wait . . . who's the Guardian?" I whispered.

YOU ARE.

SEVEN

Thursday, February 27

I ate breakfast while Mom pouted, loading our dishes into the dishwasher with a lot of unnecessary clanging and banging.

"Mom—" I tried again.

"You didn't want to talk last night. You just rushed upstairs to your room, and every time I checked on you, you were just sitting there in the dark and you wouldn't let me come in. Did I do something? Is there a reason you suddenly need to be alone?"

I opened my mouth to answer but nothing came out. *Yes,* I wanted to say, but that would hurt her, and if I tried to explain, she'd think I was having emotional problems like the doctors warned.

They couldn't have prepared either of us for this. I had looked up the word "paranormal" at school, and it meant life outside the normal senses, so it was a perfect description. I was dealing with something I couldn't explain. I had tried to stay awake last night so I could open the book once she fell asleep, because there was so much to ask and learn and school sure wouldn't cover any of it.

The last thing I remembered was hiding the book under my pillow when I heard Mom coming down the hall to check on me again. I had nodded off, still fully clothed.

A glass shattered when she slammed it into the rack. She didn't stop but just reached for the next one.

"I still get tired," I said. "And I need time to think."

"If something is going on, you can talk to me about it. You know you can tell me anything."

I could, but I didn't. I always wanted to tell her everything, but there were so many little things, overheard comments and embarrassing moments and daily hassles that I kept to myself. Changing for gym class had embarrassed me in sixth grade so badly, but Mom thought it was no big deal. I thought it sucked. Stripping to your underwear in front of someone like Candy, who was perfect, was humiliating. One time, Candy had brought the whole changing room to a stop when she pointed out my underwear.

"Sofia, are you seriously still wearing underwear with pictures on it?"

I had on my Polly Pocket panties I bought in fifth grade. They weren't cool even when I bought them, but they were on clearance and Mom loved a bargain. They had stretched out a lot, but they still fit, and I hadn't found anything else clean in the laundry that morning.

In sixth grade, girls are not supposed to wear underwear with cartoon characters on it. No one had told me. Candy made sure I knew. She was special that way.

I started changing in the bathroom stalls to avoid being seen.

So if Mom didn't understand some issues about ordinary life, even the stuff that happened last year, how could I explain this?

Fresh tears made my throat tighten, and I sniffed to chase them away.

Mom heard me and lowered her head, still holding an empty coffee mug. She didn't set it down when I walked over to her. I could tell she was still upset that I hadn't wanted to talk to her last night. I took the mug and set it in the sink, then picked up her arms, wrapping them around my waist. I rested my head on her chest.

"Are you angry with me?" she whispered. "I worry that we're not communicating."

"What? No."

She pushed me back so she could see my face.

I raised my head and kissed her on the cheek. "You wanted to get back to normal, right? Well, I'm a moody, difficult teenager. That's normal."

She rolled her eyes in mock dismay. My attempt at humor had worked.

"Let's get moving," she said. "Don't want to be late for school."

Grateful for the out, I went upstairs, but before I reached the top I glanced back to be sure she wasn't watching. It was hard to move my prosthetic leg like a real one when going up the stairs. I had to angle my torso sharply to one side and swing the prosthesis up.

When I got to my room, I dumped my book bag onto the bedspread before I packed it for the day. It was too heavy to drag around with all the books from the media center. I chose three to keep in my backpack for now and put the rest in a pile on the floor next to my bed.

A business card fell out as I picked up the books.

Hamby Animal Clinic
Andy Hamby, DVM
After-Hours Emergencies Accepted
Call Our Home Number at . . .

Billy must have slipped that into my bag while we were in the library.

I remembered seeing a new vet clinic open really close to our house. Billy had told Ms. Hochness the truth; his dad really was a vet. I suspected that was where Billy had gotten the goats.

Something scratched at my window.

The media center books about monsters were spread out on my bed. I hadn't had a chance to read them yet. I froze, glancing between them and the window. Could a monster really be out there?

Could they be real?

Not a chance. People imagine monsters, that's all.

My pillow began to glow. I guessed Xeno wanted to tell me something.

Wind rattled my window. I glanced at it, hoping I was wrong about the noise. A patch of wet fog grew on the other side of the glass. Something big had just exhaled.

I yanked Xeno's book out and turned my back to the window, feeling dizzy, like I was standing on a very high ledge looking down.

I flipped the book to the blank page where words had appeared last night. How did this work, exactly? "What's outside my window?" I asked.

Throw away those worthless books! Will I not reveal all?

I glanced at the books on my bed, then back at the window. "I just needed more information to—"

Once, I did not believe in monsters either. But the Master sent me into new lands to document every creature I found. And I found creatures beyond explanation. If I had not seen them myself, I would not have believed.

You must see them for yourself too.

A shock like the touch of cold metal shot up my spine. I wasn't ready. I thought I was, but I wasn't. It was just like the moment when they took the bandages off my stump for the first time.

Outside my window, something huffed loudly. It sounded impatient.

"Wait!" I said.

I heard a clacking like rapid-fire gunshots or teeth being gnashed in frustration.

"You haven't even told me what a Guardian is," I pointed out to Xeno. "Or does."

I can only show you what is out there, beyond your window. How you respond determines who you are. When you know that, you will also know what you must do.

The thing outside scratched at my window again. It sounded like it was testing the glass, looking for a weakness.

I heard Mom coming up the stairs.

I closed the book and shoved it under my pillow. "Oh my gosh!" I whispered. "School! I have to go to school. I can't do this right now."

Mom paused outside my room and knocked on the frame of my door. "Ten minutes, kiddo." Then she hustled down the hall toward her bedroom. Right before we left the house, she always ironed her clothes, then brushed her teeth with an electric toothbrush that was so loud and sucked up so much energy that I think it had been banned in thirteen countries.

My window slid open, just a notch.

I leaped toward it to clamp it back down, but my arm bumped the lamp shade on my nightstand, knocking it over. It tipped and fell straight to the floor, the lightbulb shattering into tiny milk-colored shards across my carpet.

I listened for my mom, but she didn't call my name. She hadn't heard anything from her bedroom.

My hands rested on the windowsill as my breath thundered in my ears.

Two red eyes glowed in the morning's darkness, framed by the rising sun. My window continued to slide open in tiny, jerky movements.

Veins instantly pinched tight all over my body, shocked by a burst of adrenaline. Huge, bumpy gray fingers slid through the opening. This was real. Xeno was real.

Monsters were real.

A hand followed, a massive square hand with fingers thick as corn dogs. The hand smeared a gray paste against the white wood trim. The hand turned, palm up, and raised the window the rest of the way. The sunrise on the horizon made a soft pink glow.

I didn't want to look. The nurses had said it wouldn't be scary the first time I saw my mutilated leg, but it was.

It was.

I looked up and saw two red eyes burning brightly, watching me frozen and alone.

The window was completely open.

I would never be able to undo this moment.

The monster growled, a gritty sound, like it had gargled rocks. It came through the window all at once, an enormous gray creature, so tall it had to stoop to avoid hitting its head on my ceiling. Its skin glistened like wet clay, and its body was lumpy with mounds of strange flesh bulging out in odd places. It looked like a rough, unfinished sculpture, as if the beautiful part was yet to be revealed, still hidden beneath all the clay.

Goose bumps pricked my skin. The awe of seeing a creature so bizarre, so *monstrous* and strange, and the shock of standing in the same room, breathing the same air, made my knees go weak. We were *both* real, living in the same world, mangled girl and monster. How was that possible?

The creature had an enormous square head with strange symbols written across the forehead and hollow places gouged out for its eyes. It didn't have eyeballs, just a dark hole in the clay, with a red fire burning inside. Where lips should have been, a gray slash created two lips stretched so thin they were almost white. The lips revealed two rows of giant teeth, each tooth the size of a Post-it note. The creature watched me, cocking its head to one side, as if I were the curiosity.

Tears formed in my eyes. I carried too many secrets in my ordinary, everyday life. I couldn't handle one more. Why had I agreed to this? I would never be able to tell anyone what I had seen. This secret would make me lonelier than ever.

It growled again and I grimaced. The monster reached its hand out to me as if to reassure me, but I shrank back. Its skin looked wet and dirty and I didn't want to touch it.

Huge tears like marbles welled in the monster's dark eyes and fell. They rolled across my carpet and burst like water balloons. Its chin trembled, and with a pitiful cry, it jumped out the window.

From my mother's bathroom I heard the whir of her electric toothbrush at full speed.

I swallowed again and breathed through my mouth, slow and steady. Every nerve in my body was on fire.

I had to shut my window and lock it. That thing was still out there. It might come back and I wasn't ready for this. I didn't want this secret.

I leaned forward to grab my nightstand for support, and a slurping noise caught my attention. It was a sound like a toddler sucking its thumb. I looked down and saw the monster, its fingers in its mouth, curled up in a ball, rocking itself right there in our shrubbery. It reached up to wipe the tears streaming down its face, then popped its fingers back in its mouth.

I started to say something, on instinct. I had hurt its feelings and I was supposed to be sorry, but I wanted to slam the window shut. It was a freaking *monster.* How did it expect me to react? Ten minutes ago I hadn't even believed they were real, and now I wished they weren't.

It looked up at me just then. Anger, pain, and sorrow emanated from its fiery red eyes. I had the unmistakable feeling I was seeing myself through them. *I* was the monster. I had hurt something because it was strange and different and ugly.

"How you respond determines who you are." Xeno's words came back to me. I felt sick.

"I'm sorry," I whispered. I really was. "I'm sorry I hurt your feelings."

The monster scowled at me and ran away through the bushes. I lost sight of it as Mom called my name. It was time to get in the car.

The first bell had just rung when Billy approached me in the hall.

"Whoa, didn't you sleep last night?" he asked, falling into step beside me. "You look tired."

I kept moving so he wouldn't know how much he was embarrassing me. I wanted to be ignored, but he stayed as close as an IV pole.

"What's wrong?" he asked. I kept walking. There was no way to answer that question.

"Are you sick?"

My heart raced as sweat broke out on my upper lip. In the hospital, a nurse would have rushed in to check my vitals at this point. Diagnosis? I think I had a crush. Plus I was still reeling from an encounter with something I shouldn't have seen and would never forget. My body felt all wrong, like my brain had to rewire itself after this morning to make room for the new information and it didn't have the energy to remind me of how to move properly.

I didn't know how to act around Billy. He was so smart and quick that anything I said sounded stupid. In the movies, the pretty girls said cute stuff and flung their hair around. I had bristles. If I swung my head, he might lose an eye.

"Look, I love that you're as fierce as I am," Billy added, "and I thought that was why we were going to be friends. But friends *talk*." He got in front of me and stopped, forcing me to as well.

He thought I was fierce? Because of an answer I wrote on a test? I wrote that because I felt sorry for myself. It was not exactly a battle cry.

I had to get to class. "I have a lot on my mind." I chose my first words carefully; then my mouth picked up speed. "And I didn't sleep well last night. I feel half dead, like a zombie."

"Don't be a pessimist," he said. "Zombies aren't half dead. They're half alive."

I grinned, and he moved back to my side. We resumed the walk to class, and a couple of girls said hi to me, loudly, while they smiled at Billy.

We passed Alexis, who stood at her locker getting a book out for homeroom. She watched us, her forehead wrinkling like when she didn't understand a question. How could I explain my friendship with Billy? Every girl flirted with him, but I didn't. Alexis knew that wasn't my style. When it came to guys, I had no style. So what was I doing walking down the hall with the best-looking guy in our grade? She might even be wondering if he was the reason I wasn't talking to her.

"So the dance Candy talked about?" Billy asked. "Will it be any good?"

I had to change the subject or be forced to admit I hadn't been to one yet. Our whole school district had a winter dance every year, even for the elementary kids. No one had ever asked me, and I didn't have the courage to go alone. Alexis hated wearing dresses—she said they made it more obvious that she had the curves of a toothpick—so it wasn't her idea of a fun night either.

"Well . . . ," I murmured.

What if Billy asked me to go? My stomach bounced down to my knees and back up. How would I know if he meant as friends or as a date? He paused, looking at me, obviously waiting for a complete sentence.

I ducked into the girls' restroom.

Once inside, I pushed the door closed and turned. Candy was there, looking at herself in the mirror. And beyond her stood the strange woman with light blue-gray eyes and blond hair. She was wearing a long black gown of a style I'd only seen in history books. The sleeves of the gown moved as if an imaginary breeze were ruffling them.

A grim smile slowly curled her lips as she glided forward, glancing from Candy to me. Clearly Candy had no idea she was there. My body jerked back, reacting before my brain could process what I was seeing, or imagining. It was the strangest feeling, like being pulled apart, my inside and outside working at different speeds. I reached out to warn Candy, my face still turned up toward the specter hovering between us.

Then her image dissolved into smoke, disappearing through the cracks of the door and out into the hallway.

"That's weird. I was just thinking about you," Candy said. She glanced at me, then went back to brushing her long straight hair in sweeping, elegant strokes, as if she hadn't noticed anything at all. Of course she hadn't. I was the only one seeing things these days. Just when I thought being the odd girl out couldn't get any lonelier. I realized my hand was still extended toward her and I dropped it to my side.

Even under the fluorescent lights of the bathroom, her hair was gorgeous, flowing under the brush like liquid.

I wanted my old hair back so badly. When Candy looked in the mirror, did she see how beautiful she was? Did perfect-looking people *feel* perfect? I almost started to ask. It would be weird if being perfect and feeling perfect weren't the same thing at all. Still, I kept my distance to avoid seeing our reflections side by side in the mirror.

Every stall door was closed, but there was no sound in the restroom except the soft whish of the brush through her hair. I refused to sit in a stall with her in here, so I pretended I needed to wash my hands.

Candy caught me stealing another glance. She shrugged as she sighed. "You're giving me the silent treatment, aren't you? Is it because of what Natalie said?"

The paper towels were on her side of the sink, so I either needed to reach over for them or walk around her. Out of the corner of my eye, I glimpsed something else in the mirror. Two brown scaly legs with claws on each toe began to slowly descend to the floor inside a stall, as if a monster had been crouched on a toilet the whole time I had been in here.

I swallowed and forced myself to breathe. Blood pounded through my veins like a freight train. I had never seen a monster at school before. Did that mean they were following me, or had they been here all along and I was only now able to see them?

Candy set her brush down with a loud clank and faced me. I glanced back at the stall as she cleared her voice, expecting me to pay attention. "Natalie isn't the brightest girl, but she didn't mean to hurt your feelings." She reached for a paper towel and handed it to me. The monster legs slid

out from underneath the stall door, slithering soundlessly across the tile toward Candy. I noticed they were covered in bumps, not scales, with a layer of fine white feathers.

I wiped my hands and crumpled the paper towel. Chances were, the monster was here because I was the Guardian, even though I still wasn't sure what that meant. I only knew that it probably wouldn't eat me. Not that Xeno had promised they wouldn't, but it was a hopeful theory. That didn't exempt Candy. I needed to get her out of here. I started to tell her we both had to go, when she interrupted me.

"Just listen." Candy rested her hand on my arm. Surprisingly, her skin was warm. I had assumed she was cold-blooded, like all reptiles.

"I know we've never been friends. But don't judge me."

I picked her hand off of me and she blinked. "We should get to class," I said. One claw scraped lightly against the tile floor right next to Candy's foot. She didn't notice. I froze, not knowing what it was going to do next.

She crossed her arms. "I know you don't like me because you think I'm superficial."

One leg extended even farther, like the monster had elastic limbs. It began slipping around the back of Candy's legs.

"Maybe I just know something you don't." She leaned forward as if she was about to spill a major secret. "Girls are judged for our looks in a way that boys aren't." She waited for me to agree, one eyebrow raised.

I nodded.

"Girls who make an effort get treated better. Life is easier for them. So being pretty is really more like being smart."

"Candy, I—"

"No! Don't argue." She met my eyes with an intense gaze. "You may not like me, but at least I won't lie to you. This is an ugly thing to say, but the truth is, life hurts less when you look good and you fit in with everyone. And, Sofia, I can't help but think that you've had enough pain already."

She moved her hand to rest on my shoulder. "The point is, you have such potential if you would just try. Let me help you."

The toilet flushed and we both jumped. The monster's two legs were sucked backward toward the bowl and disappeared.

Candy moved to the stall and used her fist to bang the door open. It was empty. The red light on the automatic toilet flashed off and on. "I hate those things," she muttered. "They always flush without any warning."

I exhaled in relief, although I felt a pang of guilt for whatever monster had just gotten unexpectedly sucked away. Monsters were old and automatic flushing toilets were new.

"Candy, we better get to class. The bell is going to ring any minute," I said.

She looked annoyed that I hadn't fallen at her feet in gratitude. "You don't even want to talk about this?"

I shook my head. I didn't know if that monster could swim. He might be back. "You might get in trouble if you're late," I reminded her. "You're on the student council. The teachers don't mind if I'm late."

"Exactly!" she said. "Because everyone feels sorry for you. But that won't last forever. You have to decide who you want to be before it's too late. You'll either go back to being the sad girl without a lot of friends, or you can use this opportunity to become everything you ever wanted to be. The whole school would get behind you! You have to decide what you want, and if you do want to change, you'll need a plan. You'll need me."

I grabbed for the door, biting my lip so I wouldn't cry. The door swung open, hard. Someone on the other side pushed as I pulled. I fell backward and landed on my rear end. Alexis stood over me, looking horrified upon seeing what she had done. Billy peeked over her shoulder. He must have been waiting for me.

Candy moved first. She grabbed me from behind, lifting me from under my shoulders, and helped me to my feet.

"I thought you two were supposed to be friends," she snapped at Alexis. Alexis inhaled like she was about to explode.

"No one here is my friend, okay?" I said. It came out all wrong. Alexis winced as if I had slapped her. Billy frowned, as if I had hurt him too.

"Think about my offer," Candy said. Then she brushed past the three of us on her way to class. "I've already started a list of things you'll need to do."

I didn't know what else to say, so I just followed her. It was the right direction to walk but felt like the wrong way to go.

I dropped my book bag on the floor when I got to the kitchen. Mom was right behind me, and picked up one of the books that fell out.

"Ewww," she said, staring at the book cover. Mom wrinkled her nose like she smelled something rotten. On the cover was a snarling monster with a body hanging limp from its jaws. Before I could stop her, she dug out my other assorted titles. I had planned on returning them all, since Xeno thought they were useless.

"I didn't even read them," I said, trying to grab the book from her hands. She lifted her hand higher, staring at me with a frown.

"Well, good, because this is not appropriate reading material," she said. "Besides, I don't want you worried about things that aren't even real."

"Why is everyone on my case today?" I groaned. *And who knows what's real, anyway?* I wanted to shout.

Mom stared at me in silence for a long moment before she replied. "I am not 'everyone.' I am your mother." She suddenly sounded tired. "And if there's something going on, we need to talk about it this weekend, okay?"

I had forgotten it was a long weekend, since tomorrow was a teacher in-service day. Normally I'd have been excited about relaxing and watching TV for three whole days, but I was heartsore from a bad day at school; plus I was nervous about what the weekend would bring. All I seemed to do was accidentally hurt people's feelings. Maybe monsters were unsafe, but apparently, so was I.

EIGHT

Forty minutes later, Mom moved to answer the doorbell when the pizza arrived. "Let me get it," I offered. "You relax."

I wanted her to think I was trying to make up for being moody, but in reality I had to make sure it wasn't a monster ringing the doorbell. I still had no idea how this Guardian thing worked. I needed to get upstairs as fast as I could without hurting Mom's feelings and figure all this out, because maybe next time there wouldn't be an automatic toilet flush to save me.

I paid the guy and carried the pizza into the kitchen while Mom stood in front of the TV. She had been searching to find a movie for us to watch but was transfixed by a commercial. As she watched, text rolled across the screen like credits after a film, listing every dangerous germ and virus that lives in the average home. The only defense was a new disinfectant conveniently priced at $29.95.

"Mom, seriously," I said. She worried all the time about me getting sick. More than once I'd caught her in the store spraying Lysol in the air and sniffing it. I worried she would make me use that instead of perfume.

She snapped off the TV and came into the kitchen to set out paper plates and napkins.

"How's Alexis?" she asked, then cleared her throat. I could tell the commercial had upset her.

I rummaged in the spice cabinet, glad to have my back to her. "Fine." When I found the red pepper flakes, I turned around and tried to think of a way to change the subject.

"I told you she was welcome to come over," Mom said, her voice sounding a little too bright. She was scared about my health, but I knew she really wanted my life to go back to the way it was, even if that meant catching colds and stomach bugs from other kids.

"She's busy with track," I replied, hoping Mom would make the connection. Alexis still had her normal life, and I no longer fit into it.

"You could call her anyway," Mom said.

She was not going to let this go. She was going to keep asking questions about Alexis, because she thought I needed a gentle push to talk about it. I didn't need a gentle push. That was like giving a nervous woman on a building ledge a gentle push to get the conversation going.

Some things are hard to explain, especially to your mom. And with my mom and me being so close, I shouldn't have had to explain anything at all. But it was just the opposite.

Maybe I just sucked at relationships.

"Can I eat later?" I asked. "I'm not that hungry. I just want to go upstairs and rest."

I tried not to look her in the eye as I said it.

"Should I wait for you?" Mom asked.

"No," I said softly.

But as hard as I resisted, I finally looked up and saw the hurt. There was a wall between us. I walked upstairs slowly, half hoping she would insist I stay downstairs and talk, but she didn't. I had put the wall up, so she was waiting for me to pull it down. I needed to find a way to do that, but it's hard to pull down a wall when you're not sure what needs to remain protected. Xeno and his monsters were strangely like chemo. I had agreed to be the Guardian, but I hadn't expected all these other problems.

In cancer centers, there are two versions of the word "unexpected." You can have an unexpected benefit, and that's wonderful, but most people get unexpected outcomes, and those are all different and usually bad. I still didn't know which version of "unexpected" Xeno's book and his monsters were. But he had asked my permission before we began. Since last October, my world had been defined by one word, and it wasn't cancer. It was "no."

Alone in the dark, I didn't really want to open his book. Monsters were the strangest, scariest, ugliest things I had ever seen, and I couldn't trust myself not to hurt them. I didn't think I was going to be a good Guardian, especially if I screamed every time I saw a monster.

But being the Guardian was the first chance I'd had to say yes to anything. Since my diagnosis, the whole world had become one big no. I couldn't walk unassisted, I had no appetite, no energy, and no guarantees about the future. Whatever I wanted, whatever I would normally do, the answer was no.

I had said yes to Xeno for selfish reasons, for a chance to escape, but the kick in the pants was that being the Guardian just brought me right back to the basic problem.

Me.

Downstairs, the heater turned on. Warm air blew from the vent over my bed, but I was still cold when it tickled the hair on my arms. I pulled the bedspread up around me and scooted down under the covers.

Dogs all over the neighborhood began to bark with a sudden urgency. Just like the other night. Had I never noticed them before, or did I now hear animals in a powerful new way?

I reached out for my lamp but then remembered the bulb had broken. Two red eyes were staring at me through the window.

It was back. My eyes adjusted to the darkness around him. In the soft moonlight, I could see the huge square outline of his head, with a face like cement that had hardened in a thick puddle, rough and uneven. The eyes were like two huge dark caves.

We just stared at each other.

He had tears streaming down his face. Again. One huge tear after the other as his breath fogged up the window.

Was he still upset about my reaction when I first saw him? There wasn't anything I could do except try to apologize again. Under my bed, the book began to glow.

If he had the courage to come back, I should find the courage to try one more time, I thought. I owed him that. I opened the window.

Like a frightened, badly scolded child, the monster crawled into my room and stood, his head hanging low.

The book's light grew brighter.

A stray snowflake swirled in through the open window. The monster and I watched it flutter in the space between us. It landed softly on the carpet, a hint of sparkle in the moonlight. The monster reached out with one foot, each of his toes as big as my fist. He nudged the snowflake. His eyes were wide with wonder, like the snowflake was a small miracle. In Atlanta, snow was always a miracle, so I grinned, but then pressed my lips together so he wouldn't think I was teasing him.

I pointed to the night sky.

It whirled with snowflakes, each one falling and landing in a dark place, like a forgotten star.

The monster stared, then looked back at the snowflake between us. I wondered why he would think that just one was special. The whole neighborhood was full of them. Why care about a single snowflake when there were thousands, maybe millions more?

The snowflake melted into the carpet and disappeared. The monster inhaled sharply, witnessing this magic. Its chin began to tremble, like a child who had lost his balloon to the wind.

I pointed to the sky again.

He stepped toward me and one huge arm wrapped itself

around my waist. His flesh was warm and hard, like a mug just out of the dishwasher. Before I could scream, he was climbing out the window. I clung to his massive body, my arms barely able to span his chest. He climbed down the side of our house like it was as easy as walking. With two great steps that shook my body, we stood under the streetlight by my house. Snow fell all around us, twinkling like fairy lights. He set me down and nodded like a child waiting for me to open a present.

I didn't move. It was so quiet. When the neighborhood kids woke up to snow, they'd go nuts. It never snowed this much here. The kids would be dizzy with the realization that impossible things still happened in the world. They had not yet learned to hate the unexpected.

The monster extended his enormous hand, palm up, catching a snowflake to give me. I opened mine and cupped them, trying to catch more. He sucked in his breath, delighted. He was so goofy I couldn't help but laugh. Maybe I could learn to love the world again too.

"Watch this," I whispered. Tilting my head back, I opened my mouth wide and stuck out my tongue. Snowflakes swirled around my face, landing on my lashes and falling into my mouth.

He tried it, but his mouth was just a black hole. Still, after swallowing at least a dozen, he stamped his feet in pleasure. I wrapped my arms around my body; the cold had started to hurt me. Without a sound, he wrapped an arm around me and we climbed back through my window.

I didn't have any magic, but he did. And he didn't just have magic; he saw it too, in the simplest, most ordinary things. I had never believed in monsters, but now I realized it wasn't just monsters I needed to believe in. I needed to believe in the extraordinary. This monster believed in a world that still had a little bibbidi-bobbidi-boo in its back pocket.

Inside my room, I shook off the snow, still smiling, then reached toward him to brush him off.

He shook his head.

"Why not?" I asked. The monster glanced at me, embarrassed, before hanging his head again. Then he turned, slowly. At first I was afraid he was going to leave, but then I understood. He wanted to show me his back. His raw red back was littered with dozens of little black-edged holes scattered all over his flesh. Each hole was no bigger than a piece of confetti.

Biting my lip for courage, I touched one of the holes. The monster whimpered. He had been so kind to me, and I hadn't even known he was in pain. He wasn't just strong in his body. He had a strong heart.

"I know what these are," I whispered.

I turned the monster around to face me. "You were shot, weren't you? Was it—a shotgun? A pellet gun?"

The monster opened its mouth and the saddest sound I have ever heard, the sound of every pain, of all pain, the pain of being alive and the pain of wishing you were dead, poured out.

"I know," I whispered.

I did.

I held my breath. Mom did not call my name. The television volume was too high for her to hear anything.

The book glowed so brightly it almost pulsed, so I dug it out from under the bed. I was moving faster than I ever had in physical therapy, but I noticed this as if from a distance. Right then, it didn't feel like I was even in my body. I heaved the book out and up in one try. It fell open to the page I needed. Elaborate edging highlighted bold black letters painted long ago. A smudged map was drawn alongside the monster's image. The names and boundaries on the map had been changed many times.

THE GOLEM

Origins: Created by a Jewish rabbi in the 1500s for defense against enemies. First documented in Prague, the largest city in the Czech Republic. Sightings now range all over the world. His forehead is marked with an ancient language and the Guardian must never touch the symbols, for they contain the mystery of creation and death.

Nature: Fiercely protective of those he loves, the Golem may be injured if humans see him and lash out in fear. If he is wounded by humans, you may use human first aid to care for his wounds. A good and kind Guardian will also do what she can for his heart too, which is the most vulnerable part of the Golem.

Of all creatures, in fact.

The page fluttered and turned over to the next. Here were more detailed notes: what he ate, where he roamed, what kinds of injuries he was prone to and how to treat them. Running my finger down the page, I found what Xeno wanted to show me:

For minor flesh wounds, do not use water. Use alcohol and be most gentle.

"Stay right here, okay?" I whispered to the Golem. "I need to get something."

He nodded and sat on my bed. It sank deep in the middle, and I hoped the frame wouldn't break. I had to move fast.

I made my way downstairs. Mom was on the couch, her face red and swollen. She saw me standing there and muted the television.

"Sad movie," she said, but I knew she was lying. Maybe she didn't tell me everything either.

"I just need something from the kitchen," I said. That's where we kept the bandages and ointments for cuts and burns. With my mom's cooking skills, the kitchen was the most dangerous room in the house.

"You hungry?" she asked. "Want some pizza?" She started to stand up and I overreacted.

"No! Just watch your movie, okay?" If she saw me getting into the first-aid kit, she would want answers. She'd demand to see the wound.

Her eyes widened and she sat back down. "Okay, then."

I promised myself I would make up for this in the morning. First, though, I had to take care of the Golem.

Once the movie was back on, I made my way to the cabinet above our mixer, where Mom kept our first-aid supplies. I grabbed a handful of bandages, Neosporin, and a pair of tweezers, stuffing them in my pocket. There was no rubbing alcohol, though, and Xeno said I needed it, but then I spied a few bottles of alcohol. The adult-beverage variety, not the kind used for first aid.

Mom rarely drank, so the bottles were full. I wasn't sure if I could use them as a substitute, and even if I could, which one? I read the labels. One hundred proof? Eighty proof? Proof of what? The labels didn't say.

"Whatcha in the mood for?" Mom chirped. I whirled around, a guilty look plastered across my face. She was standing at the kitchen counter. Her eyes narrowed when she saw which cabinet I had open.

I faked a smile. "You know. Just anything."

"You're looking at the liquor bottles?" she said, her voice deceptively flat, like a sinkhole.

"Well, obviously I'm not looking for alcohol. Why would I be looking for alcohol?"

Mom didn't reply, and I realized she was waiting for me to answer my own question. "Where do you hide the chocolate from yourself these days?"

She stared at me, her face set and blank, before she walked over and reached for the cabinet door on the opposite side of the alcohol. Inside was a new bag of chocolates.

"Busted," she said, and then laughed. The smile didn't make it to her eyes, though. They were still suspicious.

I grabbed a chocolate and pecked her on the cheek. "We'll hang out tomorrow. Promise."

I made my way back to my bedroom with a burning lump in my throat. Mom couldn't talk to me and I wouldn't talk to her, and in the middle of all this not-talking, I had to take care of an injured monster.

I sat behind Golem on the bed, my back against the wall, so I would be closer to eye level with the wounds. I had to check each little hole and remove the pellet. The Golem was quiet as I worked. I didn't want to stick the tweezers in and poke around; that would hurt. I gently pressed with my fingers on either side of the hole, hoping to ease the pellet up to the surface, where I could easily grab it with the tweezers. I did that, one pellet hole after another, until I had removed forty-three pellets and dabbed ointment on each wound.

He whimpered but I kept working, the television blaring the whole time. When I thought the pain was too much for him, I rested my hand on his shoulder and let him gather his courage. I needed some too. What made people so mean? Why would they hurt someone just for being different?

After the pellets were removed, I eased myself to sit beside him and took his hand in mine. It was like holding a big canned ham. The Golem bowed his head, unwilling to look at me. I rested my head against his shoulder and sighed, and even though I couldn't see it and he technically didn't have lips, I think he kissed the top of my head.

Then he jumped up and ran to the window, leaping into the darkness.

I hopped up and followed, sticking my head out to look for him, but he was gone. Glancing up, I saw the bright full moon above me, illuminating the street below. A woman stood under the streetlight, face turned in my direction, her long blond hair blowing in the night wind.

I ducked my head back in and shut the window, fast. The night noises grew louder—the barks and growls and howls and slithering things. I looked back out the window, but the woman was gone.

The book was open and glowing, so I turned to the blank page Xeno used for communicating. "Is that what a Guardian does? Takes care of monsters? The ones who get hurt?" I asked. The page remained blank. "Monsters need people sometimes, right?"

In truth, it is people who need monsters. How do you feel?

I chewed my lip for a second before answering. "Better, I think. It felt good to help him. And it felt good to play in the snow with him." I laughed softly, thinking about his delight in one little snowflake. "But there's a strange lady following me and there are so many questions I have for you. I have to know how everything works."

I've been alive for over two thousand years and I still don't know that. Ask me your first question.

A hundred filled my head at once. It was hard to know which to ask. How did I know which one was the most important? Mom might be coming to bed at any moment. I would run out of time before I asked everything.

"Monsters aren't like animals—your book says that. People invented them, but they aren't just stories. They're real. How is that possible?"

What is underneath you right now?

I was sitting on my bed, but didn't he know that? "Uh, my bedspread."

Your bedspread began as a thought. Someone imagined it before it came to be. The home you live in? Someone first imagined that too. Imagination made the world. Why, then, would you think that imagination couldn't make a monster too? Did you think the boundaries of imagination stop at bedspreads and buildings? Imagination is the most practical and powerful force on earth.

"But how did a monster go from being in someone's imagination to walking around on the earth?"

The entire world pulses with wonder and creation and magic. How did your bedspread go from the mind to the mill? How does the painting go from the soul to the canvas? Every one of us does some bit of magic like that every day. Do not be surprised, then, that some people can make their imagination walk out into the sun or howl under the moon. Some people perfect their magic.

"How?" I asked.

I never learned that secret. I studied what was already here, not what could be. That was what the Master asked of me.

Something still didn't make sense. "But we're frightened of monsters," I said. "Why would we make something we're scared of?"

*By creating monsters, we chose what we would be most afraid of.
We set limits to it, told it where it could live and what it would look
like. We gave fear a place of its own and we were free to enjoy our
lives once more.*

Mom turned off the television. The sudden silence made me jump. Time was running out for the night, and I had only asked four questions. There was still so much I needed to know!

"How do they find me?" I whispered urgently.

*You made a decision to love what is unlovable. They will always be
able to find you. You are a light in a dark world, Sofia. But do not
trust the darkness. Monsters are not the only things that dwell in the
shadows.*

I heard my mom on the stairs, so I closed the book, wincing. I needed more time, but it wouldn't be tonight. Mom opened my door to say good night, and I stood up to hug her. If she felt my heart pounding through my thin shirt, she didn't say anything, and so neither did I.

NINE

When I peeked out the window early the next morning, there was no blanket of snow on the ground, but only a few glistening flakes clinging to the dead grass. Atlanta weather was a real heartbreaker. I got my leg on and went downstairs in my pajamas and fluffy robe for a glass of orange juice. Mom was working in the backyard, so I lugged myself outside to sit in a patio chair and join her. There was always so much to be done in the yard every fall, but last year Mom had been too overwhelmed to care about pulling dead flowers, freshening the mulch, and pruning bushes. Now that the worst of winter was hopefully over, she had a brief second chance to get it done. Everything dead had to be cut off and cleared away. If not, when spring came we wouldn't have any blossoms.

Spring was the most beautiful season in Atlanta, but

preparing for it was hard work. I was glad Mom felt strong enough to do it.

Besides, I wasn't much of a morning person. I felt like my head had been swaddled in a thick cotton blanket, making it hard to think, maybe because there was too much to think about. I was glad Mom had gotten the day off to stay home with me. Her office friends had pooled their sick and vacation days to give to her, which not every company allows but hers did. They valued her.

I understood why.

I liked watching Mom putter around in the backyard, nothing burdening her except boring, everyday decisions. Boring, everyday decisions were a luxury we missed.

Spring wouldn't be here for at least another month, so we still had mostly cold days, but the sun shone bright and warm. Mom attacked the dead flowers from last year with a vengeance. I saw a row of loose dirt. She must have planted some bulbs.

"Hey, Mom," I called.

She straightened up, replacing her frown with a half-hearted smile, then grabbed the garden hose and soaked the bulbs she had just planted.

"Isn't it too late to plant those?" I called. Bulbs had to be planted in fall, not a few weeks before spring.

She didn't respond even though I knew she'd heard me. She concentrated on watering the dirt. I watched, and waited for her to say something.

In the cascade of water leaping from the hose, a rainbow shimmered. Above her, in our giant oak tree, still bare from winter, I saw a perfect, round bird's nest from last spring. A family of baby birds had lived right in my backyard. I hadn't even known they were there.

I closed my eyes for a moment and lifted my face to the morning sun. A bird sang in the distance, and dead leaves rustled in the breeze. I could hear a squirrel scamper across the dry grass by the fence.

I loved our backyard. I loved our little world.

Then Mom screamed, the noise followed by a hard thud. Something else was here with us.

I jumped up and lost my balance. Falling face forward onto the concrete patio, I scraped the palms of my hands. Hot tears gouged my eyes as I scrambled to get up. Then Mom screamed again. Another thud, then another. I grabbed the patio table, pulling myself up.

Moving fast, I found her around the corner by the shed. She raised the shovel over her head, then slammed it to the ground. I didn't see any monsters. I didn't see anything at all. Just Mom, a shovel, and the empty shed.

"Mom!" I yelled. "Stop! What's wrong?"

She looked at me like her mind was somewhere far away. "It was a fuzzy caterpillar. They can sting."

We stared at each other for a long moment, and my mind flooded with questions. Caterpillars didn't appear here till summer, so something must have brought one from a warmer climate like a dog carries fleas. Which meant something had been hanging around in my backyard.

Mom wasn't focusing on me; she seemed to be remembering something terrible.

I didn't feel too good about any of this.

"But, Mom?" I said. "If you kill all the caterpillars, there won't be any butterflies in the spring."

She shook her head as she stared at the pulverized blob on the ground. She set the shovel in the shed and walked toward the house.

"That's the price we have to pay," she muttered.

A dull-colored cloud rolled over the sun as she walked back inside. I hated winter and wanted it to be over.

I stayed outside because I didn't know what to do. My life was changing but hers wasn't, and I knew it was my fault. Maybe if I could explain what I was seeing and feeling and learning, she wouldn't hate all the pain we had been through anymore. Because I could see now that pain isn't a death, but a door. Everything beautiful has a violent birth: cocoons tear, seeds crack, babies come into the world with their mothers screaming and panting and sweating and people call it a miracle. All my pain, the grief of feeling so alone, the torture of feeling like a freak . . . maybe it had been not a death but a door. And who knew what was going to come through it? Doors work both ways, you know. I might find a whole new life, or a new life might come find me. And pain had been the only price. Was that really so bad? It was time to stop hating the past for tearing a giant hole in our lives. It was time to take a step into the dark passage and see where it led.

I had to try and tell her one more time about Xeno's book and the monsters.

I heard the clangs and dings of Mom in the kitchen, setting out bowls and spoons for our breakfast. As I walked back into the house, something rustled in the bushes behind me and hissed for my attention. I had no idea what it was, and I didn't want to know. Not right now. I kept moving. My mom was hurting and she needed me.

Inside the kitchen, I sat at the table, watching her. I wasn't sure how to begin the conversation. As she set out the cereal and milk, I took a breath for courage and tried to decide what to say first. She began to pour the cereal for me but then stopped, holding the box in midair.

"The night you were born, I stayed awake all night long, just looking at you," she said. I would find a way to tell her when she finished. "I was afraid that if I closed my eyes, if I even blinked, God would change his mind and ask for you back." She set the box on the table and sat down, smiling at the memory. "You were just that perfect. I was sure God had made a mistake by giving me the most perfect baby ever."

I grinned without even meaning to. I loved this story. She told it to me a lot.

A shadow passed over the sun and the kitchen lost all of its morning light. Her face darkened. "And then, when you got sick, we were back in the hospital, with you asleep and me afraid to close my eyes. One night, I heard a nurse tell another mother that it was time to let go."

She droned on, like she wasn't even aware I was in the room. This was a story she had never told. "The mom let out this wail, this howl like she was the one dying. I climbed into your bed while you were sleeping, and held on to you until my arms shook. I've never been so afraid in all my life."

Her eyes filled with tears, but she blinked fast. She pushed the cereal box in front of me and wiped her eyes. I wanted to tell her it was all going to be okay, that maybe everything had happened so that I could become the Guardian and protect the abandoned creatures of the night, but all I could think of was that caterpillar she had just smashed.

"I don't know how to protect you," she whispered, her face pale. "All I want is for you to be happy, but this world is not a safe place."

I reached my hand across the table and held hers. "It was never safe. We just didn't know that before." Taking a breath, I paused to tell her that I had found something better than being safe. "I can never be safe again. Because—"

She squeezed my hand and gave me a sharp look. "I know you've been depressed. But don't talk like that. We'll find a way. You will have a long, normal life, I promise."

I didn't want that. I didn't want to settle for any kind of normal, because that meant I might never have anything better. I needed something more.

Mom stood and grabbed her empty cereal bowl. Putting it in the sink, she ran water over it even though she hadn't used it. I think she was wrestling with big questions too, the kind of questions that have lots of easy answers but no great ones. I wanted to share my secret with her, but the answer, of course, was no. Or *not now,* which was almost the same thing.

We spent a quiet day together. She gave me some uninterrupted alone time in my room to work on homework, but I used most of the time to study the Bestiary. It wasn't just monsters I had to understand; it was geography and history and science and medicine. I swear my skull hurt from the rapid expansion of brain cells. At least I was studying important subjects, and that could help my grades. I had always liked being an A student, but recently I had begun to understand that I *needed* to be an A student. Without a scholarship, college wasn't going to happen for me.

Finally, we said an early goodnight at the top of the stairs. Mom went to run the water for a bath, a magazine tucked under her arm. She shut her bedroom door behind her; then I heard the bathroom door shut too. I had a two-door warning system.

Alone in my room, I grabbed the book for more studying. Mom could never, ever know about its existence. She had enough to handle. Normal girls didn't talk to dead men or give first aid to nature's nightmares. At least Golem was sweet. Maybe I would ask Xeno if I could just be the Guardian for Golem. I flipped through the book. Some of these monsters were terrifying; plus, they ate people. I also wanted to ask Xeno why there wasn't an entry for Bigfoot or the chupacabra. Did that mean they weren't real monsters or that no Guardian had ever treated one? It would be incredible, I thought, if I got to add a page of my own to this book.

As I turned another page, a horrid smell hooked me by the nose. On instinct, I dropped the book and threw one hand over my face to shield it from the stench.

It smelled like fish. Dead fish. Dead, rotting, stinking fish.

My room suddenly grew cold, and tiny goose bumps popped up along my arms. I exhaled slowly, trying to control my breathing and stop myself from gulping in the putrid air. White mist floated out from between my fingers, like I was breathing outside in winter.

Something wet began to slither up my calves toward my stomach. A slimy, barrel-shaped tentacle, heavy and cold, smashed against my chest, pinning me to the bed. In the moonlight, I watched another tentacle wave. It crept across my chest like a snake and struck my forehead. I couldn't move.

Little bursts of light danced in my vision. The tentacle on my chest had cut off my air. The book lay on the floor, glowing green and urgent, but I couldn't reach it.

A wet scraping sound, like a sack of wet clothes being dragged across my floor, broke the silence. A face emerged from the darkness and loomed over mine. It hissed softly, watching me. The monster had almond-shaped eyes with pupils that opened wide and black against its stark white eyeballs. It didn't have control of them, though. Each eye roved independently around the room and spun whenever the monster hissed. I didn't get the feeling this monster was anything like Golem.

I tried to turn my head. The monster smelled like it had digested something awful and dead, something that might come back up right in my face.

Thousands of scales overlapped along its skin. When it turned its head to look out my window, I saw gills along its neck, and a mouth like a fish's, with two thick pieces of rubbery cartilage for lips, which opened and closed silently. Dead leaves clung to its body. This must have been what was

in the garden this morning, and I had ignored it. Now it was mad.

The monster turned its head back to me, lips opening again, revealing row after row of tiny white triangles, each with a jagged edge. The teeth looked like they were made for tearing meat away from bone. A low giggle escaped from its open mouth as its eyes spun like loose marbles.

It was going to eat me.

Xeno would know what to do. I had to reach the book. I tried to move my right arm, but the monster pinned me tight. It looked me up and down, as if trying to decide where to start eating first. All I could do was wiggle the fingers on my left hand. I struggled to move my thighs, to dislodge the monster, but they were trapped. Had I survived cancer just to be eaten by a filthy monster with wonky eyes?

Its mouth opened, teeth emerged, and, whipping around, the monster sank them into my prosthesis. The teeth ripped through the fake skin and then scraped against the metal rod inside.

The monster snapped its head back up in a snarl of protest. I took my chance and slid to the floor. Reaching fast, I grabbed the book. It had flipped open to the blank page, glowing bright white. The words burned black.

TELL IT YOU HAVE A CUCUMBER.

"That makes no sense!" I said.

The monster tensed its muscles, preparing to pounce, its teeth like tombstones in the moonlight.

"I have a cucumber," I whispered.

It stopped.

Settling back on its haunches, if you could call them that, the creature cocked its head like a puppy, a wide grin splitting its face. Clear juice dripped from the monster's teeth. I got a good look at the whole of it. The creature had the body of a hairy man, or gorilla maybe, and a bunch of tentacles that braided together to function as arms and legs, or released and went off in different directions, like a remarkable combination of fish and man and loose marbles.

"Rrreowr?" it asked, the sound lilting up at the end like a question.

The book glowed so bright I could read the words out of the corner of my eye.

GET THE CUCUMBER.

"My mother is up here," I protested. "I'm not leaving her alone."

GET THE CUCUMBER.

Did we even have one? I tried to remember what I had seen in the fridge.

NOW.

I struggled to stand. My real knee felt like jelly.

"Please, please let us have a cucumber," I whispered. I

made it to the bedroom door, expecting to be pounced on and eaten at any moment. When I turned back, the monster was crouched on my bed, waiting. It seemed very happy.

The house was dark and no light was visible under my mom's door, but I heard water running in her bathroom. I made my way down the stairs in the darkness, cautiously testing each step. I could not trip or stumble. Mom might hear and come out of her room to check on me, and the monster would devour her. Whatever this thing was, I didn't like it.

I thought back to the girl in the hospital, her nightgown stained in blood. What had happened to her? Did she not have a cucumber? Why hadn't Xeno mentioned that produce would be involved? And why did I always have more questions than answers?

I made it to the fridge, breathing heavily. I grasped the cold metal handle and pulled. White light flooded over me like I was at the gates of heaven. I reached for the vegetable drawer with trembling hands, holding my breath.

A cucumber sat on a bed of wilted lettuce.

I was never so happy to see a vegetable in all my life. I took it out and held it above my head in triumph. "Yes!"

A growl floated down from my room. I shut the fridge quietly and quickly started my way back up. The fridge light had blinded me. I worked my way slowly up the stairs. I heard the radio playing from behind Mom's door and the water still running.

I opened my bedroom door to see the monster bouncing up and down on my bed. It seemed to like the spring action of the mattress.

It snatched the cucumber from my hands and cradled it like a baby. Then the monster lifted it and bit one end off. It stopped every few bites and held the cucumber up to the light, clicking its teeth in delight before resuming. While it ate, I noticed a fishhook embedded in its lower lip. The wound was swollen and oozy. It was infected. The poor thing had been in pain when I refused to help this morning.

I remembered when I was about five or six and went on a field trip to the lake with my summer day care. A little boy had gotten a fishhook caught in his finger when he was playing near the shore. Our teacher called the park rangers for help. I could still recall exactly what the guy had to do to remove it. When you're a little kid, scary medical procedures sear themselves into your brain.

I moved slowly, trying not to disturb the monster. It didn't have a lot of the cucumber left. In my dresser I kept my jewelry-making tools, a leftover from craft days at the hospital. I pulled out a pair of wire clippers and promised myself I wouldn't hurl if this got nasty.

As I approached the monster, its eyes swirled faster, watching me. It hugged the cucumber tightly and growled.

"No," I whispered, shaking my head. "I don't want your cucumber." I pointed to my lip and then to its lip.

The monster uncurled one tentacle, reaching up to touch the hook. It whimpered.

"I can take that out," I said. I pantomimed how I would pull it free, leaving out the part with the contorted face of anguish.

The monster looked at the cucumber sadly, then set it on the bed and nodded.

It had already tried to eat me, and it was not going to like what I had to do, but the wound looked bad. I knew how dangerous infected wounds were, and how they made doctors really nervous. If I didn't help, the monster might get sick or die.

I just wished I understood why that was a bad thing. This monster didn't seem to have any redeeming qualities.

Lifting the clippers, I reached for its lip. The monster's eyes stopped swirling and came to rest on mine. Beneath the thin green flesh, I could now see a blue heart beating inside its chest, shooting blood through the abdomen in messy squirts.

The creature's lip felt like cold rubber. Rust had begun to eat through the hook, so I hoped the next part would work. I snipped off the eye end of the hook—the end where the fishing line had been tied to it. The barbed end was still inside the lip.

I pushed with one hand and held the lip taut with the other. The monster cried as it squirmed, but I forced the barbed end of the hook all the way through and out the other side. Because I'd made the top a clean edge, the rest of the metal slipped through the hole smoothly.

I held the hook out to show the monster. It opened its mouth, flashing serrated teeth. The eyes were spinning so fast they looked like they were in a blender. It was furious.

OPEN THE WINDOW.

I obeyed Xeno immediately. The monster's tentacles reached for me.

"You're forgetting your cucumber," I whispered.

It stopped and glanced back to the bed. Grabbing and cradling it out of my view, the monster flew out the window. I slid the window shut and locked it too. I did not want any more of those things in my room. Ever. Its smell still lingered.

The letters erased on the page and new words formed as I watched.

That was a Kappa. It eats children.

Cold sweat broke out across my forehead. "What?" I said. "It was going to eat me? And you let it come to my bedroom?"

If you follow my directions, you are in little danger.

"Can you define 'little'?" I snapped. "That thing bit me."

Kappas are from Japan and have only one love greater than the flesh of children.

"Cucumbers?" I guessed. "But how did you know we had a cucumber? And what if we didn't?"

Sofia?

"What?" I said.

Close your eyes and listen.

Outside, the world was alive. I heard insects singing and cats meowing to each other through the bushes across the street. Dogs barked over fences, passing messages down the block, and a wood frog kept time with deep, happy bellows. I had spent thousands of nights in this same room, with these same noises. But only just now, tonight, my heart beat loudly, wanting to join in their song.

It was a strange feeling, one that I recognized but couldn't quite remember, sort of like when you see a friend from summer camp a year or two later. You remember them, but it takes a minute to remember from where exactly.

And then it hit me.

I was part of a bigger, mysterious, and beautiful world. It wasn't a cold and gray place unless you chose to live in the shadows. Had I only forgotten that, or were these nightmarish creatures teaching me something new?

I inhaled and exhaled in slow, deep breaths. A smile seemed to bubble all the way up from my toes and stretch across my cheeks. I opened my eyes and the blank page swirled with new letters.

You are changing, Sofia. And you are becoming a very good Guardian.

"I learned how to do that a long time ago," I said, thinking he was talking about the fishhook.

You were kind to the Golem because you realized he was sweet. But you were kind to the Kappa simply because I asked you to be. You have great potential, Sofia. A Guardian must watch over all, the terrible and the good.

"But why?" I asked. "Why protect all of them? Some of them eat people. Why not just protect the ones who are nice? It's not like we need all of them."

Throughout history, every culture created its own monsters. Why?

Social studies wasn't my best subject, but I tried to remember what Xeno had taught me. "Because we wanted to choose what we were afraid of."

Yes. A common enemy, a common dread, is a strong bond between people. It forces the most unlikely individuals to work together. It gives fear an honorable focus. Monsters made us better people.

"But no one believes in them anymore," I pointed out.

We have chosen, instead, to fear each other. Perhaps one day, people will remember the wisdom of governing through imagination instead of fear. You must protect the monsters, Sofia, because one day the world will need them. When we grow tired of war and suspicion and hate, we will need them.

Would the world really be a better place if everyone was terrified of monsters? I thought about school. If we had monsters to fight and fear, I might be thankful for the kids who were mean and strong. Bullies would actually be useful.

Maybe monsters had to be bad, I thought, so we could learn to be good to each other.

"Xeno, there's something else I need to tell you," I said. "A woman has been following me. I think she knows about the book. I didn't tell her, I promise."

I know.

"Who is she?" I asked. "What does she want?"

It is late, and that is not a story to be told at bedtime.

TEN

∼Saturday, March 1 ∼

As soon as I heard Mom stirring the next morning, I got up.
All night I had worried about the Kappa's bite to my prosthetic. How would I explain the damage? Mom was going
to freak. I got my leg on and pulled on some sweats before
making my way to the bathroom across the hall.

Wincing from the glare of the bathroom lights, I moved
to sit on the covered toilet seat and bent over to inspect the
prosthesis.

It looked pretty good, actually. The imitation-flesh material had sealed back over the teeth marks, and if you didn't
look too closely, the wound wasn't obvious. Out of curiosity,
I pried the bite marks apart to look inside. A glint of surgical
steel winked at me. I let the wound snap closed, then ran my
finger along it. I'd almost forgotten how strangely beautiful
the inner workings of the prosthesis were, like a watch.

All that incredible work inside the leg, I had told Barnes, and no one would ever see it. Why had he worked so hard to give me this leg, I wondered, if no one would ever really know what he had created? His best efforts meant that when people looked at me, nothing caught their eye. How could he be happy with pouring his genius into his work for people who only wanted to hide it? Was that what I really wanted, and what Mom had paid so dearly for? The privilege of being ignored? The prosthesis fit perfectly, but somehow . . . it was beginning to feel just a tiny bit off.

I wished I could talk to him about it, but I wasn't due to see him again for weeks, and I couldn't even think about getting a new prosthesis until I outgrew this one.

I sat back on the toilet seat and sighed. We didn't study Aristotle in school, and I'd found nothing online about Xeno or his monsters. Last year in social studies, we'd studied Alexander the Great, but only to debate whether it was right to invade and conquer other countries. Alexander had wanted to rule the world and be worshipped as a god. We debated whether he was right to force his beliefs onto everyone else. One thing we all agreed on: when countries didn't have the same beliefs and values, they usually ended up fighting each other.

Adults went to war for reasons I didn't understand, but it seemed far-fetched that monsters had anything to do with world peace. Xeno thought they held an important key and were worth saving, but I didn't know yet what I believed.

After I'd showered and dressed for the day, I went to check our vegetable drawer.

"Whatcha looking for?"

I jumped, not knowing Mom had come into the kitchen behind me. "We're out of cucumbers."

"You hate cucumbers," she said, with the tiniest trace of a frown.

"I know, right?" I tried to sound cheerful. "But I want to eat healthy. Can you buy some?"

"I guess." She didn't sound convinced.

"Like, today?" I didn't want to pressure her, but neither of us deserved to die for lack of produce.

Mom sighed. "Add it to the list. We'll try to swing by the store later."

I clenched my jaw to keep from groaning. We really needed cucumbers. Now. But if I acted too desperate, she'd wonder why. I pasted on a smile and grabbed a Toaster Strudel out of the freezer.

Mom snatched it from my hand. She threw it in the trash and handed me a mushy brown banana.

"Eating healthy," she said.

"Right. Thank you." I wanted to stab myself in the eye with the banana.

"I need to get caught up on bill paying and laundry," Mom said. "Do you mind if I take over the kitchen table?"

"No problem," I replied, sounding like the perfect daughter. In reality, this was a lucky break. "I have a bunch of homework left to do upstairs." Which was true, even though it wasn't schoolwork. I needed to study the Bestiary.

"So today will be a workday for both of us. But tomorrow

the weather is supposed to be gorgeous. If you really want to be healthy," Mom said, "we should take a walk around the park."

"Sounds great." With the price of a peck on the cheek, I had just bought myself hours of uninterrupted study time.

ELEVEN

On our walk the next day, I wore a scarf to make Mom happy, but the sun had come out and both of us took our winter coats off after a while. We walked slowly, enjoying the tiny signs of life creeping back. The tulips had sprouted thick green stalks, but because of the crazy winter we'd had, they wouldn't flower for several more weeks. The pear trees were heavy with tight green buds. Everyone in Atlanta was worried about them because one more freeze would destroy the blossoms. The tail end of winter could kill whatever was tender and new.

A woman passed us wearing dark wraparound glasses, her hair tucked under a baseball cap. She had in earbuds and was pushing a baby carriage at a fast pace. Mom let her pass and the woman waved one hand to thank us.

A half hour later, we sat on a bench, watching squirrels dart back and forth across the path. One squirrel even put on a show for us. He chattered angrily at something in the trees before dashing through the bushes. Every few minutes, he would return, his tail full and swishing, barking in protest at whatever was preventing him from climbing that tree. I didn't worry about monsters. I doubted they were out in broad daylight with so many people around. They seemed to prefer the shadows as much as they needed them. The woman with the stroller passed us again. She must have made three laps around the park by now, compared to our one.

Mom stood and pointed to the restrooms behind us. "I need to hit the ladies' room. You?"

"Nah," I said, and tipped my head back to let the sun wash over me. Squinting one eye, I smiled at her. "This was a good idea, coming here today."

Mom grinned and turned for the restrooms. Above me, cranes circled, honking loudly at each other. Mom stopped and pointed up at them, and I nodded. Cranes flew in circles, blaring like party horns, waiting for other cranes to find the right air current and join the loop before forming a V shape and flying north. Cranes migrated up from the southern beaches through Atlanta at this time of year, heading back to Canada for the spring. They were so loud that people always stopped whatever they were doing and watched them, because it was usually too hard to hear anything else.

As the V took shape and flew, the woman pushing the baby stroller walked toward me. I whipped my head to the right and looked down the path. Hadn't she just passed us? The birds must have disoriented me.

The woman slowed as she got closer to the bench.

Mom had just gone inside the ladies' room when the woman pushed her baby stroller to the side and sat next to me. I looked inside the stroller.

It was empty. She took off her glasses, but I already knew who she was. The temperature felt ten degrees colder.

My chest tightened with anxiety. "Why are you doing this?" I asked. My imagination leaped to the worst possible answer. "You're going to kill me, aren't you?"

The woman tilted her head back as she laughed. She was perfect, even up close. "What use would I have for a body? I don't want your body, Sofia." She leaned in to me and pointed to my chest with one long finger. "I want your heart."

I recoiled, and she laughed again.

"Not literally." She reached for my arm next, her fingers extending like a rake, as if to scratch me, but her hand disappeared through my arm, like a ghost. Her mouth pursed in sadness, then she looked at me and her eyes narrowed. "I'm not here to hurt you. I've come to help you. Xeno is letting you make a terrible mistake."

"I don't believe that."

We sat in silence for a moment. Then she pointed to the scarf I was wearing. "Have you ever seen anyone knit?"

"Yes."

"Our worlds, the natural and the supernatural, are like two knitting needles," she said. "We collide constantly. All that is left behind is the pattern, what we wove together when we met. The supernatural is woven into the pattern of this world. People either refuse to see that reality or they become hopelessly distracted by it." She pointed one long finger back at my face. "You do not have the luxury of denial or distraction. I need you to focus."

The invisible wind rustled like music through the trees as birds soared above. There were things in this world that I had to accept on faith, like wind. I would never see it, but I knew it was real and it affected everything. I blinked once and focused on the woman's eyes, ignoring her finger still pointed at my face. Her irises never moved as she watched me. She was alive in a vague sense of the word but with something essential missing.

"Xeno is filling your head with ideas that will only lead to heartbreak." Her voice held an icy edge. "Just as his master, Aristotle, did to him. You must understand the difference between reality and delusion before you destroy any hope you have of happiness. You are making a pattern that remains. It cannot be undone."

I looked at the restroom. "My mom will be back any minute," I said. "You should go."

"I am Olympias, the mother of Alexander the Great. I do not take orders from children."

My eyebrows shot up. I knew that name. She smiled at my reaction, her teeth bright and glistening.

"Thousands of years later and the whole world still knows who he is," she said. "Unlike Xeno, I might add. My son Alexander showed us what a truly great man can do. He would have ended all war, forever, and given us one government, with one ruler, a true and good god. There was no need for tribes and monsters and separate histories, all those identities that clashed and provoked. With my son as god and king, everyone could have lived in peace." She shook her head. "But Xeno promoted the lie that what made us different could make us strong. He even wanted monsters kept alive and recruited a child to guard them."

I glanced at the ladies' room again. Mom stepped out, cell phone pressed to her ear, and held one finger up to signal she needed a minute or two. She rarely chatted on the phone anymore. Mom needed to reconnect with her friends, but this was spectacularly bad timing.

"The monsters are in hiding," I said. "Why can't you just leave them alone?"

"But I do," she said, sounding offended. "Xeno has told you so little. I rather like monsters, my dear. If I can find the raw materials, I'll create one, to serve my cause. I made a rather special one just recently."

She sighed deeply, as if remembering a delicious memory. "Ah, yes, the old magic. So few practice it anymore. Everyone's minds are so . . . *sterile*. Except yours."

I didn't know what she meant by that, but I was more confused about something else. "So you *don't* want to kill them?"

"Monsters? No. There was an age, long ago, when that should have been done, of course, but time has passed and done the work for me. They are as good as dead now." She turned and grinned at me. A shiver crept up my spine.

Her eyes were lifeless. They were like glass marbles, hard and shiny.

"Monsters do not trouble me, Sofia. You do."

"Me?" I asked.

"Sofia, people can have their identity and their beliefs,

or they can have peace. No one can have both. Not in this world." Olympias neatly folded her sunglasses. "Watch the news. The bombings, the wars, the beheadings . . . all because we believe different things."

"We call it diversity," I said.

"I call it madness," she snapped.

Her tone was shrill, and I winced at the sound of her voice. But what really bothered me was that she was right. No matter what a person believed, it seemed like someone else wanted to kill them for it.

She continued, softening her tone. "And so what if a Guardian, more powerful than all the others, was born in this strange, soulless age? What if her courage woke a sleeping generation? What if she convinced people that their real enemy was fear? That an individual should be celebrated instead of silenced? All my work, all Alexander's dreams, would be undone. And there would be much suffering."

Mom laughed at something her friend must have said, and her nose crinkled just like it used to, when we didn't have so much trouble.

Olympias tapped my prosthetic leg with her glasses. "But what if this girl used her strength to save the world? What if she used her gifts to convince others that only in unity can we survive? Conformity is not defeat. It is wisdom. Sofia, it is salvation."

Mom had her back turned to me now, obviously relieved that I was chatting with someone as safe as a mom and her new baby.

"Take the first step," Olympias said. "Let the monsters go.

I'm not asking you to kill them or do anything cruel. I'm only asking you to stop caring for them. They are individual, personal creations, and individuality is what we're fighting. We cannot have separate identities and beliefs, because that always leads to conflict. We must become one so that wars will end. This is a dangerous time to be distracted by our imaginations. But if we let go of our beliefs, all the nations could join together, under one government, with one ruler."

She looked up at the sun for a moment, and I noticed she did not blink, not once, even though the sun was bright. Then she turned back to me and I watched as a tear slipped down one of her cheeks. It was like seeing a doll cry.

"It has been more than two thousand years since I have beheld my son's face. I long to return to him, Sofia, but I must finish what he began. Help me. Don't save the monsters. Save the world."

Then she leaned in and whispered, "Save yourself."

I pulled away, desperate for a deep breath of air, as if Olympias carried an infection, a bacteria waiting to thaw and spoil all the oxygen. Closing my eyes, I inhaled, then let my breath out slowly.

Mom must have finished her call, because she was walking toward us now, a big smile on her face. Today had been a really good day for her.

Olympias stood and loomed over me, blocking out my mother and the sun. In her shadow, the cold crept back over my body.

"Aristotle—and Xeno and the rest of his students—believed that the search for truth was a good thing. But you know, Sofia, what happens when people see the truth. How kind are people to those who are weak or different? Knowing the truth about the world, about ourselves, will never lead to peace. Xeno wants you to seek the truth, but he never explained what truth costs."

Frowning, I tried to catch a glimpse of my mom. Olympias smiled at my nervousness.

"I'm not evil, Sofia, and I am not your enemy. But I have made one last monster who will take everything you hold dear and smash it to bits, piece by piece, until you realize that what I offer the world is far better than truth."

When I got home, I locked my window and didn't take the book out from under the bed. It glowed once, briefly, but I looked away, pretending not to see it. Two weeks ago, I hadn't even believed in monsters. Now I did, but Olympias wanted to challenge everything else I believed.

Mom had dumped some laundry on my bed, so I got to work separating the pile.

Talking to Olympias had made me sick to my stomach, like that feeling you get when you realize too late that an assignment is due. When I opened the Bestiary, I hadn't known that anyone from the ancient past was going to come looking for me, especially someone like her.

I found a pair of socks and rolled them together. I hated wearing one sock; it made my phantom foot cold.

Grabbing a shirt, I replayed everything Olympias had

said, and one thing stuck with me, a thought that lodged itself in my brain as unwelcome as a seed caught in my teeth: *What does truth cost?*

I knew part of the answer: the price of truth was pain. Billy had said that too. Even I avoided it sometimes. That didn't make me a bad person. It just meant that I really loved my mom and I guess I loved Alexis too. I loved her enough to refuse to tell her the truth about why we couldn't be friends yet. I did want to be friends once I was stronger and she didn't have to worry about me. When I could be happy to see her running with someone new, I'd know it was time. Right now, it would be a lie.

And Alexis knew when I was lying. Sometimes she laughed at me for it and sometimes it made her mad. Alexis was like salt. She usually made everything better, but if her words touched on some wound I was trying to ignore, they stung like crazy. She was never mean; she was just always right.

I opened my dresser drawer and tucked my underwear inside. The socks went in next; then I'd hang the shirts and be done.

Why were relationships so complicated?

I grabbed a hanger and started the last little bit of my chore.

Was I happier now without a best friend? Could I be happy without any friends at all? I wouldn't have to worry about making mistakes and hurting people. I used to be completely alone at school. Maybe I had been happier then, even if I didn't think so at the time. Grabbing a shirt to hang up, I flinched at the memory of the day it all started.

In first grade, my mom bought a shirt for me at a garage sale for a quarter. I loved it. It had a lion made out of gold glitter, but everywhere I went, I left specks of glitter behind. When I wore it to school, Candy pretended that the glitter was germs, and all the girls took big steps to avoid touching me and the glitter germs. I kept my head down all day so no one would see the tears brimming in my eyes, and tried to avoid calling attention to myself.

Mom washed my shirt that night and hung it back in my closet, but I had vowed to never wear it again. Being the odd girl out, even for just a day, had been the most painful thing I'd ever experienced.

In the wash, the glitter got all over my other clothes. For months after that, Candy would point to a speck of glitter on me, and then everyone would talk to each other behind hands cupped at their mouths. Of course, glitter was used everywhere in elementary school, so I never escaped the teasing.

I eventually just learned to keep to myself. But if it sucked not having friends, at least I didn't have to worry all the time about hurting someone's feelings, or getting hurt either.

The last shirt was hung and I could finally sit on my bed.

So maybe truth hurt, but what hurt worse: being hurt by the truth or by someone you loved? It was the kind of question a philosopher would ask. I grinned a little and made a note to tell Xeno.

Which was more painful, truth or love?

I inhaled sharply because I had this weird thought.

What if they were the same thing?

TWELVE

Monday, March 3

Mom's alarm clock buzzed without end. She was already downstairs and refused to come up to turn it off.

She was pretty mad when I finally made it into the kitchen. I was moving slowly since I was tired; plus I couldn't find a head scarf or bandana to match my outfit and it had taken me forever to get dressed. I wasn't sure what the rule was for matching. I only knew nail polish should match on both fingertips and toes, and not to wear white bras after Labor Day or something. I made a mental note to read a fashion magazine and figure this stuff out once and for all.

Mom was stuffing papers from the table into her briefcase and tried to grab one that fluttered away. She quickly read it before she stuffed it in her bag. "Sofia, when were you going to mention this?"

I could tell it was from school by the logo at the top. My

brain raced to think of what else I had recently neglected to tell her.

"The school dance?" she said. "In sixth grade, you told me that more than anything, you wanted to go and dance with a cute boy."

"No one asked me in sixth grade," I reminded her.

"So?"

"No one asked me this year either." I faked a big bright smile. "Maybe life really is getting back to normal."

At lunch, I loaded up my tray with double the amount of cookies and a little bitty salad. Mom was making me eat plenty of vegetables at home. A lunch lady grabbed one of the cookies and put an apple in its place, giving me a wink. "We all want to keep you healthy, dear."

I walked outside to our butterfly garden, a big area in the middle of the school with a bunch of picnic tables. All the plants had been chosen by the Science Club to attract butterflies, and when it was butterfly season and the place was filled with dozens of them, it was amazing. Right now everything was dead.

I spied Alexis sitting alone at a table. I used to always sit next to Alexis on her right, because she's a leftie. My body moved toward her by instinct, seeing her with no one on her right. That was my place, ever since the beginning of sixth grade last year.

I pulled back, reminding myself that our friendship was a tangled mess and I couldn't unravel it in one day. Even if I wanted to, I would need time and space to concentrate and get my words right. I had to make sure she didn't feel guilty, and I needed to be strong enough to be happy for her that she still had her leg, her hair, and her whole life.

Happy, happy, happy, I said under my breath. So much happiness. Like stabbing a fork in your eye.

Maybe someday she would understand that I had to do it this way because I loved her. Tears blurred my vision and I blinked hard to clear them. I just wasn't ready yet.

The track team flooded outside as I stood there, and a loud-mouthed brunette grabbed the seat to Alexis's right. My spot was gone. Alexis sat with her back to me, so she hadn't seen me hesitating. I hung my head and moved toward an empty table.

I lowered myself with a soft groan, my butt sore from the hard plastic chairs in class. Why did they make desks and chairs so cold and hard? Were they afraid we might start to actually enjoy learning?

Above me, the sky was ice blue with thick white clouds. A sliver of the moon was visible, a pale shimmer beyond the clouds.

"It's a waxing crescent," Billy said, setting his tray across from mine. " 'Waxing' means 'growing.' " I noticed he took a package of carrots from his tray and stuffed them in his pocket. "I looked it up. But no more snow in the forecast. I think winter is almost over."

People were starting to claim the tables all around us. There was no place I could sit without pretending I wanted to join someone's clique.

I opened my milk and took a sip, not looking at Billy. His

knee grazed mine under the table. The butterflies I was long-
ing for suddenly appeared in my stomach. I shifted to the right
to avoid touching him in case he didn't want to touch me again.

"I looked for you all morning," he said, unfolding his
napkin and setting it on his lap. "We never had a chance to
catch up last week. You should give me your number."

I had never given my number to a guy. My mind went
blank, like the blue screen of death on a computer. What was
my number? I had no idea.

He placed his plastic fork on the left and spoon on the
right, then began scooting the cheese off his mystery slop
with his knife. "So anyway, first, don't let Candy get to you
again. And second, I wanted to apologize."

"For what?"

"Well, being the new guy sucks, because the girls always
chase me and the other guys don't like it. So I end up alone
and just try to keep things interesting until I get kicked out
again. But you didn't chase me, and I thought it was because
you were cool. But then I realized, maybe you just don't like
me. Not that I really care, but I'm sorry if you actually hate
me and I got it all wrong."

"No," I said. "I like you."

He scowled and narrowed his eyes at me.

"A lot!" I added.

His face brightened. "That's what I thought."

I felt like an idiot and changed the subject. "Why do you
do it?"

He raised one eyebrow, so I clarified the question. "Why
do you want to be the bad kid and get in trouble all the time?"

He bit his bottom lip, thinking. "I think . . . I'm trying to make a point."

"To who?" I asked.

He frowned, anger flashing in his eyes. "If you have to ask, then it's obviously not you." Shaking his head to dismiss the conversation, he picked up his fork and pointed it at me. "Anyway, we should go to the dance."

"What about the goats?" I said, pretending I hadn't heard him.

"They already turned me down," Billy said.

I struggled not to laugh. "No, I mean, what did you do with them?"

"The fire department returned them to the owner, and I gave my dad's intern a twenty for the help. Everyone went home happy."

His fork hovered over the salad that he hadn't even looked at. He was too busy staring at me.

"It drives me crazy when people get food they know they aren't going to eat," I blurted. "Why not just say 'No, thank you' to the lunch lady? Why pretend you're going to eat the salad if you know you're really going to throw it away?" My voice rose up a little at the end, and I wanted to run for the nearest exit in embarrassment.

He wiped his mouth with the napkin before answering. "You're kinda weird." He took another bite of his meat slop and jabbed his fork back in my direction. "But I admire your sense of justice. I mean, who else would stick up for a defenseless side salad? You're a vegetable vigilante."

I nodded, unable to speak. It's too bad they don't

make EpiPens for episodes of life-threatening embarrassment.

"I'd like to take you to the dance," he said, loading another spoonful of cheesy glob. "If you're not too busy saving helpless produce."

"For one thing, it's called a *dance*," I said. "And I don't dance." Why did I sound angry when I was scared? I didn't mean to. I just needed to cut him off before this got out of control. I had enough problems, like Xeno, Alexis, monsters, and my mom. I didn't want a new one called Billy and another one called dancing.

Billy opened his eyes wide, like I was missing something painfully obvious. "No, actually, it's called a date, and you should try it. You've never been very nice to me, and I'm your only boy friend." He took another bite, then paused. "I am your only boy friend, right?"

"Yes!" I said. "No!"

He grinned.

"I meant no. You're not my boyfriend. I don't have a boyfriend. I've never had a boyfriend." Why did I have to say that? I clenched my fists and considered leaping up from the table, then remembered it wouldn't be much of a leap. I'd only embarrass myself more if I tried to run.

"I am a boy and I am your friend, right? Don't make it complicated. Look, if you're scared about the dancing, I can teach you a move, if you want," he said. "I learned it from the Internet. All you have to do is bend over a little at the waist and pretend to write your name in the air with your butt. Boom! You're dancing."

"Stop," I said. "I'm not who you think I am. I'm not fierce! I'm . . ." I looked down at my lap. "Do you know what an insurance company once called me?" I asked softly. "A liability."

Billy stared at me for a long time. I could feel it by the growing burn in my cheeks.

"Maybe I understand that better than you know," he said; then he slapped his palm on the table.

"You don't need to learn to dance," he said, and with the other hand grabbed the edge of my lunch tray. "You need to learn to fight back."

"I feel like all I do is fight."

"Well, not for the right things, then. Sofia, you may need me more than you realize."

I looked up and glared at him. Why did everyone want to make me their pet project?

"I'll teach you. Let's start with your lunch." He pushed my tray a couple of inches to the left. I didn't know if he meant to do it or not, but that was still my weak side. It just took time, the doctors said, to relearn balance and counterweight, and all those daily exercises I was supposed to do at home were going to help.

I didn't move. I hadn't been doing the daily exercises.

"Come on, stop me," he said, pushing my tray a couple of inches more. "Make me sorry I messed with you."

The tray was getting dangerously close to the edge of the table. His eyes locked with mine and chills went through my whole body, even my prosthesis, I swear. I wasn't sure if I wanted to kiss him really badly or just slap him repeatedly.

Bit by bit, he pushed my tray farther off the edge. I kept my arms folded, trying not to watch. It made me crazy. When it tilted at last, I refused to look, but then, at the last possible second, I lunged.

My lunch splattered all over the ground. I slowly sat back in defeat.

"Too late," he said, and shook his head. He sounded disappointed. "I'll get you a new one. One cookie, an apple, and some wilted lettuce that you're going to eat just on principle, right?"

Everyone stared at me as he left and I got busy picking up the tray.

Sneaking a glance in his direction, I saw Billy swing the door open, but before he went into the cafeteria, he reached into his pocket and bent down.

Looking back down, I reached for a clump of lettuce. A new Sperry loafer stepped on it and I looked up.

"What is his deal?" Candy stood over me, glaring at Billy's back as he disappeared.

I motioned for her to move as I finished scooping up the remainders of my lunch and she watched.

"He's cute but psycho," Candy sighed. "I called him and he didn't even call me back, can you believe that? He told Natalie he already had a girlfriend, even though the only girl he ever talks to is you, so I know that's a lie."

I stood, keeping the tray between us for extra space. She must have applied her perfume like she was crop dusting.

"Anyway," she said, stroking her hair absentmindedly with one manicured hand, "if we're going to work on our plan, we have to start right away. I'm assuming you're going to the dance, so I'll go dress shopping with you. My aunt owns a great boutique at the mall."

More help I didn't want, though I realized that the only way to stop her was by confessing that we were broke. I took a deep breath.

Candy grabbed my arm. "I know what you're thinking, but here comes the best part. She wanted me to tell you that if you let a photographer take your picture for the newspaper, you'll get the dress for free."

"Ice cream!" Alexis stood up at her table, her voice easily carrying across the small courtyard. "Who's in?" None of her tablemates raised their hands. Only Alexis would want ice cream on a chilly day.

"Hello?" Candy said, sounding exasperated with me.

I turned my attention back to her. How could I possibly tell her everything wrong with that idea? When Candy saw a camera, her whole face lit up. When I saw a camera, I tried to shrink my body inward and turn my face away.

Candy and I lived in parallel universes and it was just too hard to explain mine.

"We're going Thursday," she said. "My mom's signing us out early, but your mom has to send in a permission slip."

Alexis stood and turned around, catching me talking with Candy. Her face darkened.

"You're so lucky," Candy said, resting her hand on my forearm. "My aunt doesn't give just anybody a free dress."

Alexis rolled her eyes and stomped off toward the cafeteria.

I jerked my arm away. "I never agreed to this!"

Candy gasped, like I had just spit on a kitten. "I'm offering you my help, and a free dress from the best store in town. How does that make me the bad guy?" Then she took a deep breath and closed her eyes, like this was hard on *her*. I wanted to scream.

"Do you know the definition of insanity, Sofia?" She gestured to my outfit. "It's doing the same thing over and over and expecting different results. We have to upgrade you. The first step is getting you a fabulous dress for the dance. People will remember it for weeks. That'll buy us some time to work on your other . . . choices." She made a face like she was trying to avoid looking directly at my clothes.

Natalie bounced up, pulling on Candy's arm. "Isabel just walked in!" she hissed in Candy's ear. "Let's go ignore her."

"Please do," I sighed under my breath.

Candy gave me a confused, searching look. I was clearly a mystery to her, but she walked off with Natalie to go ruin someone else's day.

Grabbing my tray to return it, I turned to leave through the media center doors to avoid seeing anyone else, especially Billy if he really was going to come back with another lunch. As I swung the door open, the bushes rustled beside me. I stood still, listening, but the movement was too soft and gentle to be a monster. Bending down, I peered into the gap between the shrubs. A skinny brown rabbit was chewing on a pile of carrots, its nose twitching back and forth. Poor guy looked starved from the long winter months. On impulse, I reached for the spot where my left leg had once been.

Mother Nature was nobody's friend.

THIRTEEN

After dinner that night, I tried to make up for my moodiness by tidying up the kitchen while Mom prepped for an online software class. Everyone in her office had to take it, but Mom was probably the only one excited about it. She grabbed her pajamas from the dryer while I took out the trash. Outside, dusk was settling, the night's darkness creeping in as birds with long black wings glided overhead. Several trees in the neighborhood were still bare, their spidery branches frozen in their final pose from last fall. The tight green buds on the branches were still only promises.

I looked up and down the neighborhood, at the line of lifeless trees, the brown grass, the flower beds with collapsed, rotting leaves. The world still looked dead. Who knew what would come back and what was lost forever?

I dumped the trash in the can and dropped the lid. The can shook in response, a huge dent appearing in the right side. Something was in there. Something big.

Dumb, fat possums got trapped in garbage bins all the time. Raccoons got trapped too, but they always figured out how to escape. Possums were hopeless. Even though my hands shook at just the thought of a possible bite from one of those nasty oversized rats, I popped off the lid and jumped back.

Nothing happened. Nothing moved. Maybe the possum was playing dead.

I turned to walk back into the house, when I saw two huge yellow eyes glaring at me, like twin moons side by side. With my peripheral vision, I saw tufts of brown fur, tinged at the end with white. Beneath the eyes was a snout that ended with thick black nostrils, which flared as the beast sniffed the air.

I carefully took one step back.

An enormous wolf stood before me on four huge paws with knuckles the size of golf balls and long black claws as long as my pinkie.

I knew I was seeing an extraordinary creature, one that had gone undetected for hundreds of years, maybe more. My heart beat faster.

I was alone. If I died, there would be no witnesses, except perhaps the birds that stirred in the dark trees.

Pins and needles shot up and down my arms. Maybe this was what I would feel after my first kiss, overwhelmed and unsteady. When you're terrified, odd thoughts float up from your subconscious. Why did I associate terror with my first kiss? I made a mental note to consider that at a more convenient time.

I calmed my nerves by taking a few deep breaths, but the deeper I breathed, the more I started to hyperventilate. I had to focus on the wolf, not myself. I extended one hand to reach out and touch it to make certain it was real. My hand began to shake and the wolf's gold eyes targeted it as if I were shaking a toy at a dog. Dropping my hand back to my side, I tried to take inventory, the way Xeno might have when he recorded his own sightings.

The fur on its body was a dirty brown with light tan streaks like swirls of dirt, and it smelled like old socks and blood. The skin of its thick, wide black nose was pebbly. My gaze dipped down to its mouth. Flecks of a dirty paper towel and old candy bar wrapper clung to its lips. Saliva mixed with what looked like blood, hanging in juicy thick ropes. Bits of meat, perhaps a fast-food hamburger, stuck out between its teeth. Its breath was hot in my face and stank.

Without warning, the beast lurched to the right and snapped furiously at his side. I jumped too, even though I didn't know what had spooked him. His eyes went wide and he began panting. Then he whipped toward the left, snapping at his other side, and stumbled when he landed. Something inside his stomach was punching outward, making his side expand. He growled in frustration and snapped again, but the thing inside him moved to the other side and punched. The wolf continued to whip his body back and forth. Something was at war inside his stomach.

"Wait here!" I whispered. "I'll be right back."

I got upstairs just as Mom was walking to her bedroom with her company laptop. She saw me walking as fast as I could to my room and frowned. "Where's the fire?" she asked.

"Uh . . ." My brain searched for a quick excuse. "I thought you would be on the computer already."

"Do I need to cancel my class?" she said, an ominous tone to her voice. "Are you up to something?"

"No!" I forced a smile. "Do your class. I'm not going to get into any trouble. Promise."

Mom stared at me as if deciding whether to trust me or her gut. I guess I won, because she disappeared into her room and I was only able to see the top of her feet as she stretched out on her bed to watch the video.

Once in my room, I grabbed Xeno's book and flipped until I found the page with the monster's picture on it. It was at the end, and the paper and handwriting were different from the rest of the book, as if someone had made this entry later. How many Guardians had there been? Did they quit, like Claire, or did they get eaten?

Bending over closely to read, I kept glancing at my window, straining to listen for new sounds, any howl or growl that would alert the neighbors.

THE BEAST OF GEVAUDAN
Origins: Gevaudan territory, France

The Beast terrorized France in the 1700s, eating over one hundred villagers. He first appeared on a spring morning in 1734, attacking a young girl tending to her sheep. He ate the sheep too. The King of France sent the army after it, but the Beast made his way across Europe to England, killing as it went, evading the troops. Finally, it boarded a boat in the fog, hoping to sleep and digest its last meal,

which was a rather fat baker. Aboard this ship, the Beast ate two
passengers and several crew members. To avoid panic, their deaths
were attributed to sickness.

    The Colonists had brought the Beast of Gevaudan to the New
World.

I studied the picture carefully. This was definitely the
monster in our driveway. If any of our neighbors saw him,
Mom was going to get a strongly worded letter from our
Homeowners Association. Unless he ate them all first.

The Beast has poor digestion because he does not chew thoroughly.

I was beginning to get a bad feeling. I read the rest of the
entry, which contained a map of the Beast's natural habitat
and a few notes about his behavior.

A low growl erupted outside. I opened my window and
peeked down at our driveway. There was no sign of him, but
I knew he was there. The dogs in our neighborhood were
barking furiously.

"Shhh!" I whispered. "You're going to get us both caught!"

A moth flew toward my bedroom light. The Beast lunged
out from the bushes, his white fangs glistening in the
moonlight as he snapped up the moth before falling back to
the pavement with a crash. Mrs. Cranston across the street
turned on her porch light and I panicked.

Sliding my window open, I motioned to the Beast below
to climb inside, fast. He made the jump to the second story
easily, like a dog leaping onto a couch.

Mrs. Cranston opened her front door and squinted into the dusky evening. She had rollers in her hair and was wearing a white robe that made her look like a giant marshmallow.

The Beast whined and lifted his paw, knocking my bed against the wall with it as he clawed at his mouth frantically.

Why had I opened my window? Now I had Mrs. Cranston outside and a Beast inside. I didn't know which one was scarier.

The Beast couldn't fully close his mouth and he panted heavily, his saliva dripping onto my carpet.

"What do I do?" I asked, and flipped to the blank page Xeno used. The page remained empty. I tried shaking the book, like it was an Etch A Sketch, but still nothing happened.

The Beast tried to circle me like I was prey, but he barely fit in my room. He scooted his butt across my wall as he turned and knocked the *Doctor Who* poster off center.

The book began to glow at last. I exhaled, my knee going weak with relief.

The Beast will bite you if you are not careful. You might not survive.

"Isn't it your job to keep me safe?" I snapped.

I do. I give you advice.

I scowled. "I don't want advice! I thought being the Guardian would give me superpowers or something."

Following good advice is a superpower.

I rolled my eyes. "So how do I help him?" Maybe I shouldn't help at all, I thought. The world needed monsters, but this Beast had eaten lots of people.

He must be restrained. It will require a special rope.

"A special rope? What kind?"

A rope made from the beard of a woman.

"You're not helping," I groaned. *And you're not funny,* I wanted to add.

Are you sure you trust me? Remember, it is the only thing I asked of you.

"I didn't realize what that meant," I said, my voice getting high-pitched. "I'm trying."

I don't want you to try. I want you to trust. This is not about monsters. This is about you. Answer one question and I will help.

The Beast whined, a pitiful sound like someone who's had the stomach flu for two days and just wants it to be over.

"Okay," I said, "I trust you. I have a million questions of my own and you never give me all the answers, but I trust you."

The Beast belched, causing my hair to blow back. I clasped one hand over my mouth as a shield against the smell; it was worse than fish-stick farts.

To survive, monsters must hide. You do not have to hide, yet you do. Why?

The Beast retched, and a squirrel flew out of his mouth still wearing a wide-eyed look of shock. The squirrel ran toward my bed, then back toward my closet, then back to my bed. The Beast and I watched as it made one more zigzag, before the Beast ate it again. It made a little barking noise as it went down the Beast's neck and into his stomach.

The Beast swallowed animals whole! There were live animals inside his stomach, fighting to get out! I had to get the Beast out of my room. Whatever came up next might be harder to handle than a squirrel.

I glanced back at the book. "I can't answer that right now! I have to help the Beast."

And I have to help you. You are not meant to live in the shadows. And because you are a rather difficult student, I must try a new method of teaching. I will refuse to say anything else tonight. Your help will not come from me.

I gasped. I wasn't stubborn!

The Beast's stomach changed shape again when the squirrel hit the bottom. It looked like animals fighting inside a pillowcase. He slammed his side against my wall and the fighting stopped for a moment.

"Sofia! Keep it down!" Mom hollered from her bedroom. "I'm trying to concentrate!"

"You've got to get out of here," I whispered to the Beast, panicked.

The Beast slowly turned away from me. He knew I had failed him. I saw it in the way he moved his legs. Sadness made them heavy. I couldn't help him.

"What do I do?" I asked Xeno.

The page erased itself and remained blank. I waited for as long as I could and realized Xeno meant what he had said: he was not going to help me. I had the world's most dangerous wolf in my bedroom, the one who had started the legend about the existence of werewolves.

I couldn't handle this alone.

Billy's dad was a vet. A veterinarian would know what to do. But what if I called and Billy answered? I had left the butterfly garden before he could replace my lunch and ask me about the dance again.

We only had one phone in the house, not counting Mom's cell phone. It was the landline downstairs.

I reached for my book bag and pulled out the business card tucked in the front pocket. I had fished it out of the trash earlier, feeling guilty about tossing it. Billy deserved a good friend even if I thought he had chosen the wrong person.

The Beast moved to the window, a groan escaping his closed lips as his stomach rumbled again.

"Wait!" I said to him. "I can help you. Just follow me downstairs and do not make a sound. Not even one. Do you understand? Not a peep!"

He lifted his lips to reveal huge canine teeth. They were

as long as steak knives. I don't think he liked my tone. I stepped back carefully and crooked my finger, indicating that he should follow me.

Adrenaline was making me light-headed, and I took each stair as carefully and as quickly as I could without risking a fall, his snout edging along me next to the wall.

We made it into the kitchen, where the landline was. I left the lights off and grabbed the phone, sitting on the couch before I dialed.

The Beast stayed in the kitchen, his snout wrinkling as he sniffed loudly. I whirled around, one finger to my mouth in warning. He snapped his teeth at me. I gulped once and dialed fast.

In the dim light, I could barely read the business card. It listed an office phone and a number for after-hour emergencies. This was an emergency.

Billy picked up right away. I closed my eyes in agony and every other painful, delicious feeling that came from hearing his voice. A cereal box flew out from the pantry, ripped to shreds and empty, as it skidded across the floor. Then I heard another box being ripped open.

"Billy, it's Sofia," I whispered.

Nothing but silence.

"Billy?"

"Why are we whispering?" he whispered.

An empty box of crackers hit me in the head. I swirled around and glared at the Beast. He had one paw poised over a can of tomatoes, preparing to use his claw to pierce it open. I shook my head.

"Billy, what should I do if my . . . dog . . . has swallowed something he can't digest?"

"That's why we're whispering?" Billy said loudly, sounding disappointed.

The Beast punctured the can of tomatoes. He jerked his head back, then leaned in and sniffed the can. Knocking it to the side, he grabbed another.

"I swear, Billy, this is important," I pleaded. "I need your help right now."

"You should talk to my dad, not me," he said. "He's the vet."

"So get him," I said.

"Say you'll go to the dance with me."

It was my turn to be silent. The Beast was now on his third can. He was opening each one just to smell what was inside. I held one hand over the phone and hissed at him, making that little hissy-snappy sound that the Dog Whisperer uses on bad dogs. It had no effect.

Billy repeated the demand, slowly. "I'll get my dad if you'll be my date to the dance."

The Beast turned from the pantry and began using his giant teeth to pull open a cabinet. He grabbed a coffee mug and dropped it to the floor, then sniffed the shards before moving to open the next cabinet.

"Okay! I'll be your date. Now get your dad."

I heard him drop the phone and yell for his dad.

"This is Dr. Hamby." A deep, fatherly voice came on the line.

"This is Sofia, a . . . friend of Billy's from school. Sort

of. I mean, definitely from school." I giggled nervously. "Anyway, my . . . dog . . . has really bad indigestion."

"Did he get into anything he shouldn't have?" Dr. Hamby asked.

"No, just the usual, I think. But too much of it."

"Have your mother bring him over. Can I speak to her? She'll need our address."

"No! I can't. I mean, she can't. Talk to you. She's too upset. And the dog can't come over. Never."

A bright light temporarily blinded me. The Beast had opened the refrigerator. I heard him make a happy noise in the back of his throat, in between a bark and a whine.

Oh, no, no, no.

"Because?" Dr. Hamby asked, sounding patient. He was probably a really good dad. Not that I would know how to judge one.

"Because . . . he . . . hates men. He, like . . ." I tried to think of the absolute worst thing a dog would do. "He bites crotches. He's a really horrible crotch biter. So . . . maybe you could tell me what to do? I can do it here, by myself."

"Well . . ." He sounded unsure.

"I'm sure I'll be fine. He never bites my crotch or anything." I rolled my eyes. Had I really just said that?

The Beast poked his snout around in our fridge, using his teeth to open our cheese drawer.

Dr. Hamby cleared his throat, like maybe he was trying not to laugh at me, then spoke slowly. I could tell he was thinking this through in his head. "Is he acting normal right now?"

I watched as the Beast swallowed a block of cheddar whole, the wrapper still intact.

"It's hard to define normal for him," I replied. "But he seems okay."

"Is he drinking normally?"

The Beast now had his head tilted back, drinking straight from the milk carton. Mom didn't even let me do that. I hoped he didn't leave any hairs.

"Yep."

"No vomiting or diarrhea?" Dr. Hamby asked.

I hadn't realized that was a possibility. "Not yet," I said, my voice getting weaker.

"Well," Dr. Hamby said, "I'd watch him for a little while. You might try withholding any more food until tomorrow to give his system a chance to settle down. If he's not better by then, bring him by. I'm not afraid of a cranky patient."

"You should be," I whispered under my breath. Louder, I said, "Okay. Thanks for your help. Bye." What I wanted to say was, *Thanks for nothing,* because I had no useful information and I had just agreed to be his son's date.

Could this night get any worse?

The Beast lifted his tail and expelled a big cloud of gas that shimmered like a rainbow in the refrigerator light. Lifting my shirt over my mouth and nose, I marched into the kitchen and grabbed the Beast by the scruff of the neck, just like I had seen mother wolves do on Animal Planet. I had to stand on my toes to do it, and stretch my arms until they burned, but it worked.

The Beast whined and cowered, his big yellow eyes blinking at me innocently.

"To the backyard," I said through gritted teeth. "Right now."

I opened the back door and he followed me obediently. In the moonlight, protected from the neighbors' view by our fence, I collapsed onto a patio chair to think, my muscles burning. The Beast sat on his haunches beside me. He was so big he blocked out the light of the moon, but I could still hear strange and awful noises coming from inside him. I stroked the Beast's fur, trying to think of a plan. A Heimlich maneuver wouldn't work, since I couldn't wrap my arms around him. It wasn't safe to get him human medicine either.

The Beast's breathing slowed. Under my palms, his muscles released and elongated. A little burp escaped his mouth.

"You shouldn't swallow things whole," I scolded. He pressed his body against my hand, and it gave me an idea. Didn't mothers burp their babies by patting them on the back? I pushed myself up and stood next to him, running my palms down his side, trying to position them near his stomach. When I felt the trapped animal push back, I began gently slapping his body in that spot. The Beast turned and lifted an eyebrow, curious but unaffected and slightly condescending. He was French, after all.

I took a deep breath, made two fists, then punched him twice in the side. His eyebrows shot straight up in surprise. I did it again. This time I remembered to suck in my abs, because the physical therapists had told me that whenever I needed physical strength I should move from my core. I landed another one-two punch, and his mouth popped open, so I let more punches fly, until I was working up a sweat.

The Beast looked up at the moon and his body trembled. I realized, almost too late, what he was about to do, and I scrambled to move away. His jaws opened wide, his giant pink tongue flopping to the side as he dry heaved once; then the squirrel popped back out, followed by Newman the cat, and then a coyote. The Beast opened his mouth wider, his head jerking back and forth, until at last a huge hawk, wings spread out in either direction, emerged and flew into the sky.

The terrified animals looked around, then fled into the night.

The Beast sighed and lay down, obviously exhausted. He coughed once more, and a can of Cheese Whiz rolled across our patio.

The light came on above our stairs.

I froze. The Beast leaped into the darkness and disappeared.

I stood up just as Mom turned on the kitchen lights. Our eyes met through the glass of the patio door; then she turned her head and surveyed the damage.

I walked into the kitchen without saying anything. Opened cans, shredded boxes, and torn wrappers were everywhere. Cabinet doors stood ajar. The sweat on my face was cold as it ran down in little drops from my forehead.

"Well" was all Mom said. I started to clean but she waved me off, the heat of her anger and frustration rolling off her in waves. I went upstairs and got into bed, not even bothering to open the book. Xeno had said he was done for the night. My mom clearly was too. I wasn't worried about that.

I was worried about tomorrow.

FOURTEEN

Tuesday, March 4

"I'm in," I said to Candy. She was sitting with her little coven of friends at the center lunch table. The source of so much frustration was now the answer to my problems. It's too bad that colleges don't give out scholarships for irony. I was in the accelerated program.

Candy nodded in smug satisfaction, then took a long sip from her water bottle, her eyes never leaving mine. Xeno probably wanted me in this situation. He was using monsters to push me out into the open and ask others for help. Everyone around Candy smiled blankly, waiting to resume their private conversations.

Walking away, I could hear them gossiping about Billy asking me to the dance. News spread fast in this school. I tossed my cookie wrappers into the trash on the way out the door.

The intercom blasted my name. "Sofia Calloway, come to the office for early checkout."

My stomach lurched, and not just because I had eaten three oatmeal cream pies. There was only one reason I had ever gotten checked out early: the doctor.

Mom was waiting in the office but refused to give me any details. She was amazed that I had been hungry for breakfast that morning, and even a little suspicious that I was feeling so good. Plus, I wasn't due for blood work for another month and I'd already had my teeth cleaned a few weeks ago. I started to go a little nuts in the car, but Mom's only response was reaching over to pat my leg, except she patted my prosthesis, not me.

When we arrived, she parked under a big magnolia tree that cast a dark shadow across the lot. Gray clouds hovered above. I had another odd feeling, as if something were not right. I glanced around, expecting to catch a glimpse of Olympias. Xeno had been so wrapped up with me asking questions that he hadn't told me what to do about her.

We walked toward a plain one-story building. The lobby was brightly lit by a harsh blue light that buzzed overhead. In front of the elevators, Mom pulled out a piece of paper from her purse, checking it, then walked down the hall to the left. She kept looking from her paper to the signs on the doors. Finally she stuffed the paper back in her purse, straightened her posture, and took a deep breath.

MARIE INEZ CAPISTRANO, MD, PhD

The sign on the door was thick gray plastic with black letters. Mom was already turning the knob before I could stop her.

"Who is that?" I asked, pointing to the sign.

Mom ignored me and walked to a receptionist's desk with a frosted glass window made to slide open. Nobody was there.

"All my labs came back normal," I protested again. "I'm not due for any more tests until the end of the month."

An old woman, with white hair swept all around her head into a big fluffy bun, opened the door into the waiting room from the inner office. Her hairstyle looked like it had been shot out of a can of whipping cream.

"Sofia?" she asked. She had on an embroidered shawl with fringe that swayed when she moved, and big doughy cheeks that swelled up around her eyes. "Come with me. Your mom can stay out here." Her body moved from side to side as she turned to walk down the hall. I followed, only stopping once to turn back and glare at Mom.

The woman led me into an office. A movie poster from the old black-and-white *Frankenstein* film was on the wall behind the desk. I counted four diplomas hanging on either side of it. A plastic dragon sat next to a box of tissues. I leaned forward to examine it closely.

"Like it?" she asked, waddling around to her chair.

"It's kind of dumb," I replied, without thinking. What I wanted to say was that I was wondering how accurate it was. I hadn't seen one yet.

"Good," she laughed. "You're honest."

I felt my cheeks get hot. I hadn't meant to insult her statue. The rest of the office was decorated in normal adult fashion: practical, uncomfortable, and beige.

She settled down into her chair with a wiggle. A pile of

mail sat unopened on her desk, including a newspaper. The front page had a photo of the girl from the hospital next to an illustration of odd-looking bite marks. I hadn't had time to ask Xeno what had happened to her or which beast had attacked, but the marks didn't look like they'd come from anything normal. Beneath the photo I read the words "Animal Control Warns the Public: Unknown Animal Still on the Loose."

She caught me staring at the article and I glanced away. We took turns stealing glances at each other, sizing one another up. This definitely did not feel like a normal doctor's appointment. Looking anywhere but at that paper, I noticed she had a big cooler next to her on the floor. This lady packed some extremely large lunches, but there was no medical equipment in sight. She had several black-and-white movie posters: *Dracula, The Wolf Man, The Mummy.* I looked back and caught her staring at me.

"What are you?" I asked. "I mean, obviously you're a doctor. A doctor of what, though?"

She glanced out the window to my left, craning her neck and frowning, as if checking something. Turning her attention back to me, she smiled politely. "I'm a psychiatrist." She tapped her forehead as if I didn't know what a psychiatrist was. "I'm on staff with the hospital. I teach at the university. I'm a specialist in childhood fears and post-traumatic stress disorder. Your mother thought you might benefit from my services. She found a paper online that I wrote on the role of monsters in the history of mental health."

It was hard to pay attention. She had huge white eyebrows

that jumped and batted each other like kung fu caterpillars when she spoke.

"I don't need a psychiatrist."

Dr. Capistrano shrugged. "Your mother thinks you do. And the only other psychiatrist here who treats children works with functional constipation."

It was my turn to shrug.

"Children who refuse to poop." She glanced out the window, then scowled slightly. She turned back, smiling at me next as she folded her hands, resting them on her big pudding-bowl belly. "Don't be embarrassed by your interest in monsters, my dear. It's all very normal."

It was anything but normal, I wanted to yell.

"You see, by fearing monsters, we stay in control of our emotions. We use our fear of monsters to distract us from what we cannot manage ourselves. Monsters are a beautiful illusion, a dream that protects us from feeling pain."

The hair along my arms stood up, the same uneasy feeling creeping back: something definitely wasn't right.

"But what if you're wrong?" I asked.

The air around me turned cold.

"What if they're not an illusion?"

The doctor was rummaging through the cooler, grumbling beneath her breath, not listening to me. Did no one ever listen to what I was trying to say?

A monster hovered outside the window, watching us both. It had huge red feathered wings, each feather three or four feet long. Its body looked like a man's, but with bulging muscles. Its skin shimmered like gold. The skin on its face was black and lumpy and hung in folds. Instead of a mouth, the creature had a long beak, so white that it made its black eyes sparkle like a scalpel. I searched my mind for images from the book. What was it? What did it eat? I hope it didn't eat people, but if it did, my odds of survival were pretty good with Dr. Capistrano sitting there.

The monster floated outside the window as it watched us.

Nodding as if she was satisfied with something, Dr. Capistrano sat back and picked up a pen. Didn't she see the monster? She scribbled thoughtfully in my patient file, her head down. And how could she diagnose me so fast? She had no idea what the real problem was.

I looked back at the window. She might be about to find out.

"I have a patient waiting," the doctor said, smiling to herself as she recapped her pen. I knew she was lying; the waiting room had been empty. "This was a brief consultation, but I think I have all I need to make a recommendation for therapy." She snapped the folder closed and pointed to the door. "Let's go find your mom."

This monster must have followed me here. It needed me. I couldn't leave it floating outside, but I couldn't go out into the parking lot with my mom either.

"Go on." Dr. Capistrano motioned with her head for me to leave. "I'll be right behind you."

I stood still, goose bumps popping on my arms, my stomach flipping in every direction. I couldn't let it get inside. What if it tried to eat her? If a monster attacked a human, whose side was I on?

"I can't leave," I said weakly. "You might need me."

She paused and her eyes grew wide. "You see him, don't you?"

"Of course," I said, then looked back at her in surprise when it hit me. "*You* see him too?"

"Cover your eyes, quickly," she demanded. I did, just as the creature crashed through the plate-glass window. I tilted my head down as glass flew everywhere, followed by a sharp cold wind. I opened my eyes to see its red wings spread and open, creating a dark screen that blocked out the sun. Fear rooted me in place.

"That's the third time in a month," she muttered. "By the saints, those windows are expensive."

The monster chirped and then clicked his razor-sharp beak at her.

"Excuse us a moment," she said, then pulled a human foot from the cooler and tossed it to the monster. He caught it in midair and took a step toward her, chirping again.

"Who's a good boy?" she cooed.

She pulled out another foot and tossed it. The creature craned its head, catching it easily and swallowing it whole.

Then it took a step toward me, talons on each foot scraping against the carpet.

"Don't be afraid, dear," she said. "He's not bad. He's just hungry."

The monster cocked its head and bobbed side to side, making clicking sounds in its throat.

I tucked my good foot under the chair to keep it safe. I was beginning to get a little protective of it after the Kappa. I

used my prosthetic foot to scoot away from the creature. Without the Bestiary, I couldn't be sure, but it looked like the Native American monster the Thunderbird. A Jesuit priest had written of its existence in America back in the 1600s.

The monster danced from foot to foot, coming closer. I held my breath, my spine pressed against the back of the chair. It cawed loudly right into my face, the fetid burst causing my bandana to slip backward on my head. The smell of nasty, dead feet made my eyes water. I reached up to adjust the bandana, blinking back tears. The monster nudged my hand with its beak, like it wanted to be petted. I shrank back.

Turning, it looked out the window before flying out, eclipsing the gray sky with its red feathers.

"So you're a believer too." Dr. Capistrano clapped her hands together and studied me with delight. She closed the curtains to disguise the shattered window and sat back down. "Well, this changes everything."

"You're treating it like a pet," I said quietly. "You shouldn't do that."

She paused, studying me. "But I'm not afraid of it. *We're* not afraid, right?"

I wasn't sure how to answer that. I helped monsters, but I didn't trust them. They were shadowy dreams and nightmares, but it was my job to protect them, not make friends.

"You keep body parts in there?" I pointed to the cooler.

She pulled the cooler closer to her knees and opened it. I stood and peeked inside.

"Most monsters are carrion eaters, and they like roadkill. A few prefer human flesh, so I buy cadaver parts from the medical college, or I just steal medical waste. You wouldn't believe what an arm and a leg cost."

I didn't laugh.

She frowned, obviously disappointed that I shared her secret but not her sense of humor. With a sigh, she set the arm back in the cooler. I sat back in my chair.

"We used to live in perfect harmony, you know," she said. "All over the world. Every monster had a tribe, every tribe lived in peace. Monsters were created to be scapegoats for the human race, and they accepted their job with grace."

She sighed as if the story hurt her to tell.

"Then medicine killed the monsters, in a manner of speaking. People don't have to feel fear anymore; we could take a pill. But science can never change the human heart. Without monsters, we're cruel to each other. We still need these creatures, Sofia. And they need us, because what could be worse than knowing you are invisible? That no one sees you?"

She leaned back in her chair and opened the desk drawer. Pulling out a bag of M&M's, she tore them open and tilted her head back, pouring a few in. I watched her chew, and then she spoke. "We'll save the manatees and protect forest snails, but no one gives a rip about monsters."

"I give a rip," I said, leaning toward her desk.

"When did you first see one?" she asked, her eyes narrowing. She was testing me, I think. But how much was I allowed to reveal?

"Recently." Vague answers might be best until I knew if I could trust her.

She jerked her head back. "Recently? That's odd. Little

children sometimes see a monster, or the telltale signs that one is near, perhaps even under the bed, but no one takes them seriously. That's why adults rarely witness these miraculous creatures. Adults are not willing to believe, so they are not able to see." She clasped her hands together as if she were praying. "As a doctor, I was trained to set aside my personal prejudices, to listen and observe. Medical school made me curious about mysteries, not afraid. I had been a doctor for eight years when I saw my first monster." She lowered her voice. "So what happened recently? Something must have changed you."

I looked down at my knees. Xeno said not to share his secret, but Dr. Capistrano already knew it, didn't she? And what else did she know? I needed a lot of answers. Relief washed over me. I hadn't realized how hard it had been to do this alone.

"I was given a book," I said. "It belonged to Aristotle's last student, Xeno, and he uses it to communicate with me. He understands the monsters and helps me take care of them. But I'm not the only one who knows about the book, or the monsters. There's a ghost of a woman following me, or the book, but I don't know why." My words spilled out faster. "I don't think she wants the book or she would have taken it by now. I don't know what she wants, and I never have enough time . . ."

Dr. Capistrano's eyes were as wide as saucers. "It exists?" she whispered breathlessly. "The Bestiary? And you have it?" She paused. "You're the Guardian, aren't you? Their very survival depends on you." She began furiously scribbling notes in my file.

"I don't do much for them," I said, embarrassed.

"It's not what you do, it's who you are. This is extraordinary."

In the distance, a scream split the sky. I turned toward the window, once again frightened. The doctor didn't flinch; she must not have heard it.

"I'll help you in any way I can," Dr. Capistrano said, suddenly smiling. "You don't have to do this alone."

But I was alone. For reasons I couldn't quite explain yet, I knew that.

The door swung open. "I am so sorry," my mom said. "I was reading a magazine and looked at my watch and was shocked by how the time had flown. I know you said twenty minutes, tops, since you had to work us in between your other appointments. You should really hire a receptionist."

Dr. Capistrano stood and maneuvered herself to block my mom's view of the broken glass on the carpet, then turned to smile at Mom. "It's hard to keep good help." She took my mom by the arm and steered her back toward the door. "You have a wonderful daughter. Her mental health is excellent, but I do believe she would benefit from a few sessions."

"To talk about her recovery from cancer?" Mom asked.

Dr. Capistrano cocked her head to one side and looked back at me. We hadn't talked about my other problems at all. We'd both forgotten about them entirely once the monster had shown up.

"Yes, of course," the doctor said, then focused on me. "Sofia, I want you to consider me a friend. Call me anytime, day or night."

Mom treated me to dinner at the cheap Italian place we both loved. It had an aquarium in the middle of the room. There were huge fish in brilliant hues of green and blue, but my favorite had always been a yellow fish with bulging eyes and big white lips, because he looked startled every time he finished another lap around the tank.

On the way to our table, I checked all the windows and exits. I glanced toward the front door before sliding into the booth. I picked the side with a great view of the aquarium and studied the fish while Mom went to the buffet. She returned with two fully loaded plates.

"Look, Sofia, about the doctor, let me explain," she began.

A monster floated in the aquarium. He looked like a swollen, colorless frog, with huge gills that opened and closed while he swam, all six eyes watching me. He must have recognized me as the Guardian, because he merrily waved with his fin.

I frowned, trying to remember his classification. An Afanc, maybe—a British water monster. Before I could decide, he opened his mouth and ate my yellow fish. My jaw fell open in outrage. The Afanc continued to swim in lazy circles around the tank, selecting his next fish to eat.

Mom shook her head and talked faster. "No, no, let me explain. I'm worried about the changes in your behavior, that's all. I thought a neutral third party could help you open up about what's been bothering you."

"I have a date," I blurted. Ugh. What made my mouth disconnect from my brain like that? But it worked.

She set down her fork and changed the subject. "What? Where? Who?"

The Afanc hovered next to the sucker fish on the wall and opened its gaping maw. The sucker fish clung to the glass and didn't budge.

"The school dance on Saturday. A new guy named Billy asked me." The Afanc's lips made a sucking motion and the sucker fish flew in, along with most of the gravel along the bottom of the tank and a few more fish. The hostess stood in front of the aquarium checking her phone, oblivious.

I buried my face in the plate of spaghetti.

Mom sat back, a big smile fighting to bust out across her face. Her mouth twitched and she tried to stop it. "Is that what you didn't want to tell me? You have your first boy-friend?" She grinned. "That's wonderful."

This was so awkward it hurt. "No, not my first boyfriend."

She grinned even wider. "Do tell."

I hung my head. "The new guy asked and I said yes and I guess it's kind of a big deal. Everyone's going."

"Alexis?" Mom asked. I reached for a bread roll and tore it into four pieces, ignoring the question.

Mom sighed. "Well, we can talk about her later. I guess we need to go shopping for something to wear. I get paid on Friday. Maybe we can find something before then and ask the store to put it on hold."

"You won't have to pay for a dress," I said. "Candy's aunt owns a boutique at the mall. She's going to give me a dress in exchange for letting the paper take a few pictures. Candy really wants to help me with my new look. It's all she can talk about."

Mom frowned. "Candy?" She chewed her lip. "You've been hanging around Candy, instead of Alexis?"

"No, Mom, this has nothing to do with Alexis."

Mom looked confused. She had heard my stories about Candy for years. I could tell she wanted to ask more, so I took another big bite of spaghetti, and reached for another roll too. I hadn't eaten like this since before the diagnosis. She always worried that I didn't eat much. She looked happy and confused at the same time.

"I don't know how I feel about the paper taking pictures of you," she said finally.

"No one's ever asked to take a picture of me before."

"That woman I talked to in the grocery store," Mom began, her voice drifting as she thought about it, "she said something that stuck with me. She said girls who make an effort to look pretty and fit in with their peers have an easier time in life. I don't think that's always good, but I think it's true. If you're going to the dance, you need a nice dress."

"So you think I should take Candy up on her offer?" I asked.

Mom groaned. It was a tough decision. "So much has changed. Maybe Candy has too. All I know for certain is that I want you to be happy. You may have to try new things to make that happen."

Neither of us had anything to say to that. To avoid talking any more, I polished off my spaghetti, plus a salad and two breadsticks.

Mom paid the check and tucked the receipt into her wallet with all the others. When we stood to leave, I saw the hostess throw one hand over her mouth, having finally noticed the fish tank. It was completely empty: no fish, no plants, no gravel. The Afanc was gone. The hostess glanced around the restaurant wildly, like one of us had done it. I kept my head down and made for the front door. Mom was busy checking her cell phone and didn't look up.

On the way home, I had to move the seat belt away from my abdomen. I felt like I'd swallowed a bowling ball. This made Mom laugh. I kept my eyes closed, pretending to concentrate on my digestion.

I had never been a girl anyone wanted to take pictures of. I didn't think Candy was going to embarrass me or do anything cruel; she genuinely seemed like she wanted to help me. Her logic was probably twisted but right. People were nicer to me now because they felt sorry for me, but that wouldn't last forever. The medical term for it was "compassion fatigue." Soon everyone would be ready to forget my trauma and focus on their own problems, and they'd need a place to put me, a label for me to wear just like everyone else. I would go back to being the outsider . . . unless I changed.

I knew we couldn't afford a nice dress, but Mom wouldn't have to worry about the money. She'd be excited to see me dressed up to join my classmates for a fun night out. Mom would be relieved and happy and hopeful.

But what would *I* be?

FIFTEEN

We stopped for gas on the way home. I tilted my head back and closed my eyes, glad for one quiet moment alone. The acrid smell of gasoline stung my nose as the clicking noise of the pump kept ticking on. I hated the sound of money flying out of Mom's wallet. I wished now that she hadn't bought me dinner, but I was glad I had made the right decision about the dress.

I certainly wasn't going to tell her that a monster from an ancient bestiary was largely responsible for my first date. There's only so much a mom can take.

Mom was having trouble with the pump. I heard her arguing with it and opened my eyes to watch her pressing the button for a receipt over and over. No receipt came out. She marched off toward the cashier inside the store. I closed my eyes again.

Her door opened. I opened my eyes to tell her how unbelievably fast she was when a smell hit me, worse than the gas smell before, if that was even possible. It was the Kappa. It slid into the driver's seat, eyes swirling fast in every direction like two pinwheels. Tentacles slithered out, then braided together as it reached for me.

I pushed back in my seat as far as I could go. "I don't have any cucumbers," I whispered. "Go away!"

Its tentacles were cold and wet as it grabbed my arms, pulling me toward its face.

"Please, no!" I glanced around and saw my mom waiting in line to talk to the cashier about the stupid receipt. "I'll get you a cucumber, okay? Just let me go."

The Kappa's jaws opened wide, saliva stretching like gummy rivers between its lips. Its mouth opened wider and wider, revealing a darkness with the stench of dead fish. Fog burst from its nostrils, and little tendrils of slime ran down its face. Its eyes slowly came to rest on me and I recognized something in them, my face only inches away from that awful mouth.

I tried to see why it had come back. Another fishhook? An accident? A craving for human flesh?

The Kappa whimpered, but I was the one helplessly trapped. Then I realized what it was. It was fear.

The Kappa was afraid.

"What is it?" I asked. I needed Xeno here. These beasts couldn't talk, at least not to me.

The Kappa whimpered again; then it released me and used its tentacles to cover its eyes. It wasn't here to eat me. It was here to be saved, but from what? I took a deep breath for courage and gagged. Kappas really stank. Steadying my nerves, I took another look at it. The body looked normal, at least for a Kappa. Nothing was wrong there. The face was still horrendous, which seemed like a good sign. So what was wrong?

It opened its mouth wider.

I peered inside. The smell was worse than spoiled shrimp left in the car trunk. My stomach closed like a hard fist, threatening to send my dinner spewing out.

Inside its mouth were hundreds of tiny Kappa babies. They squealed in terror when they saw my gigantic face looming in front of them, sounding like a hundred tiny balloons deflating at once. The Kappa snapped its jaws shut, nearly giving me that perky nose job I had always wanted.

This thing was a mother? Suddenly mine didn't seem so bad.

A low growl tore across the sky. People at other pumps looked up, as if they had just heard thunder. I knew it was something much worse.

I heard the car door close and turned back around. The Kappa was gone.

My heart was thumping twice as fast when Mom got back in the car. She wrinkled her nose and looked at me. "Whew! Garlic bread does not agree with you," she muttered, putting her finger on the button to roll down her window.

"No!" I said. "Don't." I didn't know what was happening or what was outside the car. "It's cold outside."

"Sorry," Mom said. "Turn on the heater if you want. You won't freeze to death."

"It isn't the weather that I'm afraid of," I muttered under

my breath, but the night air was already whooshing into the car as we left the gas station. The stench of the Kappa faded away, and something new was being carried on the wind, vaguely familiar, a stale musky scent, one I remembered from visits to the pet store.

It smelled like a snake.

"Wow, you're getting good on the stairs," Mom said, trailing behind me. I hadn't realized I was moving so fast or that she would notice the difference. Being the Guardian was paying off in unexpected ways: as I pushed my body to work and move faster, it responded with grace.

"I work my core every day," I said, omitting the part about monsters being responsible for that too. Pausing at my bedroom, one hand on my doorknob, I smiled awkwardly. "Um, well, good night, then."

"You understand why I did it, don't you?" Mom asked, taking a step toward me. I didn't want her to come in my room for a late-night heart-to-heart. Something was wrong, and I had no idea what it was. Something awful was out there, something that scared even the Kappa.

Mom tried again. "You understand why I wanted you to talk to Dr. Capistrano?"

"I'm not mad at you," I said. "But I am really tired."

She opened her mouth, then shut it and smiled. "Good night, then. Sleep well."

The book was glowing dark green when I got inside the room and shut the door.

"I get to ask the questions tonight," I said. "And I need answers. About the woman who's been following me, Olympias, and a doctor who sees monsters too. And the Kappa, because it has babies in its mouth and it's scared and I think there's something awful lurking out there. Something that's not in your book. Something you didn't tell me about."

Flipping to the blank page, I saw that it was empty. He was there but he wasn't speaking. "I've done everything you asked, haven't I?"

The Kappa is a mouth brooder. Mothers keep their young inside it when a bigger predator is near.

"A bigger predator? A monster that other monsters are afraid of?"

Xeno was silent. Did he not know the answer or was he afraid to tell me? Letters etched slowly onto the page as Xeno responded with small, frightened marks.

Yes.

"What kind of monster? How can there be a new monster? I thought your book listed all of them. How could a brand-new monster suddenly appear?"

Your birthday wish—do you remember it?

I did. On my thirteenth birthday, the nurses had put a candle in a hospital cafeteria cupcake and brought it to me. Mom was asleep in the chair by my bed. I leaned forward, and just before I pursed my lips to blow, I made a wish. I didn't want to seem ungrateful, because being alive was, after all, the best possible way to start another year, but birthday candles are made for big, selfish wishes.

"I don't know if I'll ever have another birthday, or another chance to make a wish," I whispered. "There are a lot of things I want to experience, and if I get to grow up, I will. But there's one thing that more time isn't going to give me. I've never been pretty. I've never been the girl who could star in the story. I've always just faded into the background of a crowd. So if I could have one wish, it's to look in the mirror and smile. To see myself as strong and powerful and . . . *exquisite.*" That word surprised me as it tumbled out, but it was perfect. It made my imaginary self seem beautiful and rare. That's what I wanted to be, really, not just some model in a magazine.

Opening my eyes, I blew out the candle and made the wish.

The flame flickered as if deciding, and just before it went out, the lights dimmed in my room, like my wish had interrupted some unseen electrical current.

The next morning I looked in the mirror, sighed in defeat, and decided to shave the rest of my hair off.

That moment shook the supernatural realm. In the age of science and doubt, how could any child wish with such power? Every cell in your body vibrated and pulsed with the desire for what existed only in your imagination. You are so different from every Guardian of the past. You are a Guardian that neither Olympias nor I knew could be born in an age of unbelief.

I picked up the book and shook it. I had to grab his attention. "I don't understand what you're saying! Who created the new monster?"

You did.

My body revolted; my mouth dried up and my stomach tensed as his words sank deeper into my brain like some poisonous arrow. It couldn't be true; this couldn't be my fault.

His dark shadow has haunted many girls. They feel him near when they look in the mirror, when they walk alone down the school hallways. He is the voice which whispers that they will never belong, that they are unloved. His presence is often mistaken for the human emotion of shame, but it is something much worse: it is a monster begging to be born into the world, waiting for the one person who still remembers how to call fear into existence.

If you have read about Olympias, you know she practiced a terrible and cruel magic. Like me, Olympias felt the power of your imagination when you made your wish, and knew you would make a strong ally. You would convince people to see the world through her eyes. Your fears, which were many and dark, gave the monster its form, and when you chose to become the Guardian, Olympias granted him life. He was created not to kill you, but to convince you.

"Convince me of what?" I asked.

That you cannot be at peace with yourself, that you will never see beauty when you look in the mirror, that you will see only what you lack. You will see a void. He whispers that you must hide the wound because the world is not a safe place. Those who do not belong suffer.

My tongue felt like sandpaper in my mouth, and it was hard to speak. "Olympias used my fears against me."

The words erased slowly and a new message appeared, as if Xeno was carefully thinking as he wrote.

She calls him Entropion.

"En-*tro*-pee-on?" I repeated. "What kind of name is that?"

Xeno didn't reply. I guessed he wanted me to figure that part out on my own.

I thought about what Olympias had said in the park about differences leading to war. If everyone was alike, there would be no more suffering. Nobody likes different. The only way to stay safe in this world is to look like everyone else, to act like them and want the same things.

It reminded me of how weird it was to go with my mom to vote. She had to stand inside this box with privacy screens all around so no one knew who she voted for. And we were a country founded on the idea of freedom. So how come adults had to hide who they voted for?

But what Olympias didn't understand was that no one wanted to be like me, so I had no power or influence. It wasn't like I could convince anyone that being more like me was a good thing.

What good would I be as an ally?

"She said she was going to take things away from me, though." I paused. "Xeno? I'm scared."

I do not know what waits for you out there. But, Sofia? I know what lives within you. I will put my hope in that. Now, you have work to do.

"What work?" I asked.

First, you must create one last entry in the Bestiary. Entropion must be documented for future generations. And then you must find a way to overcome him and the power of his lies.

I suddenly realized I was now part of history. The thing about history, though?

Everyone's dead.

SIXTEEN

Ms. Hochness was sipping a cup of coffee when I hustled into the library the next morning. I had fifteen minutes until the first bell. Nothing else had come to my window last night, not even a moth, and Xeno hadn't said any more either. I had begged Mom to do me a favor later today, but I didn't know yet if she would come through.

I threw my book bag on a table and went to the row of books Ms. Hochness had shown me earlier.

"Whoa, where's the fire?" she asked.

"I think I missed something," I called to her. "I need to know more about Alexander the Great and his mother."

I grabbed the dictionary that sat next to the computers and looked up the *E*s while she gathered a few books and carried them to a table. "Entropion: from the Greek word *'entropia,'* meaning 'a turning inward against oneself.'"

"Entropion" also described a medical condition affecting the eyes. So Entropion was created by the part of me that had turned against myself, the way I saw myself.

"You're working on a special project?" she called as she pulled books for me.

I looked up. Our eyes met and I nodded. "Very special."

She got my meaning. This was important.

She motioned for me to stand, and when I did, she took my place in front of the computer.

"I'll rummage around in the university's database. Sometimes they upload research articles. It's good stuff."

"Thanks," I said. I immediately sat at the table, opened one of the books, and dug in.

Fifteen minutes later, I had discovered nothing new. I dropped my head onto the book, groaning. There had to be something on how to stop a monster like Entropion, and Olympias probably held the only clue. Sucking in a deep breath, I sat up and went at it again. If I knew what sort of rituals she used, or magic she practiced, maybe I could find her weakness too. But it seemed like people had hated and feared her so much they'd been afraid to write about her.

By the time the bell rang, nothing new had turned up, and my shoulders hurt from bending over the books.

"Cool beans!" Ms. Hochness yelled.

I jumped up and made my way over to her. "No one says that anymore, Ms. Hochness."

"I just did." She smirked, hitting a button on her keyboard with a flourish. I arched one eyebrow.

She grinned. "An academic piece that someone at the

teaching hospital was working on," she said. Behind her, the printer whirred to life. "It's not even finished," she continued. "I'm shocked that a professional would upload anything before it's finished."

I didn't care about any of that. I just wanted it.

The tardy bell rang.

I grabbed my book bag, then snatched the two pages from the printer. The second hand on the wall clock swept around again.

"Last one," Ms. Hochness said.

"Thank you!" I yelled, grabbing it from her as I hustled, making it to homeroom just in front of Ms. Forester, who was carrying a steaming cup of coffee. She tsked at me for brushing past her so fast. I apologized, but secretly I was pleased. It meant I was getting faster.

After I settled into my seat, I pulled out my textbook and laid the papers from the library over it. The little writing at the top of the page didn't catch my eye at first.

I had to reread the front page twice before it really sank in.

The Mysterious Death of Aristotle and His Last Student
By Dr. Inez Capistrano

I stared at the name in disbelief, vaguely aware that Ms. Forester was passing out a pop quiz on bathroom etiquette. Apparently, the janitors were refusing to clean the boys' bathrooms unless the boys learned some basic skills, like how to put paper towels in a waste basket. And aiming, I suppose.

The tiny time stamp at the top of Dr. Capistrano's paper showed when it was uploaded into the system. It read 4:36 a.m.

And today's date. So at 4:36 a.m. this morning, just a few hours ago, in the middle of the night, Dr. Capistrano had uploaded it, before it was even finished. But why?

The paper began,

In investigating the history of Aristotle, in hopes of verifying the legend of his last student, Xeno, and reported sightings of a book popularly referred to as the Bestiary, a scholar must be able to separate fact from fiction. Fiction, however, would surely offer scholars a better story, because fiction holds the promise of a happy ending.

As I have tonight learned, there can be no happy ending for the student who possesses the Bestiary. The book is cursed and should never have been opened again.

I am sorry I could be of no further help, but I have chosen to move on to safer subjects.

May the one who reads this take every precaution.

Ms. Forester grabbed my book and shut it. She then tapped her finger on the pop quiz now in front of me on my desk.

I was going to pass this quiz, but the bigger question was, what else was I going to fail, and who would pay the price?

After school, Mom turned out of the parking lot and headed in the direction of Dr. Capistrano's office.

I cleared my throat so I wouldn't sound too anxious. "Thanks again for getting an appointment."

"I didn't. No one answered the phone," she replied. "We'll just stop by and see if she can fit you in."

It was hard to tell if she was still frustrated with me or just really tired. Either way, this was not the moment to confess that I had helped create a super-monster that just might try to eat us both. *Sometimes,* I told myself, *good relationships are all about timing.*

Mom turned up the volume on the radio, listening to a report on a new variety of drug-resistant, flesh-eating bacteria. *Besides,* I thought, *she has enough of her own monsters to deal with.*

Mom glanced into the rearview mirror and pulled to the right. A police car zoomed past, lights flashing and sirens screaming.

We watched it take the same turn we were about to make toward Dr. Capistrano's office. A bad feeling deep in my bones grew stronger. The doctor had uploaded that paper at 4:36 a.m., but it hadn't been finished. Why couldn't she wait? What had she discovered? Had Entropion interrupted her?

I reviewed the paper in my mind one more time. The facts were simple. But the meaning escaped me. I knew enough from history to remember that Alexander the Great was still considered a military hero. But not many people knew about his mother. Bile flooded my mouth as I read on;

Olympias was believed to practice a dark, evil magic, and snakes were said to be her closest companions. In fact, she told Alexander that he had been fathered by Zeus, who came to her one night in the form of a snake. That's why Alexander was worshipped as a god. And during his travels, he sent letters to Aristotle, detailing all he had discovered, so he had contact with his former teacher for years. Dr. Capistrano added one last note:

> Here the historical record ends, and we must imagine what other letters Aristotle received. If indeed a student had discovered fierce and terrible creatures in the new world, Alexander would not be able to force his troops to march upon them. The men would have been too terrified. And if Alexander as a god was not able to defeat a monster, he would be revealed as a fraud and failure. Alexander would have faced a difficult decision, to either send his men to their death or he himself die in dishonor.
>
> And then suddenly, Alexander the Great, the god, was dead. Some believe he was poisoned. Some believe that he had epilepsy and tried unsuccessfully to hide it, lest his men see him as weak.
>
> Olympias went mad with grief and surely must have craved revenge. Some wonder if Olympias blamed Aristotle for her son's death. We will never know, but within a year, Aristotle was found dead, then all his books mysteriously disappeared. Forever.
>
> Legend holds that Aristotle's last student, Xeno, saved a book documenting the existence of monstrous creatures,

but no trace of him or the book has ever been seen. The last student who so dearly loved the truth has become a legend.

And legends do not die. They are extinguished, often violently, in the name of progress.

Dr. Capistrano's paper ended abruptly with that detail. The sirens continued to race past us as an ambulance rushed toward the highway exit ramp.

Crime scene tape stretched across the entrance to Dr. Capistrano's building. A police van blocked my view of the doors, and four police cars were parked in front, their lights silently swirling. Dozens of people in uniform walked around with walkie-talkies.

Mom slowed the car and reached for my hand, finally stopping at the end of the street. Neither of us spoke.

A news van sped around the corner and raced right to the edge of the tape. A woman with a perfectly styled helmet of hair jumped out, a cameraman following. She tried to get a police officer to talk to her, but he gestured for her to back up and get out.

The police didn't want anyone knowing what had happened inside.

"Wait here," Mom said, getting out and walking away before I could argue.

Pressing a hand to my mouth, I rocked back and forth in the seat.

When Mom got back to the car, she opened the door and slid in, locking the doors and checking the mirrors. She cleared her throat and put the car in reverse.

"What happened?" I asked.

"Dr. Capistrano is dead," Mom said. She glanced in the rearview mirror, then sideways at me.

It felt like a block of ice had crashed into my chest.

"What happened?" I asked, my voice hoarse.

"Let's go home," she said.

"What happened?" I asked again.

She stopped at a red light, knuckles white, wrapped around the steering wheel.

"Mom. Please."

"It's better not to know."

"You can't protect me from this," I said.

She turned to look at me, and frowned. "Yes, I can," she said.

The light turned green but she didn't press the gas pedal. Her eyes were glazed over.

The car behind us honked twice, startling us both. Mom floored it and I jerked back in my seat. The city became a smudge, a blur racing across my window, trees whipping past, houses looming and then shrinking, people weaving in and out of focus.

Mom shook her head, as if giving up, and spoke quickly. "Dr. Capistrano's first patient this morning found the office door torn off its hinges. The police found a sweater that had been slashed to bits," she said. "They think, when the doctor came in to work, her murderer was waiting."

I swallowed down the sick feeling in the pit of my stomach. Entropion had been there.

Mom shook her head. "Plus . . . the police found a cooler with a leg in it." She glanced at me again and reached a hand out to rest it on my thigh. "Not a body. Just a leg. I am so sorry to have to tell you this."

I sighed in relief. That leg didn't mean Dr. Capistrano was dead. She'd uploaded that paper to warn me that she was getting out of this before Entropion got to her.

I settled down into the seat to think. Mom looked angry. "Sofia, you've watched too much TV. This is reality, not make-believe. A woman has lost her life."

"I'm just trying to understand it," I said, and it wasn't a lie.

Dr. Capistrano was the only person who knew my secret, and now she had fled, probably forever, because of the dangers. I should have obeyed Xeno and kept my mouth shut. Thankfully, I hadn't said anything to my mom. Now I was certain I had to carry this burden alone.

All I could do was wait for Olympias's next move. If I asked anyone for help, they would get hurt. Olympias wanted me to give up being the Guardian and let the monsters die. Xeno wanted me to keep the monsters alive until the world needed them. But neither of them had really answered the most basic question: why me? Did they think I was powerful because I survived cancer? That had been a battle, true, but I hadn't really won. Cancer had taken my leg and could still return for the rest of me. Every day, it took other kids, ones who really were brave and strong. Heroes are supposed to defeat the enemy, not just stay alive. If Xeno and Olympias expected the most powerful Guardian in history, they had picked the wrong kid. I knew how to fight, but I didn't know how to win.

Only Entropion knew I wasn't a hero. He knew the shame and fear I carried, because he was born from those foul thoughts, a secret truth that he and I shared. But Xeno was teaching me about the other truths that shape the world. One thing was clear: the truth could be a tool to build or a weapon to destroy.

Everything depended on the one who wielded it.

SEVENTEEN

Thursday, March 6

Facing my own possible death, I knew the only logical next step was to go to the mall.

Mom had insisted I keep my shopping date with Candy the next day. Because that was "normal" and would be good for me, she promised, after the shock of hearing about Dr. Capistrano. I wasn't too worried about the doctor. I hoped she had made her escape safely; I just didn't know if I would.

I left fifth period early as planned and headed down the empty hallway to the front office to meet Candy. In the music room, the chamber choir was practicing a classical song with lots of long, high notes that gave me the chills. As I glanced down the opposite hall, a door at the end of it slowly closed, hinges squeaking like a haunted-house sound track. The choir continued chanting.

Something small and white floated past my head, and I brushed at it instinctively. A little clump of Styrofoam clung to my bandana, so I picked it off for inspection. I gazed at it, frowning, until I realized it was a piece of the ceiling tile. I snapped my head up to see the tiles shake and warp as something crawled above them.

Panicking, I walked as fast as I could to the office. My stump burned as it chafed against the prosthesis, but I didn't care. Moments like this were the reason I didn't feel guilty for skipping my rehab exercises. I got a good workout just trying to stay alive each day.

Candy smiled when she saw me swing the door open.

"Ready?" she asked. Before I could reply, she handed me a huge stack of books. "Can you put these in your bag? I only brought a purse today."

"I didn't know you studied so much," I said, struggling to adjust my stance under the load, the top book threatening to spill over.

"I don't," she said. "I just have to look like I do, to keep my dad off my back."

She turned to finish signing her check-out card. Her mom waved to us through the office windows as she stood beside her SUV.

The top book slid to the right, and I thrust my hips to the side to catch it. I couldn't carry all these without dropping one. I decided to adjust the stack, and set everything on the counter.

I opened my book bag to see if there was any room.

"Hey, Sofia. Hey, Candy." Alexis stood there watching

me, a bottle of Pamprin in her hand. Girls could keep it in the nurse's office for their period if their parents approved.

Alexis stuffed the Pamprin in her pocket. "What are you doing?" she asked.

I just stood there, mute.

"We're going shopping," Candy said, stepping closer to me. "I'm giving Sofia a makeover."

Alexis looked at me like I had just kicked her grand-mother in the crotch. "Seriously?" she said.

"Sofia, we better go," Candy said. "My aunt is waiting. I can't wait to try on the dresses she picked out." She acted like Alexis wasn't even in the room.

Alexis glanced again between me and Candy, then frowned. She was judging me.

Alexis always used to worry that she might not ever get her period, especially because of all the running she did. What if she never got curves, she said, and was always as skinny as a stick? Getting her period was hugely important to her. She wanted her body to change so maybe her sister wouldn't resent her anymore.

Turns out Alexis kept secrets from me too. She had got-ten her period and never told me, and who knew when it had happened? Maybe when we were still talking, even. Everyone kept something hidden, even Alexis, but it felt like I was the only one being pushed out of the shadows. It wasn't fair.

"Sofia," Candy snapped, "we're wasting valuable shop-ping time."

Alexis's face clouded over again, darker this time.

"I can't wait," I replied, and followed Candy out.

As for Alexis? Our friendship was officially dead. I knew I should be sad, maybe even devastated, but mainly I was relieved. It's weird how someone can be so important to you that sometimes it's easier to let go than to hold on. If everything had to change, I guessed my friends would too.

Everywhere I looked, headless women were frozen in unnatural poses. Some had heads, but then their faces were all white, no eyes or mouth, nothing to tell any of them apart. I wanted to enjoy the mall, especially since I didn't have to pay for the dress I was going to get. Everyone loves free, right? But I had never noticed how creepy mannequins were, maybe because I had always been double-checking how much cash I had. The worst feeling in the world was not having enough money when you were at the register and adults were in line behind you, tapping their feet impatiently.

Candy's aunt, Mrs. Baker, had a whole rack of dresses already selected for us to try on. They were gorgeous. I lifted the tag on one that caught my eye. Black, mid-length, form-fitting to create some serious curves. It was $355. I dropped the tag.

"Don't be silly, Sofia, that one is for me," Candy said. She pushed it farther down on the rack, separating the dresses into two sections. "It wouldn't work for you anyway. Not with . . . just trust me."

I looked down at myself, then shrugged. It was hard to

ignore the stinging in my throat, the warning that I was going to cry. But Candy was probably right. What did I know about fashion?

The dresses for me were all long and straight, like Popsicle wrappers. I had never worn a long dress, except maybe a nightgown when I was little.

Mrs. Baker stood in front of the rack and studied my body. Then my face. When she pointed to my bandana, I shook my head.

"That's all right," she said. "You can remove it when you're ready."

"I won't be ready today," I countered, frowning to make sure she took me seriously.

"Well," she said, turning back to the dresses, "let's take this one step at a time."

I didn't hate her, which was a surprise since she was related to Candy. She was sweet and soft-spoken, and I liked how she wore loose black pants with a fuzzy sweater. She also wore little pearl earrings and a plain silver necklace. Mrs. Baker was like an elegant librarian. It seemed to be an achievable fashion goal, even for someone like me.

Candy grabbed her selections and disappeared into a dressing room.

Mrs. Baker chose the first dress for me to try. It was shapeless. Just a straight gray tube of shimmering fabric. But gray could be a good color, I tried to tell myself. Gray was the color of useful things, like knives and scissors and surgical instruments.

No, I corrected myself. Instruments like the flute. Shrill

and annoying when badly played. Good grief, why was I even here? I was a thrift-store shopper. This was not my world.

Mrs. Baker followed me to the dressing room, making polite chitchat about how my day was and whether I wanted a soda or bottle of water. If she could tell how nervous I was, she didn't show it.

Outside the dressing room was a table with several trays on top. Inside two of them were different pieces of jewelry. The other three held cosmetics and hair products and accessories like ribbons and barrettes.

My stomach bounced down to my knees. I didn't have enough hair to use ribbons or barrettes. I would look like an idiot if she decorated my head.

Mrs. Baker waited outside the door while I stepped into the dressing room.

The inside was pretty. It had striped wallpaper, a chair, but no mirror. Was that good or bad? I wondered. Did she give me this room on purpose?

"The photographer called," she said.

I had almost forgotten about that horror. In real life I could get away and escape from people staring at me, but in a photograph I'd be frozen. I wouldn't be able to hide.

I struggled to get into the dress. The zipper was in back. Sweat broke out on my upper lip as I writhed and wriggled and yanked at it. If I braced against the wall with one hand to keep my balance, I couldn't quite get the zipper to hold still.

"He's stuck at the airport in Boston," Mrs. Baker continued. "Would you mind if we took the pictures at the dance instead? The lighting won't be as good, but I'll make him promise to take an extra shot of you and Candy together."

Wonderful. Something for the fridge.

I didn't answer, because I knew it was a rhetorical question. After a few more embarrassing grunts, I defeated the zipper. Before I could celebrate, though, I realized I had to use the big three-way mirror at the end of the dressing-room hallway next.

Maybe in these fancy stores, it wasn't your own opinion that counted. Other people had to approve too. I ran my hands down the front of the dress, feeling the weak spot where the Kappa had bit me.

Opening the door slightly, I motioned for her to come in. Instead, she reached for my hand and pulled. I felt like a turtle getting yanked from its shell. Mrs. Baker was surprisingly strong.

Standing there in a six-hundred-dollar dress that covered me from neck to ankle, I had never felt more exposed.

Mrs. Baker slapped her hands to her cheeks.

"I'll change," I said quickly. "It probably looks bad."

"No," she gasped. "It's perfect! Just wait." She disappeared for a minute, then reappeared with two boxes of shoes. When she opened both boxes, I saw that the two pairs were the exact same style. She grinned and pulled one shoe out of each box. "You're not my first customer with a prosthesis," she whispered.

Squatting at my feet, she helped me into the shoes. "Since you probably haven't worn heels yet, let me tell you a little secret. Sometimes you'll need a different size for each foot when you buy high heels. A prosthesis has a different fit in heels, even if it's the same size as your natural foot."

If I wanted to wear anything but tennis shoes, that meant I'd have to buy two pairs. We could never afford two pairs of new shoes at one time. I'd have to cry later; Mrs. Baker had already started on my face. Soft brushes tickled my chin and nose. Then a cold metal necklace circled my neck. Next, she reached for my bandana.

My hand caught hers in midair.

"Time to take a leap of faith," she whispered.

I didn't know if that was a joke but I let go of her hand and closed my eyes.

The bandana slid off. A light comb pulled through my short stubble up top. A cold spray followed, then more combing. The combing felt good, like my mom's fingernails on my back.

"Ready?" she asked.

I took a deep breath and opened my eyes.

"I want to see!" Candy squealed from her dressing room. I heard her door handle turning.

Mrs. Baker stepped to my side. Candy stood in between me and the mirror.

Candy stared at me. She didn't move. I had never seen that expression on anyone's face when they looked at me. I didn't know what it meant.

I walked around her to the mirror, holding my breath. There in front of me stood someone I had never met.

She was beautiful.

I was beautiful.

The long dress hid everything I hated about my body. My toilet-scrubber hair was slicked back and stylish. Mrs. Baker had draped me with blue and silver jewelry, and my eyes reflected the glittery shine.

"I look like a model in a magazine," I said softly. "Exquisite, even."

"I know," Candy said. "You look amazing. You don't even look real."

I turned side to side, admiring myself. This was what I had wished for, wasn't it? I wouldn't blend in and be forgotten, ever again.

I used to hate that no one noticed me. Then I came back after I got sick, and it was like I was doubly invisible, because people still didn't see me. They just saw a new label: cancer. That was the loneliest feeling in the world, to realize that despite everything I was going through, and all the ways I was changing, people just saw a different label. But now I realized that on my birthday, I had wished for the wrong thing. I had wanted to look in the mirror and like what I saw. I should have wished to look in the mirror and see someone else.

That was what Candy was trying to help me understand. I didn't have to show anyone the real me, ever.

I could show them something *better.*

I thought of Billy suddenly and blushed. What would he see? Would he think I was beautiful too?

"All you had to do was trust me," Candy said. She moved to stand side by side in the mirror. The air around us turned cold. "I knew you'd like what you saw."

I suddenly thought of Entropion. If I wasn't ashamed of myself, his lies held no power. Maybe this was the way to defeat him, by beating him at his own game. I didn't have to like the real me. I only had to be someone different, and I had just learned that it wasn't really that hard.

Mrs. Baker walked up behind me on the other side and put her arm around my shoulders. She shivered and glanced at the thermostat on the wall.

"Well, thank you, Mrs. Baker," I finally said. "And . . . thanks, Candy."

"This is going to change everything," Candy replied.

A rumbling noise echoed in the air-conditioning vent above the dressing rooms.

"We should get going," I said, glancing up. "I have a ton of homework." I didn't know what that noise was, but I didn't want to find out. Had something followed me from school, maybe the thing that had been hiding in the ceiling?

After I changed, Mrs. Baker took the dress and put it in a bag with the hanger at the top, and she put the shoes in a velvet bag too. I had never owned anything this expensive. At the store where I shopped, all the clothes got thrown together into one plastic bag. Walking out, I passed by the faceless mannequins again. One head swiveled slowly as I passed, and out of the corner of my eye, I saw it watching me with light gray eyes, just like Olympias.

I walked so fast Candy was breathing hard when we got to the car. I took a moment to tie a bandana back on my head, even though Candy rolled her eyes when I did. I wasn't ready for anyone else to see my hair.

Candy talked the whole way home about everything she still had to do before the dance. I tried to listen, since she had just scored me a dress and shoes, and her aunt had thrown in a bunch of makeup samples. Thankfully, we had a short drive to my mom's office.

I opened the car window to allow cold air to blow onto my face. A bunch of plain brown sparrows sat on a telephone wire. We had studied the life cycle of sparrows in science last year. The birds looked at us when we were stopped at a light. Not one of them was beautiful. No one went to the zoo to see sparrows; they weren't special. My science teacher said most sparrows don't even survive after they hatch. If they do, they only live a few years.

"So if you're one of them, what's the point of living?" the teacher had asked, obviously hoping that a student would have some profound insight about the circle of life. No one did. And the teacher didn't even answer her own question, so it hung in the air all period like a dark cloud. We didn't want to try and explain the meaning of death. Most of us were still trying to figure out if we needed to start wearing deodorant.

I was still staring out the window at the sparrows when a shiny black SUV drove past. A woman with long blond hair and sunglasses was driving. She didn't look at me or turn her head, but somehow I knew she was smiling. And I knew exactly who she was.

EIGHTEEN

I slept fitfully and awakened early to the sound of weeping. I pushed myself to sit up, groaning with the effort. I hopped to the window and looked down to where the noise was coming from. Caitlyn, my next-door kindergartner neighbor, stood at the edge of the street, in tears. Her father said something to comfort her that I couldn't hear.

"But I told you!" she wailed. "I told you that we shouldn't let Newman go outside last night. There was a monster in the bushes!" When he shook his head, she stomped her foot. "I saw it!"

He wrapped his arm around her shoulders, trying to nudge her home. Behind his back, he held a collar with a dangling tag. It looked like it had been ripped from the cat's neck.

Caitlyn refused to move, and stood with her head bent

down to her chest. Her father finally had to pick her up and carry her home. That's when I saw it.

A huge red bloodstain was smeared across the road. It must have been Newman . . . or what was left of him.

I glanced up and down the street but saw nothing. If a car had hit Newman, there would have been a body. But Caitlyn wasn't crying over a body. Newman was dead, and it wasn't a car that got him.

The little hairs on my neck rose. If Entropion was out there, why had he attacked Newman? Cats weren't monsters. I mean, most cats weren't.

"Sofia! Breakfast!" Mom called from downstairs.

I grabbed an outfit and got dressed. "I need to see if I left something in the car," I called when I got downstairs. The street was quiet and empty. I walked to the stain in the road and bent down to inspect it. It didn't look like blood—at least, not animal blood, not if you really stared at it. It had a greenish-blue tint. It looked like . . .

Newman meowed at me from the bushes.

Turning, I made my way to him, relief flooding through me. He pranced out, looking offended that he had been forced to hide. Poor Newman; he had been eaten and vomited up by the Beast of Gevaudan, and now this. I reached to scoop him up and carry him home to Caitlyn. I couldn't wait to ring the doorbell and see her face.

As I reached for him, I heard a little squish. I lifted my right foot and looked down. Part of a tentacle clung to the sole of my shoe.

Entropion hadn't killed a cat. Entropion had killed a Kappa.

He wasn't going to let any of the monsters get to me. Even if they needed help, he'd stop them. I would be useless as the Guardian.

Newman hissed when he saw the bloodstain, and leaped from my arms. There weren't going to be any happy endings today.

Hijacking Darwin: The Science of Evil

The banner in front of the Natural History Museum hung lifeless in the morning light. I'd forgotten all about the science field trip, just like I'd forgotten my paper on evolution was due in less than a week. I needed this. My assigned topic was on how evolution impacted the balance of power in any ecosystem. I wasn't even sure what that meant. The bus ride here had been fairly miserable, with Mr. Reeves having us sing the school song twice to fire up the track team for their meet on Saturday.

I avoided looking anyone in the eyes.

When the bus doors opened, Billy called out my name and told me to wait. Mr. Reeves had assigned Billy a seat with a chaperone in the back. I pretended I didn't hear him and hustled down the steps, scanning the area for Entropion. I didn't know what he looked like yet, but there was nothing else I could think of to do.

Inside the museum, the exhibit was cold and dark. There were black-and-white pictures on the walls, and war relics from all over the world in square glass boxes. A lot of the exhibit had to do with Nazi Germany. I saw pictures of children with Down syndrome sitting on an examination bench without any clothes on, so skinny their ribs were visible under the skin. They were smiling, as if the bright camera flash were a sparkling promise that these men in uniform were humans too, and weren't all people basically good?

The Golem came to mind, his back riddled with buckshot. I dropped my head, my heart suddenly hurting. Had he been shot out of fear or for fun? Would either answer make it right? Not all humans were good. And even good people could do bad things. The monsters were gone from our lives, but we had never felt less safe.

An old guy in a crisp museum-guide uniform clapped his hands to signal the beginning of our tour. He had white hair trimmed into sharp clean lines at the temples, and a deep sadness that haunted his eyes. When he turned his head to one side, I saw a red scar, old and flat, that ran from ear to mouth.

Our first stop was an exhibit called "Survival of the Fittest?" As we filed in, Candy caught my eye and smiled. "What did your mom think of the dress?" she asked. "I told everyone you're going to look amazing in it."

The museum guide was talking, so I turned to listen.

"As you see, the natural world is extraordinary in its diversity. Whether we are looking at a lowly insect or an apex predator, every creature is wonderful in its own way. Some would have you believe that these creatures"—here he waved to all the pictures—"must destroy each other to survive. Survival of the fittest, they call it. I call it utter nonsense."

We all glanced at each other, confused. Wasn't that what evolution was all about? The strong gobbling up the weak?

The museum guide continued. "Competition does *not* determine survival, not in the way you may think. Species survive by being *different,* not stronger. The dinosaurs? So strong the earth trembled beneath them." He lowered his voice as he spoke and made fists, imitating a strong beast. Then he shrugged. "And today, of course, quite dead."

A gloomy feeling settled among us. He pointed a finger, sweeping it past all our faces, then jabbing it at the pictures of the strange creatures from nature.

"To survive, one must adapt, change, do the unexpected."

Candy nudged Natalie and whispered something to her. Natalie just shrugged.

He cleared his throat. "The mistake that Hitler's men made was in not understanding the true power of evolution. Survival does not go to the strong or the beautiful, not to the fast or smart. Only the *unique* live on, those with the rarest of strengths: the ability to stand alone for the sake of the greater good." He pulled out a linen handkerchief and dabbed at his mouth. The corner of his mouth drooped when he talked.

"He's saying it's better to be a freak," Candy whispered, but loud enough for us all to hear. A bunch of people giggled. "Good luck with that."

The guide stared at Candy. Something in his eyes told

me that he was too tired to argue with her, like maybe he had already fought that fight a thousand times and knew how it ended.

The guide waved his hands, motioning for us to line up to walk to another exhibit. He made a wide path around Candy.

Without warning, Billy was right next to me, his shoulder grazing mine. I pretended not to notice. I worried he might sense the way I had been thinking about him when I looked at myself in the dress.

"Good grief, I can't leave you alone for a minute," he said. "I just heard you went shopping with Candy for a dress."

"I had to," I said. "Long story."

"We have the whole bus ride back."

Thankfully, the guide continued the lecture. "The Nazis tried to create a superior human race. Those inferior were identified by what made them different: religion, disabilities, artistic gifts, sexual orientation, being left-handed or just noticeably strange."

Several people snuck glances at me. Instinctively, I reached up and touched my bandana to make sure it hadn't slipped.

"Hitler wanted to control evolution to gain power," the guide said. He pointed to a picture of a soldier shooting a mother cradling an infant in her arms. Some of the girls in our class started crying. Hitler was a real monster, I thought, the kind even Xeno would be afraid of.

I looked down to where my leg should have been.

How could anyone believe they could control nature?

The exhibit had more photographs, but my brain shut down. It was an eternity before we got the signal to head back to the tour buses. I was the first one out the door, and that was when I saw it.

The first flower of spring.

The first real, growing flower I had seen up close since last fall, when they admitted me to the hospital. The world had been feeling gray for so long. But here was a perfect tulip shooting straight up from a bulb buried in the cold dirt, its thick red petals a signal to the others to do the same. None of the flowers were blooming yet, but there's always one that can't wait to feel the sun.

Mr. Reeves made me keep moving, but I turned just before getting on the bus for one last look at it.

Candy hovered, casting a shadow over the tulip. Then she reached down and, using her fingernails, severed the blossom from the stalk. She held it in her hand, showing it off as her friends gathered. A teacher yelled at them to get moving. Candy tossed it aside as she walked onto her bus, and the first bloom of spring was trampled by the rest of the seventh grade.

NINETEEN

I swallowed hard, trying to keep my tears from spilling.

Billy climbed onto the bus and was just about to sit down next to me, but with a shake of his head, Mr. Reeves shot his long arm out and pointed to the back of the bus. Billy huffed in protest but the kids in line pushed him down the aisle. He took his seat about six or seven rows behind me.

Mr. Reeves sat in the row across from mine and turned toward me, giving me a kind smile. He almost looked like he felt guilty for making me see that exhibit. I turned to look out the window. Everyone knew I would have been chosen for extinction. Why did evil people pick on people who were different? Why were they so afraid of us? I was different because I was less than perfect. How could that be a threat to anyone?

I was directly behind the driver, with his seat blocking most of my view. Mr. Reeves had plenty of extra space, with no rows in front of him. He was busy making notes in his notebook.

Mr. Reeves got up to borrow the driver's intercom mike. "Traffic may be a little heavy as we head back to the school. Please talk quietly so we don't disturb our driver. If you brought a snack, you may eat it, but remember to pick up your trash."

I looked back at the museum as the windows darkened in the afternoon sun. No one was safe. Not if we were different, out of order . . . or just the first to sense a change coming. My eyes began to fill up again.

Billy cleared his throat loudly. I refused to look back.

"Sofia!"

I jerked my head around to face him.

"What's wrong?" he asked.

"I don't want to talk about it." The last thing I wanted was for everyone on the bus to know why I was crying.

The bus rumbled forward and I settled farther down in my seat, resting my head against the window. The sun warmed the glass and my eyelids grew heavy.

"Sofia!"

I sat up and turned around again. "What!" I snapped at Billy.

"Is it what I said in the museum?" he called back.

In the rearview mirror, I saw the bus driver raise his eyebrows, irritated with us. Mr. Reeves turned around and warned Billy not to get out of his seat.

Facing forward, I refused to look back again. Then I realized I could spy on Billy by looking in the driver's mirror, and snuck a glance.

Billy caught me. Before I could look away, he held up an

orange. He had used a Sharpie to draw a smiley face in what I think was supposed to represent me.

I turned around. "Am I supposed to be flattered?"

"You're supposed to laugh. I'm trying to cheer you up."

We were pulling into the school lot when Billy sent the orange rolling, fast, straight up the center of the aisle toward me.

A dad on his cell phone drove his SUV too close to the bus, and our driver had to swerve to avoid him. Instead of landing in my hand, the orange shot forward and lodged itself under the brake pedal just as the bus driver slammed his foot on the brakes.

The orange exploded.

The bus skidded to a stop, fleshy bits of orange pulp dripping down the driver's face. He pulled the lever to open the doors and stumbled down the steps, collapsing like someone had kicked him in the back of the knees. When he caught his breath, the driver shouted an impressive list of four-letter words at us.

I heard Billy gulp.

No one else made a sound.

No one even dared to breathe.

Carefully, quietly, Mr. Reeves bent down and retrieved the burst orange, holding it up for us all to see. If I had ever wondered what my face would look like if it was orange and completely smashed in, now I knew.

I was standing by myself as the rest of our class gossiped, their backs turned, eyes darting back and forth between me and Billy. Alexis was listening to her friends from the track team. A few of them had been on my bus, and they were filling her in on the incident.

Parents started to arrive. I could tell the story was traveling fast by the adults' expression when they looked back at me. As if this were my fault.

Alexis turned away from her friends and stormed toward Billy.

"What is wrong with you?" Alexis snapped at him. Mr. Reeves raised his eyebrows, but he made no move to stop Alexis. I think he was hoping she would punch him.

"What, because I'm her friend?" Billy asked, like Alexis had asked the most obvious, ridiculous question ever. "Something's wrong with me because I care how she feels?"

"Something's wrong with you because you won't leave her alone! She doesn't want you bothering her! Anyone can see that, you moron! Look at her!" Alexis shouted as she pointed at me.

I looked away.

Billy took a step toward her. He got right in her face.

"Who cares what you think?" Billy shot back.

Alexis shoved him, both hands on his chest. "I'm her *best friend*!" she shouted.

My heart felt like someone was squeezing it. Billy looked down at the ground. I could see his jaw muscles flexing as he cleared his throat.

"I didn't know you already had a best friend," Billy said

to me when he finally looked up. His eyes were hard and cold.

Why did it matter if she was a best friend instead of just a friend? Was it against the rules to have more than one?

"You should have said something," Billy said. "I don't want to get caught in the middle. I don't want to be a *liability*."

My toes curled in my shoe. If I had a zipper on my back, I would have unpeeled myself from my body and run.

Alexis held her ground, arms crossed. They both looked at me like I owed them an explanation.

"She *was* my best friend," I finally said. I wanted to look at Alexis, but I couldn't. "It's complicated."

"Why are you doing this to me?" Alexis uncrossed her arms and moved closer. She moved like an athlete, strong and confident, even in short strides. "Just give me one good reason."

"To save you the trouble," I said. "You don't want to be friends with me anymore."

"Yes, I do," she said, and stomped one foot. "Why don't you believe that?"

"When we were friends," I said, "and we would run together . . ." I had to stop. My throat burned from the sobs I kept swallowing back. Saying each word was like chewing razors. I took a breath and tried again. "We'd be racing, and your shoes would be rubbing a blister, and then I'd have to stop and vomit because I always ate the wrong thing for breakfast, but you never let us stop or give up. If there's one thing you really hate in life, it's pain. You said there was too much of it already. You always said you refused to let pain win."

"Because I'm not a quitter," she said. "I don't quit on races . . . or friends."

A tear burned my cheek and I wiped it away, fast. Billy frowned in concentration as he listened and watched.

At our very first cross-country practice, Alexis and I hadn't even known each other's names. The coach had divided the girls into two groups to encourage teamwork, and Alexis and I weren't in the same group. The average pace for a middle school runner is twelve minutes and fourteen seconds per mile, so our goal was to run a 5K in under thirty-eight minutes. That would qualify us as average, our coach said, but he wanted better-than-average runners, so he would be standing on the track, clipboard in hand. We had twelve laps to impress him.

I knew I was going to do that.

I hadn't trained much; I wasn't a great runner, so I didn't see the point of training really hard. I sprinted from the start line and ran until my sides burned in agony. Before the first lap was even done, Alexis blew past me in the lead for her group. On the third lap she saw me: my hands on my knees, breathing hard and crying. I knew I wasn't a great runner, but I hadn't known that I would humiliate myself in front of everyone. I couldn't even finish all twelve laps unless I walked.

Other girls passed by but Alexis circled back for me. "We'll run together," she had said. "If you run with a friend, it doesn't hurt as bad."

We introduced ourselves when I stopped to stretch out a cramp in my calf.

Alexis never left my side after that. She was strong enough for both of us. Even when it meant she had to run extra portions of a race just to keep me company. I didn't know why she wanted to be friends with me. She kind of dazzled me, but after I found her crying in the bathroom, I knew she had issues at home so she needed a good friend. I decided to keep my mouth shut and hope that a little of her strength would rub off on me. She really only had one rule: it didn't matter if we lost, as long as the pain didn't win.

Remembering it all, I took a deep breath that made me shudder. "You tried to visit me in the hospital, right?"

Alexis glared at me, but I saw tears in her eyes. "You know I did."

"But you didn't come back after that. Maybe you knew I wasn't strong enough. The pain won, Alexis. Look at me!" I gestured with one hand to my body. "How could I be your friend like this? You'd feel guilty that you can run and I can't, and then you might even stop. I would ruin the one thing you love most."

"Are you crazy?" she yelled. She looked like she was trying not to explode. Billy stepped toward her, raising his arms in case he needed to grab her. I shook my head at him angrily. This was my fight.

Alexis chewed her lip, rolling the bottom one under her front teeth, mentally working something through before she said it. She started three separate times before she finally spoke.

"When we raced, there were rules," she said, holding her hands out, palms up, for emphasis. "If we followed the rules, we might win. But if we broke the rules, we got disqualified. *No matter how hard we ran.* Your cancer? That was a race that you had to run without me." Tears slipped down her cheeks. "Yeah, I love running. But I love you too."

My own tears were building. Big swallows of air kept me from completely disintegrating when she continued.

"And I didn't want to hurt your chances," she went on. "I left you alone in the hospital, because that's what your mom wanted me to do! She said I might give you another infection. And then suddenly you didn't want to be my friend anymore. I didn't know why and you wouldn't even talk to me to explain it, but I would never, ever quit on you. So I waited for you to circle back for me this time. And you never did!"

"Because I can't!" I screamed. "You have to go on without me. You *get* to go on! And I can't be happy for you, not yet. I'm angry! It's not fair, not to either one of us. Every time I look at you, I feel sad and angry, and every time you look at me, you feel guilty."

She briefly looked away, then shook her head, but we both knew I was right. I knew how she felt when her sister looked at her and how much Alexis hated having the one thing her sister wanted more than anything else. I knew the truth, and it cost us our friendship.

So what hurts worse, truth or love?

Both, because they end up being the same thing.

I buried my face in my hands and bawled.

Alexis held out her arms to wrap me up in a hug, but instinctively I took a step back. I knew that the cracks around me weren't the good kind. If she touched me, I would break into a thousand sharp pieces.

Billy stepped between us, holding his hands out to keep Alexis back, like he knew what it meant to be shattered.

"Leave us alone," Alexis said to Billy. "Go find someone else to stalk."

Billy's face turned red and I watched Mom's car turn in to the lot.

"You abandoned her," Billy said. "I would never do that, no matter who told me to. A *real* friend stays."

Alexis pulled one arm back to shove him, just as I tried to twist around and push Billy out of her path.

Mom got out of the car and waved just as my hand hit Billy's face. He fell, hands covering his face, blood seeping out between his fingers. I had accidentally smashed his nose with the flat of my palm.

"Wow," Alexis whispered. "Just . . . wow." She slowly walked off and glanced over her shoulder at me, once.

I stood there, my head swimming. Everything about the moment had gone wrong. I had finally spoken my truth, and it wasn't a beautiful thing, not at all. My truth was not something to write poetry about or frame on a poster. It was ugly and small and screaming in pain, but it was mine.

So what was I going to do about it?

I watched from the passenger seat of our car as Mom and Mr. Reeves talked. Billy was holding an ice pack to his face, and a girl was laughing at something he had just said. She flung her hair and must have said something witty, because he laughed next. It hurt to watch them. Why had he completely shut down when he learned that Alexis and I were best friends? And were we best friends, even now that she knew how I felt? She'd have to be either strong or crazy to be my best friend after today.

My attention snapped back to the adults deciding my fate. Their discussion involved a lot of finger-pointing. Mom straightened her back and went toe-to-toe with Mr. Reeves to stare him down.

But then she said something and his whole face changed. He softened and reached out to touch her arm. He pulled out his wallet and showed her a picture. She smiled and nodded, and touched his arm in the same spot. I had never seen my mom flirt. I rubbed my eyes, trying to stop the damage, but it was no use. The image was seared on my retinas forever.

She walked slowly back to the car. The expression etched on her face was a work of art, a delicately balanced composition of shock and fury.

My life was a constant loop of misunderstanding.

"Well, you had a memorable field trip," Mom chirped after a few minutes of silence. She merged the car onto the highway. Apparently there had also been some confusion as to whether I had tried to stage a mock explosion of the driver's head, and whether I had meant to punch Billy. The car was cold and she reached for the heater, but accidentally turned it to AC.

Her knuckles were white but she didn't notice the drop to subzero temperature and I didn't dare move. Or speak.

"I should probably blame myself," she said. "I pushed you to be a normal kid again. Perhaps I should have been more specific. A normal *law-abiding* kid with good grades and nice friends!"

She hit the wheel with the palm of her fist. "Mr. Reeves felt sorry for me," she sputtered, like the words left a bad taste in her mouth. "Like I need pity, since I'm a single mom."

Pity rubbed us both the wrong way. We didn't speak again until she pulled into the driveway and turned off the engine.

"What is going on with you?" she demanded.

I shook my head and looked at my lap. If I said what I was thinking—that she was only getting a little taste of my everyday existence—we'd end up in a huge fight. Should I tell her that the boy I had just injured might be my first boyfriend? That I had recently been a beacon of hope for terrifying monsters from all over the world? That what I wanted more than anything right now was to be able to talk to a dead man? Or that I had accidentally helped create a new predator?

"Where is the Sofia I know?" Her voice got quiet. "I want that girl back. I miss her."

"If I told you the truth, you wouldn't believe me."

"Try me," she said.

I folded my arms. "I didn't like the old me. No one liked her, Mom."

"That's not true."

"I'm not saying I was bullied, not exactly. But no one

paid attention to me, except to make sure I wasn't in their clique," I said. "No one wanted me around, and just because people feel sorry for me now doesn't mean they suddenly like me. I still don't belong anywhere."

"But you can't live like this. I can't live like this! Not one more day," she said. "Something has got to change. I just want you to be happy."

I turned my face to the window. "I'm trying," I whispered.

My mind went back to everything in the museum exhibit. If all the animals in a species were exactly like each other, eventually they all died. But if one was born different? It died first.

And that wasn't the worst part. I had learned the worst part in the last exhibit.

Change was useless unless it was the right adaption for what was about to happen—and no one ever knew what that would be.

Evolution was so unfair.

We pulled into the driveway a few minutes later, and I glanced up at my window. It was open, the curtains fluttering in the early evening breeze. I was sure I hadn't left my window open. Mom got out, lugging her briefcase from the car, and I followed.

She turned the doorknob and nudged the door open with her shoulder. A small brown package sat on our doorstep with a return label that read "Germs-B-Gone." Mom bent down and tried to hide it behind her briefcase, knowing I would probably say something snarky.

That was why I saw the inside of our house first.

The couch was standing on its end against the living room wall, where huge chunks of drywall had been ripped out. Our pictures were facedown on the floor. Papers and books had been thrown everywhere and torn to shreds.

Mom saw my face and turned slowly. She dropped her package and briefcase as she slumped against the door. I stepped over her, picking my way through the debris until I was in the kitchen. The phone base was empty but still plugged in, which seemed like a miracle. Instinctively, I hit the page button and listened for the beeping. I found the phone inside a soup pan resting by the TV. The TV was lying on its side by the back door.

I held up the phone. *We still have this,* I was trying to say, *if that helps.*

Mom's face went blank, the way people look in the movies just before they pass out. She clutched her cheek with one hand.

I dialed 911.

The emergency operator stayed on the line with me and told me what to do, which was not much. I propped Mom's head up and fanned her. If she had been a monster, I might actually have had a clue as to how to treat her.

Police and paramedics arrived seven minutes and eighteen seconds later. One of the paramedics checked Mom's vitals, then, after a few tests, smiled brightly at us both. I rested my head in my hands, relieved. Mom was okay. They use a very different smile when it's serious.

A police officer tried to get me to answer questions while

the paramedic wrote on a clipboard. It was hard for me to form words. My brain was like pudding.

"Do you have any valuables that a thief would want to steal?" he asked again.

I shook my head. "We don't have anything valuable."

I suddenly remembered: we did have a valuable book, one of the greatest treasures in history. Dr. Capistrano was the only one who had known about it, but she had wanted to help, not stop me. Was she so worried about the curse on the Bestiary that she'd try to steal it?

I looked around the place again, seeing it for the first time: ragged edges, scrapes and tears covering everything.

This wasn't the work of a thief.

And it wasn't a monster who had come here looking for help either.

This was Entropion.

Olympias had told me she would destroy everything I held dear. She was angry, maybe because I had weakened Entropion's power when I looked in the mirror and liked what I saw. She was punishing me for fighting back.

A shudder rolled through my body like a wave. Right behind it something else rose too: anger. Entropion had no right to come into my house.

I made my way to the stairs as fast as I could, stumbling twice over the debris. A policeman caught me gently by the arm when I tripped for the third time.

His name badge said "Officer Lopez."

I jerked my arm free. "I need to check my room!"

"Let my partner go first," he said, his eyes searching mine.

He had soft brown eyes, with a few deep wrinkles around the edges, the kind from laughing a lot. His warm, steady hand was still on my arm.

I nodded.

After his partner had gone up and declared it safe, Officer Lopez helped me up the rest of the stairs. At the top, he placed one hand on my shoulder, forcing me to pause for a moment. I needed it. Each breath hurt, like my lungs were filled with glass shards.

"I'm sorry this happened to you," Officer Lopez said. "People do ugly things sometimes."

TWENTY

All my clothes had been ripped from the hangers, torn to shreds. Even my track trophies, which had been hidden in their box, were in bits and pieces. The bedspread was in ribbons, but hanging neatly in the closet was the gray dress.

Why hadn't Entropion destroyed that?

Looking around, I saw a scrap of shredded purple-and-gold fabric on the floor in front of my nightstand. Disbelief drowned out all my other thoughts.

These were the remains of my track jersey. It looked staged, like I was meant to find them only after I had seen everything else around me destroyed. The edges glistened with saliva.

I sat on my bed, focused on taking one breath at a time.

That was the jersey I had worn on my very last run, the one when I fell, literally, into another world called Cancer. Alexis had injured her knee that week, so she was using our run-a-minute/walk-a-minute technique. She had urged me to run ahead. "Not without you!" I argued. "You have to!" she yelled back. So I ran, *fast.* Running with Alexis had made me strong. I had been right: a little bit of her really had rubbed off. My legs were like springs attached at my hips. I bounded, I leaped, I *flew.*

For the last time.

Entropion had shredded the memory, torn apart any last hope of wearing that jersey again someday, and almost killed my mother from shock.

Olympias had won.

I never wanted to see my mother collapse from shock and pain again. I never knew I could hurt like this again either. The track jersey was a scar that Entropion had split wide open. Unless you've spent weeks watching your body slowly knit itself back together in ragged seams and thick red scars, you take healing for granted. You get a paper cut and don't worry. A few days later, without any effort or thought, you notice that your body has quietly healed itself, one more little magic trick for an audience that forgets to applaud.

But sometimes healing is like being taken hostage in a violent siege. You have to survive each hour passing on the clock. You pray to make it until the next one, or the next pill, without losing your mind, telling yourself that relief can't be far.

I couldn't survive another open wound. I didn't have the strength to wait for it to close.

Officer Lopez stood in the doorway while I began searching through the rubble. He was short but really muscular and had thick, dark black hair. "Can I help you find something?" he asked. I shook my head. "Are you sure? You look pretty upset."

What could I say? I was looking for a two- or three-thousand-year-old book? That it was the connection to a dead guy and all the monsters in the world? Careful to keep my back turned to him, I bent down to check under the bed. My breath caught in my chest.

"How about you take a break and I'll get you a glass of water?" he asked. "Or a Coke if your mom says it's okay."

The book was gone. It really was over. Entropion had everything he wanted. He'd granted me a tiny bit of mercy, though, because he'd left me that gray dress.

I sat on the bed and cried, opening my mouth to take in big gulps of air. I wanted to be angry, but strangely, I felt as if a big weight had been lifted off my shoulders. I hadn't been a great Guardian, not like Xeno wanted, but at least I hadn't quit. Someone stronger had beaten me, and that was different. I wished, for one second, to be the kind of girl who would get angry and vow revenge, but that type of girl would never really be me. At least I didn't have to try anymore.

Officer Lopez offered me a fresh tissue. When Mom came up to see the damage, he rested a hand on her arm and was really nice to her too. She looked like she wanted to collapse against him. He seemed like he could handle it. She held the phone in her hands, as if she needed to call someone but couldn't remember who it was.

I wiped the tears from my cheeks and took the phone, setting it on my bed. I wanted her to scoop me up in her arms like she used to when I was little. But she didn't look at me, not really. She picked her way through the stuff on the floor, looking around in dismay.

"At least they didn't get this," she said, touching the gray dress and stroking the soft fabric with her fingertips. Empty hangers swung on either side of it, but she seemed mesmerized as it sparkled in the ruins of my closet. She didn't act like she knew I was even in the room, so I didn't reply, neither of us understanding why the dress hadn't been destroyed. It didn't make sense. Olympias had promised to destroy everything I held dear, and I loved that dress. It made me look flawless.

"You are going to be so beautiful. I can't tell you how happy I am that you still have this." She turned to me and smiled, tears shimmering in her eyes. "We still have that to look forward to."

"I'm so sorry," Officer Lopez said again. "Strange things have been happening ever since this little girl showed up at the hospital with bites from an animal she couldn't—or wouldn't—describe. Then an animal attacked an office near the hospital. Weird, even by Atlanta standards."

Mom dabbed at her eyes. She wasn't listening, but I was. They thought an animal had broken into Dr. Capistrano's office? No animal could tear a door off its hinges.

"Do you think we should get a dog?" Mom asked. She wrung her hands, looking around like she was lost, even though she was standing in my room. Officer Lopez stepped closer and gently nudged her toward the stairs before he gave me one last reassuring smile.

"Please let me get you a glass of water or something," he

said to her. "You should sit down and take all this real slow."
They walked out of the room, speaking in hushed tones.

I kicked one of my broken trophies with my prosthetic
leg. A piece of it cut through the material and got stuck right
in my big toe.

The fake stuff is never as strong as it looks.

Neither of us wanted dinner. Mom poured herself a glass
of wine and wrapped herself up in a blanket to sit outside
on the patio. I don't think she wanted to look at the house
anymore.

It was strangely quiet. Without monsters, the world felt
dead.

I grabbed another blanket off the tattered couch and followed Mom outside. I scanned the night sky.

"What a day," she muttered. She was standing in front of
our patio swing, staring straight ahead.

I nodded.

"The locksmiths will be here in a few hours. It's nice that
they agreed to come out so late." She didn't sound like she
was really talking to me.

"Yeah," I said. "Officer Lopez was a big help." He had
called in a favor to get them to agree to do the work after
hours—it was already past dinnertime.

Neither of us said anything for a while. Things had been
so awkward between us lately. Mom didn't understand why
going right back to our "normal life" had felt like a death

sentence to me. And all I knew was that the old me was gone, and I had been trying really hard to find the new me.

Mom broke the silence. "Girls your age push their moms away. It's normal," she said. "Healthy, the experts say."

"I'm not pushing you away."

She laughed under her breath and sat down on our patio bench.

I groaned. "I'm really not."

"I can't understand everything you've been through," she said. "I know that."

I touched my prosthesis, without even meaning to. She and I locked eyes.

"I just want to try," she said softly.

"I'm not pushing you away, I promise." I sighed. "I just can't explain everything to you right now. Some things I can't even explain to myself."

She gently waved a hand to dismiss the conversation and took a sip of her wine.

"It's okay," she said. "I'll wait till you're ready. That's what moms do. We give you everything we ever wanted for ourselves." She took another sip. "We give you the life we once wished for, and then we discover it's not what you needed after all. My worst fear is that you're nearly grown and I've wasted all my chances to be a good mom."

I sat beside her as she opened her arms to wrap the blanket around me too. She never really talked about her mother or childhood. I wondered if she had her own secrets.

"You've been through so much," she whispered. "You deserve a Cinderella ending to your story."

I giggled softly. I had been Cinderella for a while, hadn't I? Except that songbirds flocked to her window, but man-eating monsters slithered through mine.

An owl flew above us, hunting something we couldn't see. The bats were still hibernating, so the owls currently ruled the skies at night.

The phone rang, but Mom didn't move. She just stared at the sky, so I went inside to answer it.

"You broke my nose."

I gasped. "Billy?"

"Who else did you punch today?"

"Did I really break it?" I cringed. "I didn't punch you. I smushed you. Accidentally."

"That's why I'm doing this over the phone. In case of another accident."

"Doing what?" I asked.

"Officially breaking up."

"You can't break up with me. We aren't dating."

"Not anymore we aren't. My dad won't let me take you to the dance tomorrow night," Billy said. "He thinks you're a bad influence. Seeing as how you nearly killed the entire student body on the bus today and then broke my nose. You were supposed to catch the orange, you know."

"But I got a dress!" I blurted. "I went shopping with *Candy* for it!" He couldn't back out now. "We made a deal," I added.

"The deal was you would agree to go with me. And you did."

"Is this because of the fight with Alexis?" I said. My body tensed. I wanted to punch him for real now. "You *told* me to fight for myself, and now you don't want to go to the dance with me?"

"Try to pay attention. I *do* want to go with you," he said. "My dad won't let me. I have to stay out of trouble at this school. My mom is threatening to send me to military school if I get expelled again. I think she's only mad that I've ruined the illusion of having a perfect son."

"I didn't know you had a mom," I muttered. That came out wrong, like everything else I said. I had seen his family picture, but he never talked about her.

"Did you think I was hatched? Of course I have a mom."

"I just didn't know if she was still around." I moved to sit on the couch, searching for a cushion that was still intact.

"She's not. But at least now she might feel guilty about it."

Neither of us said anything for a long time. Silence made talking again even harder. A thousand thoughts went through my mind all at once. Nothing I wanted to say sounded right. The longer we were silent, the more important it seemed to say something perfect.

"On Christmas morning two years ago," Billy said, "I opened a present that didn't have a label. I just assumed it was mine. My mom got this funny expression on her face. She hadn't meant to put it under the tree. It wasn't for me. It wasn't for my dad either. When New Year's rolled around a week later, she was gone. She had a whole new family."

"I'm sorry," I said weakly.

"That's not the worst part," he said. "She always told me I was the ideal son, and we had a picture-perfect Christmas that year; she even said so. Everything in our house looked like it came out of a magazine. We had all this amazing food, we went to a candlelight church service, we sang Christmas carols at the neighborhood party . . . and it was all a lie. Maybe she thought she could have both, but in the end she had to choose." He sighed. "The funny thing is, it wasn't her lies that nearly killed me. It was finding out the truth."

"So you wanted a friend who saw what was real." I thought about my test answer and why he loved it so much. "So you wouldn't get hurt again."

"You were supposed to be my early warning system," Billy replied. He sounded exhausted. "As long as I could see the truth about people, I wouldn't get hurt."

"You know what's funny?" I asked. "The only part of me that doesn't hurt is the fake part. It doesn't feel anything at all."

I could hear him exhale.

"Billy, I think that, sometimes, getting hurt is the only way we know what's real."

"Tell that to my nose."

I laughed so hard I snorted.

"My dad says I have to go," he said, "but remember, I said you had to learn to fight for the *right* things." He paused before going on, like what he was going to say next would cost him something. "Alexis is one of the right things. You need to fight to hold on to your friendship. Don't worry about me right now, okay?"

Then he said good night.

We had just broken up, and now we were closer than ever. How was that even possible? Boys were the strangest discovery of all.

The locksmiths left a little before ten. Every hour or so, a police cruiser silently rolled past our house, and the walls lit up in red and blue. When Mom and I hugged good night, she held on for a long time. Or maybe I held on to her. She wanted me to sleep in her bed, but I was worried that I might start crying if I thought about the house, and I didn't want to upset her. She found an old quilt for my bed and then a couch pillow downstairs that was still in one piece.

An hour later, I lay there, unable to sleep, waiting for the next wave of lights, staring at the silver-gray dress hanging in my closet. The price tag twirled whenever the heat vent turned on.

A noise startled me. I turned my face to the window.

Thick fingers gripped the windowsill, followed by a hand the size of a dinner plate, the skin rough and gray.

"Golem!" I whispered, sitting up and reaching to open the window the rest of the way. My heart bounced in my chest. I scanned the street below. No police car was in sight, no stirring in the trees or bushes. Entropion wasn't there, but he had already made his point. Maybe he didn't think I would be strong enough to care about anything but myself now.

One massive foot, which looked like a big gray brick, came through the window first. Then the leg followed. He repeated the process slowly with the other leg, and I tried to see what was making him move so carefully.

When the Golem was completely in the room, he wasn't able to stand up to his full height, but instead hung his head.

He was holding his left hand against his chest. I looked him over quickly but saw no wounds or marks.

"If you're hurt, I won't be able to help you, Golem," I said. "I'm not the Guardian anymore. The book is gone."

I braced myself to stand up by grabbing his arm. With one hand, I lifted his chin up so I could look at his face. A tear from one of his dark eyes splashed near my lip. On impulse, I licked away the tear with my tongue. It tasted salty, just like every other tear.

"Oh, Golem, what is it? What's happened?" I asked.

He lowered his left hand, opening it to let me see.

A baby sparrow lay in his palm. It was bald and raw, and then I saw what made Golem weep.

A sharp white bone protruded through its leg. The leg was swollen twice the size of the other one and bright red, filled with blood. The baby had its eyes closed, taking shallow rapid breaths.

I could feel its tiny heart beating under my fingers. It was strong. The bird refused to give up, even if the battle had already been decided.

An ant crawled through its feathers and I picked it off, crushing it between my fingers, angry. Outside, a mother bird called, a sharp *chirrup* sound. The bird was so small, so fragile. It had never even flown and it wanted so badly to live.

Golem and I sat together on my bed. Golem held the baby bird in his palm as I rested my hand in his, cupping mine around the bird to keep it warm. We kept vigil over it as the heartbeats slowed, then became irregular and soft . . . and then stopped.

Forever.

A star shot past my window, the darkest hours of the night still unfolding. I rested my head against Golem's massive arm and went right to sleep.

When I woke, I was lying in bed with the covers tucked neatly around me. Golem and his sparrow were gone.

The sun rose in hot pink and orange colors above the dead landscape. Winter was lifting; out of the cold, dark earth, millions of forgotten seeds were breaking open. New life would finally rise through the darkness.

The dawn illuminated the frost on my window. In it, Golem had etched a heart. I stood and used my finger to trace its outline. I remembered how when I had first seen him, I was repulsed by his appearance. Then I began to see his heart, and I realized that the heart was all that really mattered.

I placed my hand over my chest, feeling my own heartbeat, hoping it would tell me whether I had changed in the right ways, whether I had finally made the right choices. It just kept its rhythm. Nothing had slowed it: not the tumor, not Entropion, not my own stupid fears and flaws and mistakes. Nothing had convinced it to stop beating.

It was strong, and, maybe, so was I.

TWENTY-ONE

Saturday, March 8

Mom had gotten up to work on the house while I slept in. It looked a lot better. Big chunks of drywall were still missing, but at least all the broken things were picked up. We went out to eat fast food for lunch, which was unusual for us, but I think she wanted to get out of the house for a little while. We'd need to do a lot of work to get it looking good, and more work wasn't what we needed right now.

Alexis was at her track meet, so I couldn't talk to her yet, but I was feeling a little better. Maybe telling the truth, as ugly and selfish as it sounded, had opened a wound that desperately needed air and light before it could heal. In the hospital, the nurses had always said sunlight was good medicine as they opened the curtains in my room every day. So maybe there was hope.

I still wasn't sure how I was going to coordinate hanging out with her and Candy, though. I owed Candy for the dress, even if it was free. Billy was right about one thing: sometimes sharing didn't work.

Late in the afternoon, after she had taken a long, hot shower, Mom pulled a box out of the freezer and rubbed the frost off with her palm to read the instructions. It was what she called "cooking from scratch." She scratched off the frost and read the directions.

I excused myself to get ready. I couldn't eat anyway. My stomach was a mess from nerves. I didn't tell Mom that Billy had canceled. I just said I wanted her to drive. She thought that was a good idea for a school dance with a date she hadn't even met yet. I think she wanted to add "and one that you assaulted." She had already set out all my stuff for tonight, plus some of her own cosmetics and a fragrance called Eternity. I wondered if anything would really change when I slipped into that dress and did my hair and makeup. All I knew was that once people saw me like that, there was no going back. I had to keep up the look. No one would want the other me. Was that why Entropion had spared my dress? Olympias had promised to destroy everything I held dear. . . . Did that include my real self, the part of me that shone through my heart instead of the mirror?

And was evolution always this terrifying?

"Set out the plates anyway," Mom said, waving toward the dining table. She had chewed her fingernails around the edges. I wished we had time to talk. She handed me two glasses. "You're going to be beautiful. I can't wait to see you come down those stairs."

She turned on the radio and moved her head to the rhythm of an old song. I watched her, a soft smile spreading on my face. We needed music in this house again.

I knew what I had to do.

I shut my bedroom door softly, then rested my forehead against the cold wood. Finally I made myself let go of the doorknob. I turned and faced the dress.

It was still perfect. The silver-gray threads winked at me in the late afternoon light.

Was I supposed to get dressed and then do my makeup? Or the other way around? I had no clue. Part of me didn't want to do anything at all. I looked down at my feet, willing one of them to take a small step forward. I wasn't sure which would move first, the fake part of me or the real.

A bright flash blinded me. I winced and started blinking to clear my vision. From under the bed a fierce white light blazed.

Goose bumps spread over my skin, each of them a sharp protest. A thousand thoughts exploded inside my head.

The book scooted out from under the bed, approaching in slow stutters across the carpet, just like on our first morning.

I looked at the dress, and a wave of panic hit me, like I was being yanked out of a really good dream.

"Entropion stole you!" I said. "And you can't come back now. I already made up my mind."

There was a burst of light and a ripping noise, like fabric being torn. I was again momentarily blinded, as if someone had flashed a camera in my face.

"I have made up my mind too," said an unmistakably male voice.

I rubbed my eyes fast. Who was talking? None of the monsters had talked. "The book was stolen. I checked under the bed."

"As it happens," the voice said, "being stuck between worlds provides for an excellent hiding spot."

My vision cleared. The book was on the carpet, but it wasn't glowing. Instead, the letters flowed into the air. I watched, transfixed, as black letters hovered around me, some of them grazing my hair, flattening little strands as they flew past. Then streams of gold and red and blue, every paint color I had seen in the book, poured out in shimmering rivers, circling the letters in curls.

I reached out a finger to touch a letter hovering near my nose. It stung me.

"Ow!" I said, and stuck my finger in my mouth. The letters softened their shapes as if they were melting, until I was looking at an inky black cloud surrounded by the rivers of color. It was like watching a painter assemble their paints before starting on a canvas. Then, with a noise like someone snapping their fingers, the ink and colors flew into an image that took shape and began to move.

An old man made of moving pixels sat on my bed. I could see light between each of the dots as they moved. His hair was pure white, and long, almost as long as his beard, and he had a mustache so big and bushy it reached across each cheek to his ears.

"Xeno?" I whispered. Only my gaze had moved; my body was still pinned against the door.

He smiled. "You were expecting someone else?" His clear blue eyes sparkled. The pixels around the edge of his body were softer than the rest, more like smoke or mist, and a few drifted in my direction. I inhaled and caught the scent of pine and old books and the sea. "The world will go on without its monsters," Xeno said, crossing his legs and smoothing his robe. "But, oh, my dear, how will it go on without the real you?"

It was, I realized, the way I thought a father should smell. I smiled softly, staring at him in wonder.

Then I suddenly remembered what night it was.

"Do you not see that dress?" I blurted. "I'm starting over with a *new* me. You're interrupting the most important night of my life!"

He held up a hand to stop me from talking. "There is no time to thank me."

My mouth dropped open. I wanted to throw something at him, but he wasn't really there, was he? I could still see the outline of my nightstand through the dots that made up his body.

"I thought being the Guardian would help you to discover who you really are," he said. "You would find all those wonderful seeds of the bizarre and beautiful, and grow into all you were meant to be. But you are afraid, Sofia, much more than anyone realized."

His words burned and I knew they were true. I also knew they didn't matter anymore. "I'm not the Guardian now," I said.

Xeno's face softened into a smile. "You will always be the Guardian. I'm not here to convince you of that."

"Then why are you here?" I asked. "I told you I've already made my decision."

"Because you do not understand the choice you are making," he said. "Aristotle gave me more than one chance to choose the correct answer, and so I will do that for you."

"I'm just putting on a dress and going to a dance," I said.

"You do not understand what you are throwing away." He looked out my window at the darkening sky. "And you do not understand what you are inviting in."

A cloud rolled over the moon.

"When I first discovered monsters, I thought everyone would be as thrilled as I. I had much to learn about the human heart. Olympias used fear to destroy courage, and suspicion replaced hope. People forgot what they were capable of."

He shook his head, as if lost in memories. "And then you became the Guardian. You were so very different from the others. You are one of the extraordinary ones, and yet you hate yourself for that. You want to hide what makes you different. You are ashamed. Olympias worried that you would become her greatest enemy, and then she realized the truth: you could be her most powerful ally. Everyone's eyes are upon you right now. If you conform, the others will follow." I got the feeling he was talking about more than just the kids at school.

A bitter taste rose in the back of my throat. His words burned like matches held too long. Maybe that was what real truth felt like. I swallowed hard, trying to push the pain away.

"Olympias wants me to fit in," I said, my voice hoarse. "It's better than killing me."

Then it hit me.

Candy's sudden interest in me; the disappearance of Dr. Capistrano, the only adult who knew my secrets and could help me; the loss of Alexis, the best friend who had loved my real self; the shredding of my old track jersey. Nothing was left but a gray dress that hid all my imperfections, every feature that made me different. Olympias didn't care what I saw in the mirror after tonight, as long as I didn't see the real me. She was afraid of who I really was. So was I.

Xeno glanced at the dress on the bed between us.

My cheeks grew hot, as if I was guilty of something.

He pointed to the dress. "If this is who you want to be, put it on. Just understand the choice you are making." His chin quivered. "You are the only one who can decide who you will be."

I had to know the truth about one thing, but I needed time to think too. "The other Guardians, the ones in the past?" I asked. "I bet they were afraid sometimes. They didn't always like who they were or what they looked like. No one is perfect."

"Of course."

"And you let Claire out of being the Guardian."

Xeno sighed, and a little puff of pixels floated from his

mouth. "Of all my daughters, you were the only one who had already faced death, and it held no fear for you. I thought that meant you would be safe from Olympias. I thought you might become the most powerful Guardian of all. But I was wrong! You, Sofia, do not fear death. You are terrified of life."

I sank down to the floor. His words had finally burned through me and I was as light as ash.

Everything Xeno said was awful and true. I had always been the odd girl out, and hated myself for that. I thought I was the sparrow that no one cared about.

Xeno crossed the room and held the dress out to me. I couldn't lift my arms. I didn't want the dress anymore. I shook my head and a teardrop landed on my thigh.

"Then become who you were born to be!" he yelled. I gasped and looked up. The edges of Xeno's body burst into a white flame. A mist rose from his feet, and he dissolved into a swirling cloud; the book fluttered open to draw the funnel into its pages.

The book closed and all went dark.

The dress rested on the floor at my feet.

I thought of Golem and his little brown bird. He needed me. The weak and the forgotten and the ugly, they needed me, the real me. Whatever it cost. One person had to be alive to see and love the forgotten things in this world, the sparrows and the monsters and the freaks. They mattered, even if I couldn't always explain why.

My fingers rested against my prosthesis. They ran back and forth over the uneven bite mark as I sat still, staring at my legs, thinking. I knew how much tonight meant to my mom. It was a new beginning for us both.

My index finger dug into the wound. Without thinking, I ripped off a piece of the fake flesh. It was soft and rubbery. The metal frame underneath it was hard and shiny and beautiful in a strange way. I stared at it, mesmerized; then my fingers began to frantically pick off the fake stuff.

I shuddered, trying to catch a deep breath, and realized that pieces of fake flesh were all over my carpet.

You should hurry. You have a dance to go to, Cinderella.

I laughed out loud, but I didn't know if that was my conscience or Xeno speaking to me inside my head.

"But . . ." Words failed me. I looked at the metal of my leg. Why had I done that? It was like my body knew something my brain didn't.

I got this weird feeling that Xeno was smiling, watching me. Instinct made me reach for the phone Mom had left in my room, without even knowing what I was going to say. I punched in the old familiar numbers.

"Hello?" Alexis answered, breathless.

"It's me," I said. She was silent, and I didn't know how to continue. I guessed she hadn't checked caller ID.

"Sorry, I was busy changing," she said. "I thought you were someone else."

"That was the problem. I wanted to be *anyone* else," I said, then paused. "I'm so sorry."

"Um . . . ," she said, "okay."

Closing my eyes, I prayed I was doing the right thing. "Listen, I know we need to talk more," I said, the idea forming in my mind even while I spoke. I needed something, but if I went looking, Mom would get suspicious. "But first . . . can you come over right now? And . . . bring scissors?"

🌿

Alexis and her mom arrived fifteen minutes later. When Mom opened the front door, Alexis hesitated, looking at the ground and chewing her lip. My mom immediately pulled her into the house and into a big bear hug.

They hugged for a while. I had to clear my throat a few times at the top of the stairs for Mom to let Alexis go. Alexis looked up at me and frowned.

"You're not even dressed yet!"

"You look amazing!" I said at the same time.

We both broke into big grins.

She was wearing a fitted pink dress that made her muscles pop and her boobs look huge. I tried not to stare, but I hadn't known she had boobs. Since illness had interrupted puberty, Mom said I had to wait for the Boob Fairy to visit. With my luck, the fairy would be eaten by a monster.

"Come up and help me, okay?" I asked.

Mom and Alexis's mom wandered over to the couch and sat down, talking like they were afraid of running out of oxygen before they said everything.

"Don't take too long," Mom called up to us. "I am so excited to see you in that dress!"

Alexis carried a cute beaded purse up the stairs with her. Once we were in my room, she opened it, pulled out the scissors, and held them out to me. I reached for them, but she didn't let go.

"Not yet," she said. "First you have to tell me what you're going to do."

I smiled, my hand on top of hers. The metal of the scissors winked at us.

"I'm *not* going to hurt myself, but you just need to trust me right now, okay?"

She considered that for a minute and then released her grip. I took the scissors and held them.

There would be no turning back.

Ever.

I took the blade's edge and lowered it to the prosthesis, then looked up at Alexis. Our eyes met and she nodded. Somehow, she knew. Best friends are like that. A little lump formed in my throat; I was so grateful to have her with me for this.

Working fast, we cut and pulled and picked all the fake flesh away from the leg, revealing the metal skeleton underneath. Alexis ran and got a washcloth from the bathroom and rubbed the metal down, removing the last bits of flesh material.

I stared at my leg, transfixed. "Now the dress," Alexis said. She grabbed it while I shimmied out of my shirt and skirt.

"Oh my gosh!" Alexis yelled, seeing the price tag.

"Candy," I muttered.

"Say no more," she replied. She snipped it off and the tag fluttered to the floor. "Good riddance," she said. Next she handed me the dress. I slipped it on and smoothed it down.

"Wow" was all she could say. I think she meant it in a good way this time. She set the scissors down on the nightstand.

"Not yet," I said.

I grabbed the hem of the dress, so long and lovely, the perfect length to disguise what made me feel different from everyone else. I looked at Alexis. Her eyes went wide.

People were going to see. They were going to stare at me, just like she was doing now. I narrowed my eyes at her to tell her I was ready.

Alexis gave me a serious nod.

"I'll do it," she said. Taking the scissors back, she approached me and knelt down. Grabbing the hem, she stopped and looked back up.

"You want to know a secret?" she asked.

I nodded, too nervous to speak.

"When we ran together, I was always jealous of you," she said.

I frowned. "Why? You're a better runner."

"Yeah, I know," she said. "But I never had to fight for it. I knew I would finish every race. You had to fight for each one." She plunged the scissors into the fabric and cut.

I inhaled, holding my breath as she worked and talked. "I always watched your face when you crossed the finish line. I was jealous of how happy you were." She cut and motioned for me to turn. I did. "It's why I pushed you so hard, because I knew I would never get to feel anything like that.

I loved running because it made me feel free and I never wanted the runs to end. But you? You weren't like me. You weren't running away from anything. You were running *toward* something. I guess that secretly, I hoped I would get to do that someday too."

After two more cuts, she stood up. We grabbed hands and each took a few deep breaths. There was still so much to get caught up on, but I knew this: when we faced life together, it hurt less.

I turned toward the door.

She grabbed my arm. "Wait," she said, then swiped off my bandana and gasped.

Alexis used her fingers to tousle the fringe on my head. "Wow. Just . . . wow."

I giggled.

"I—I'm sorry," she stammered, waving her hands to make me stop. "I know I need a new word. But . . . wow!"

"Come on!" Mom yelled from downstairs. "You girls don't want to miss the dance!"

Alexis pointed a finger at me to stay right where I was. She went to the top of the stairs and hollered sweetly down at my mom, "Down in a sec!" When she returned, she was all business. I closed my eyes as she fluffed and brushed and sprayed.

When we walked out of the bedroom, Alexis nudged me toward my mother's room. Mom had the only full-length mirror in the house, fastened to the back of her bedroom door. Alexis leaned against the doorjamb and smiled. I took a deep breath and walked.

Everything led to this private moment between me and the mirror. The cold, familiar twist of fear snaked through my body. I had always hated the mirror because it reminded me that I was the odd girl out, and didn't nature prove that the weak were only safe in a pack? Those who got separated were eaten alive. Olympias had made sure I understood that my only chance at a happy life was to hide my true self and go with the herd.

But she was wrong. The difference between humans and animals is that any human can become an alpha. Being pushed out of the pack isn't a death sentence. It's an invitation.

I opened the bedroom door and stepped inside, ready to look in the mirror with fresh eyes.

I had finally figured out what was worth standing alone for.

I can't lie, though; at first glance I felt a tiny, familiar lurch of disappointment. I had wanted to see perfection. It was an old habit, I guess. But really, what *is* perfection?

Then that feeling was replaced slowly, sweetly, by a strange awe for this new creation. I reached one hand out and gently grazed my reflection with my fingertips. The cocoon had torn and here I was. There had never been anyone like me in a magazine or on a billboard. I had learned that the world is full of people who are both unusual and stunning, but they have to find the courage to see themselves with new eyes. Because when they do, when they see who they truly are, they catch a glimpse of what they might yet become. And the world needs a new generation that is unafraid to change.

Breathing quietly, I studied my reflection and listened as the din of old lies faded and the howl of the alpha began to rise. This was not who I had once so desperately wanted to be.

This was *far* better.

And then, yeah, I bent over at the waist, just a little, and wrote my name in the air with my butt. It totally worked.

Minutes later, at the top of the stairs, Alexis whispered for me to go first. I descended and waited for Mom to glance up. When she did, her mouth fell open, her eyes wide and unblinking.

Alexis's mom turned to look up at us too, and froze.

I wanted to go back upstairs, but Alexis kept her hand on the small of my back. The tiniest of nudges told me I had to keep going. This was me, the real me, on display.

"Your dress," Mom whispered.

I nodded. Sliced off at an angle, it deliberately exposed every inch of my prosthesis, and that was all that caught your eye . . . at first.

"Your hair," she murmured.

I reached up and tried to smooth it a little. Alexis hissed at me. "Don't you touch it!"

She had moussed it into white, spiky perfection. It resembled a medieval weapon.

Then Mom stood and screamed, "Your *leg*!"

I guess her brain had random disconnects too. She'd just realized that I had destroyed all the fake flesh.

I hurried down the last three steps before she could keel over or yell at me again.

"Mom, calm down! It's only a fake leg anyway. You let them cut off my real one, remember?"

I was the only one who found that even a little funny.

Mom was opening and closing her mouth like a fish that's been yanked out of the river and thrown into a chest of ice.

"Anyway, it still works," I said. I did a little jig to prove my point. She sank back onto the couch, shaking her head.

I took a deep breath, knowing that what I had to say next was the most important thing I might ever say to her. "I just can't hide anymore. I can't hide who I am. I don't want to be afraid when I look in the mirror or when people look at me."

"I don't want you to be afraid," she whispered, sitting forward on the couch. "All I ever wanted was for you to be happy."

Neither of us moved.

"So . . ." Alexis came down the rest of the stairs. "Maybe we should go."

Her mom stood and rested a hand on my mom's shoulder.

"I've never seen you look more beautiful," Mom said finally. Every word seemed to cost her something, as if a little piece of her ached as she said it, but the bigger part, the deeper part, kept pushing those words to the surface.

"I forgot one thing upstairs," I said. "Be right back."

TWENTY-TWO

I made it up there in record time. I was free, and free felt
fast and light.

"Xeno?" The room was dark, the sun outside gone. The
moon had claimed her place in the sky, a delicate silver crescent.

"Thank you," I said. "For helping me choose something
better. For helping me choose myself."

Silence.

The book was open, but no words appeared. Maybe even
philosophers struggled for words sometimes.

"If Entropion shows up tonight, what do I do?" I asked.

"Do I have to come up there?" Alexis yelled. "Let's go!"

I stood closer to the book, speaking quickly but keeping my
voice down. "Can the Guardian kill a monster if she has to?"

"Sofia, hurry up," Mom called.

Xeno's words came fast.

Entropion was made from fear, and fear does not die. But nature teaches us that even things that cannot die can still be done away with. For example, an apple cannot be killed. It can only be transformed, forced into another state of being.

"How do you transform an apple?" I asked.

It must become part of something or someone else.

"Like possession?" I said. "When a ghost takes over your body?"

Like digestion.

The problem with getting advice from a philosopher is that most of it doesn't make sense. Plus I had a vague suspicion he was mocking me. But we'd deal with that later.

If I survived.

Alexis's mom offered to drive. I said goodbye to Mom with one last hug. Alexis opened the front door. The night air took our breath away.

It was sharp and brittle, a mean-spirited cold, like winter was hanging on, forcing spring back into hiding. The full moon cast a ghostly pallor on our faces, making us look like corpses.

"Is it too cold?" Mom called from the doorway. She sounded hopeful, like maybe I wouldn't go through with this.

I shook my head, not wanting to look her in the eye.

I sat in the backseat next to Alexis. My foot kept tapping the floor. What had Xeno meant by "digestion"? My heart beat too fast, and I willed it to keep time with my foot.

Alexis smiled at me.

If anything went wrong tonight . . . I groaned a little, and Alexis's mom glanced at me in her rearview mirror.

"Just nervous," I said to everyone.

Alexis laughed. "Don't be nervous, Sofia. Enjoy it. Think of this as a finish line. I'll be right beside you to cheer you on."

She reached for my hand, and I let her take it. We clutched hands and nodded to one another; then she realized how sweaty and cold my palm was. She giggled and let go, wiping her hand on the seat between us.

We were still giggling when her mom made the final turn. We were almost there. White clouds huddled together in the sky, covering the moon. Floodlights lit the school entrance, and we saw police barricades set up around the perimeter. Uniformed police officers stood in front of the school, holding leashes.

Two German shepherds, one of them smaller than the other, paced in front of the main entrance. Everyone had to walk past these two animals to get inside.

"Whoa," Alexis said. I looked at her, one eyebrow cocked. She shook her head. "It's a different word entirely," she insisted.

Her mom slowed the car and rolled down her window. "Since there have been reports of strange animal attacks recently," she said, "the PTA voted to pay for extra security."

She pulled closer to the barricade, but a police officer held up his hand.

The dogs paced and panted, watching us.

The smaller shepherd was probably a female. She tilted her head back and sniffed the air to read my scent. She did not blink. Or bark. She just held my gaze, and something in my soul understood.

It was a warning.

The police officer was explaining to Alexis's mom that only students and faculty were allowed past this checkpoint.

Alexis's mom hesitated, but the officer nodded at her warmly. "Ma'am, I have a daughter in there too. Nothing is going to hurt those kids on my watch."

With that, Alexis and I got out of the car and walked in. In the bustle and confusion of the unexpected drop-off, I forgot about my appearance.

The disco ball and dimmed lights disoriented me for a moment, and Alexis grabbed my arm to steady me. People were staring. Slowly, one by one, everyone on the dance floor stopped moving. Friend nudged friend, and girl whispered to boy, until every set of eyes was glued to me. Only the boy taking our tickets didn't seem to notice me; he was too busy staring at Alexis's boobs.

I took my first step forward.

Everyone looked different tonight, not just me, and they all looked nervous. Change wasn't easy for any of us. As people caught sight of me, they stared, eyes wide, a few of them actually letting their jaws drop open.

And then I understood.

Xeno hadn't chosen me. My peers had. They sensed I was different and pushed me outside the protective circle of our little herd, but my mistake—and maybe theirs—had been assuming that my difference was a weakness. I was suddenly thankful for the heartbreak. I might never have become this strong. For a split second, I pitied everyone who had stayed in the circle, protected and popular. Maybe one day they would discover this same strength, if they could endure the loneliness that comes before the understanding.

Music boomed all around us, sending vibrations through my whole body. I made my way over to the punch bowl, with Alexis behind me. Walking on heels took a ton of concentration because my center of gravity shifted forward slightly. I wouldn't feel so triumphant if I face-planted on the floor. A couple of guys moved to get out of our way, one of them looking at my leg, the other looking at Alexis's chest.

A cluster of girls surrounded the refreshment table, their backs to us.

"So I was at my grandmother's and I wanted some milk, but she was out, right? So I went home and opened my fridge and there was no milk! I was like, noooo! And my mom just said, 'Sorry, we're out.' I was so sad, I was about to cry. Really. That's how bad I wanted a drink of milk. Because on this diet, liquids are all I can have." Candy gestured to the cup of punch she was holding and sighed.

"Uh, Candy . . . ," the other girls murmured. They must

not have seen me enter, but they saw me now. Alexis grabbed my hand protectively. Everyone stared, mouths open. Candy put her hands on her hips, ready to scold them for not taking her problem more seriously, but first she glanced back to see what had distracted them.

She looked at my leg. The disco ball spun over us, reflecting little circles of light that washed over their heads. Candy's face morphed from confusion to disgust to anger.

I dropped Alexis's hand. I wasn't going to hide anymore, not from myself and not from Candy.

"Do you know how expensive that dress was?" she hissed. "Is this how you show your gratitude? By turning this into some kind of joke? Who's going to want to see a picture of that?" She gestured at my dress, or my leg, or maybe both.

"Candy, let me explain," I said.

"What happened?" Natalie asked breathlessly. "I mean, to your leg?"

"Everyone knew it was fake," I said with a shrug, keeping my eyes on Candy. Her face was a swirling vortex of anger.

Several football players, including Matt, swaggered up to us. Candy handed Matt her punch and he drank it in one gulp. I guessed he was her date.

"Her leg looks like a vegetable peeler," Matt whispered to his friends, but we all heard it.

Natalie's face brightened. "Ohmygosh, my mom just got one of those automatic ones. It can shred a carrot, like, really fast."

Billy saw me from across the gym. He was alone, wearing

a dark shirt and nice khakis with a belt, his hair combed back neatly. He looked scrubbed and fresh and nervous.

His eyes met mine and he didn't look away. He didn't just see the leg, or the dress, or the hair . . . he saw *me*. A warm, bright joy surged from my heart into a smile.

He pushed his way through the crowd. Candy noticed him and smiled too, maybe because he looked so good. Matt watched her, then glared at Billy. When Billy lightly touched Candy's arm to nudge her out of the way, Matt shoved him on the shoulder.

"Not tonight, okay?" Billy said, raising his hands like a shield.

Matt pushed him again, but Billy stepped back just in time, causing Matt to trip and ram an eighth grader in the back. The eighth grader turned, punch running down his chin onto his shirt. He shoved Matt into Billy. In a flash, it looked like a swirling mass of fists and hair and legs.

Everyone was yelling, but a shrill scream pierced my ears. I whipped my head around, searching for the sound. No one else heard it. Sweat beaded my upper lip.

Candy was hyperventilating, glancing wide-eyed between the pile of boys and me. "I can't believe you ruined that dress," she said. "After everything I did for you."

"Look, I'm sorry," I said, backing away. I needed to find out where that sound had come from. What if Entropion was here and he attacked the wrong person? "I appreciate your help, but that wasn't the real me."

"That was the whole point," Candy said.

Mr. Reeves ran up and called for more teachers. They

separated the boys, and I tried to make my exit. Strange new vibrations moved up both my legs. Something heavy was moving through the hallway outside, coming closer. I cut across the dance floor through the couples. Candy and Alexis shouted at me, but I didn't turn around.

I burst through the gym doors and looked in either direction, listening for the sound again. Two teachers and one security guard stood in the hallway. I turned to the left.

"That hallway is closed," one of them called to me.

"Just need a bathroom!" I hollered back. "Gotta adjust my leg."

Neither knew how to respond to that in a politically correct way. They didn't try to stop me.

Around the corner, I paused to listen, but all I could hear was the pounding of my heart.

A low moan, like the sound of an injured animal, rose from somewhere deep within the school.

I closed my eyes and strained to hear with everything inside me, everything that had gone into creating this last monster: my heart, my mind, my fears. I wanted to face Entropion at last.

He was in the library.

An officer was down.

I opened the main door to the library, but Entropion was already dragging his victim out the door on the opposite side of the room. The body disappeared through the door, two limp hands dragging across the floor. I heard the wet thud of the body being dropped. Carefully, I made my way to the door and glanced out of the windows built into the top.

In the hallway, only the emergency lights were on. The little bulbs gave a flickering, unreliable light, casting strange moving shadows. I stepped out of the library and looked in either direction.

The dog was on her side, panting and whimpering. Blood seeped out from underneath her body.

A thick, musky odor hung in the air. I took a deep breath anyway. I could see the dark shadow of Entropion looming.

A low, soft laugh echoed in the darkness as the air around me turned bone-numbingly cold, like a door to a giant freezer had been opened. Olympias stood before me while her body separated in two, dividing down the middle like curtains being pulled apart.

And there was Entropion. Blood froze in my veins. He looked like a giant serpent with a misshapen human head. He had no lips, only thick pink gums mottled with blood, like the mouth of a great white shark. His arms and legs were short and scaled, like a crocodile's, with clawed hands and feet. It was as if someone had tried to create a monster, taking the worst parts of every creature imaginable and setting them at odd angles. Then I remembered that that someone was me. He was all that I had feared, the misshapen, the broken, and the scarred.

Vomit crept up the back of my throat. My vision dissolved at the edges; the sight of him disoriented me, like I was looking at a face inside a kaleidoscope. His eyes were the eyes of a wolf, bright yellow with a hollow black center that glowed with rage when he looked at my dress. In the flickering shadows I saw rows of shiny white teeth as he growled. I fled back inside the library and shoved the door closed.

Two cold hands curled around my shoulders.

I spun around, arms flailing.

Candy grabbed my shoulders and pushed me against the metal door handle. It crunched against my spine.

"Let go," I begged. "You've got to get out of here!"

"I don't have to do anything," she replied. She looked around the library in disgust, as if I had only retreated here to hide from the dance. "I didn't have to help you, but I made a plan and you agreed to it. This is how you repay me?"

Natalie was behind her, shaking her head.

"This isn't about you," I replied. I couldn't hear anything moving in the darkness around us. "Let me go."

"A newspaper reporter is waiting in the gym to take your picture. You will smile and pose, just like we agreed. Natalie and I will stand just a little in front and on either side so no one can see what you did to the dress."

"You go," I said. "I *promise,* I'll be there as soon as I can."

Candy tried to pull me, but I planted my good foot and braced against her.

"Like I would ever listen to you again," she said.

"You never listened to me at all!" I yelled, slapping her hands away. "You have no idea who I am!" A terrible realization hit me. "You have no idea who *you* are either."

She sneered, but a flicker of sadness in her eyes told me I was right.

My voice hardened; she *had* to get this. "We're not packages, or illusions, or magic tricks. We're not just girls . . . we're *humans,* and we're supposed to want things that can't be found in a mirror."

She shook her head, refusing to listen.

"Candy, some people can't change how they look, or disguise who they are. They're just born different, and this world is not a safe place for people who don't fit in. And I'm one of them. You think that makes me a loser, but I think that might make me a hero. I'm not afraid anymore that people won't love me; I'm afraid of hurting the ones who really do. So you can keep the limelight, because I've learned that not everyone is like me. *Not everyone is strong enough to face the shadows.*"

"You don't know anything about life in the shadows!" Natalie snapped, pushing both of us to the side. She swung the door open, expecting Candy to force me out into the hall. Candy and I stood face to face.

A flickering shadow moved across Candy's pupils.

Natalie's body flew backward, crashing into a bookshelf. Books scattered around her, pages flapping. Candy and I screamed at the same time.

Entropion stood in the doorway. His lips lifted to show rows of white teeth as he reached his arms out wide to either side, claws scraping down the metal doorframe. I winced from the sound. Olympias stood behind him, delight etched across her face as she watched her creation at work.

Entropion lowered his head and hissed.

My good foot was wet and warm. Glancing over, I saw a

dark stain spread across Candy's dress. She had peed all over us both.

Entropion shifted his head back and screamed, the sound piercing my ears. I shook my head, trying to stop the pain.

Above us, the ceiling tiles shuddered, flakes of insulation fluttering down. Something else was up there. I had seen this a thousand times on Animal Planet. It was a hunting strategy. One animal bared its teeth and scared the prey while the other circled behind and attacked.

Xeno was wrong. I hadn't made just one monster.

I'd made two.

I grabbed Candy and shoved her to the ground with all my strength. I was the one they wanted, not her.

But it was Golem who crashed through the ceiling. He opened that beautiful, thick dark mouth and roared. Windows shattered and books flew through the air. I hadn't created Golem, had I? No, but I had loved him, and that was maybe close enough. He was mine, and I was his.

Entropion lowered himself on his haunches and lunged.

Golem caught him in midair before he reached us. One of Entropion's claws shot out for me from under Golem's arm, slicing my skin. Blood bubbled up beneath the long mark.

Golem had Entropion pinned down, his mouth open, thick teeth snapping in fury. Every second, Golem seemed to grow bigger and bigger. Entropion thrashed, lifting his knees to knock Golem off. Golem flew up and back, crashing into the lockers outside the doors. They burst open, papers flying like a snowstorm.

Free now, Entropion turned toward me again and

jumped, throwing me on my back, one clawed hand around Candy next to me, the other around my prosthesis. I bent my good leg and kicked him. He clung to my prosthesis, trying to regain control. I tried another tactic and spun onto my stomach. The prosthesis came off in his hand.

Confusion flashed in Entropion's eyes.

Behind him, Golem rose. He grabbed Entropion by the waist and lifted him into the air, and then Golem's eyes met mine. A softness shone within them, something like love.

He slammed Entropion to the floor, and Olympias released a bloodcurdling scream.

Entropion didn't move again.

My breath came out in spurts like short laughs. Golem had done it. He had killed Entropion. Golem looked at me and pointed to his heart.

With a trembling hand, I pointed to my own.

Olympias raised her arms like a puppeteer commanding her creation.

Entropion rose and shifted, sinking his claws into Golem's chest. The tender monster slowly fell backward with a mighty sigh.

"Golem!" I screamed. "No!"

Entropion was on top of him now, claws twisting inside Golem's chest, sunk to the knuckle. Golem lifted one shaking arm and rested a finger against his own forehead. Then he opened his mouth wide, inhaling. Locker doors swung in his direction, books and papers careening toward him. He inhaled harder, chest expanding, mouth gaping wider and wider.

Entropion trembled and yanked at his arm to free it, but Golem had caught it with his other arm, pinning Entropion to himself. Golem inhaled so powerfully that Candy and I began to move across the floor toward him.

Olympias collapsed, her hands covering her face as she shrieked.

With Golem's final mighty inhale, Entropion exploded into a cloud of ash that was sucked into Golem's mouth. Golem snapped it shut and looked toward me.

With one raised finger, he smudged the last symbol on his forehead.

Golem's head rolled to one side, limp, his eyes blank holes.

He began to fade, and the air between us shimmered and danced like snowflakes falling softly at midnight. Then he was gone. I pressed my hand to my heart, expecting it to break, but instead, it was stronger. Golem was still with me somehow. He was not lost, not as long as he lived inside me. I knew I would see him again.

My focus shifted to Olympias. Underneath her hands, her face was shifting, the skin rippling between her fingers. She turned her back to me and stood.

Then she looked over her shoulder at me, and I could see her profile. I didn't recognize her anymore; if I passed her on the street now, I wouldn't know who she was.

"The first chapter of our story is finished," she whispered. "But oh, what surprises await!" Like smoke floating up from a candle, she vanished into the night.

TWENTY-THREE

"What happened?" Natalie sat up, rubbing her head.

At some point, Candy had fainted, and she was still flat on the ground. Natalie stumbled over to her and shook her awake. Candy pushed herself up, her eyes glazed over. I grabbed my prosthesis and wrestled it on, feeling the suction that secured it into place, then wiggled the stretchy support bands over the top to secure it.

Mr. Reeves burst in from the opposite set of doors, and his mouth fell open when he saw the mess of papers and books lying everywhere.

"Don't be angry, Mr. Reeves," I said. "They saved my life."

"We did?" Natalie asked.

Candy nudged her, hard. "We did," she said.

"I ran away from the dance," I said. "Candy and Natalie followed me. They were worried because I was so upset. We found the library like this, and a big animal—a dog or wolf,

I think—jumped out and Candy shoved me to the floor to protect me."

Candy looked at me, suspicion lingering in her eyes. I didn't know whether she doubted my story or her sanity.

Mr. Reeves tapped his notebook. "Is what you're telling me true?" he asked. I nodded.

Billy and Matt ran into the room and froze. Billy looked at me first, checking me up and down, then exhaled so hard his upper body caved forward. Matt ran over to Candy and she let him put his arm around her.

Resting his hands on his thighs to catch his breath, Billy looked up at Mr. Reeves.

"Somebody called for an ambulance and it just pulled up," Billy said. "Who's it for?"

Outside the school doors, the familiar blue and red lights were flashing in all directions. Every police car and ambulance in the county must have been there. Parents were calling their kids' names and jumping out of cars with the motors still running. Cell phone rings came from all directions. Teachers were shouting about the strange animal that had been sighted in the school.

A beehive of EMTs and police officers swirled around the fallen officer. He was alive—Entropion had only knocked him out—but he had a nasty gash on his hand. One of the paramedics said it looked like a defensive wound; another one said it was a bite mark. Either way, something was wrong. A hand injury couldn't cause the amount of blood I had spied on the floor.

I pushed past the kids peering into the library and found a new trail of blood drops leading toward another hallway.

Billy saw it too. He grabbed my arm and propelled me forward, his strength carrying me along. The trail led to the drinking fountain. The smaller, female German shepherd had collapsed in the recessed area under it. Red slashes crisscrossed her fur. She must have tried to protect the officer when Entropion attacked.

"Is she dead?" I asked, hand over my mouth. "Please don't let her be dead."

Billy gently rested two fingers on the inside of her thigh. He was still, waiting for a pulse. And I swear, in the silence, my own heart stopped and listened for hers.

"She's alive."

"Call your dad," I said.

"There's no time." He scooped his hands under the dog's body, and she whimpered when he lifted her.

I was already moving toward the school's front doors, where all the adults were.

"We can't," Billy said. "It's crazy out there with all the cars. They won't move fast enough."

We had to get help. We couldn't handle this alone.

Billy turned and staggered toward an emergency exit. "We'll take my golf cart."

He glanced back at me. "It was the only way I could get here. I snuck out."

I kept moving, following behind Billy and the dog faster

than I thought possible. My brain was screaming, but all my thoughts were jumbled. Billy pressed his back against the exit doors and burst through them to the outside, carefully cradling the dog.

"The key's in my pocket," he said, and turned to present his rear end to me. With no time to argue, I grimaced and stuck my hand in his pocket, feeling for the key. Billy had a gift for putting me in awkward situations.

"You'll have to drive," he said, while carefully lowering himself into the passenger seat. A golf cart only went about ten miles per hour, I knew, but we were desperate. I put the key in the ignition and the engine roared to life. It sounded like a jet engine had been dropped under the hood.

"Take Main Street down to Milton," Billy yelled above the noise.

I hit the gas and the cart burst out of the lot, gravel flying behind us. There was no speedometer, so I had no idea how fast we were going, except that it was somewhere between Crazy and Dangerous. I glanced at him in amazement.

"My dad let me tinker with it. I upgraded the motor. But be careful!"

I narrowly dodged an elderly woman setting out her trash can. She yelled at me, shaking a fist in the air.

I made the turn onto Milton Street, smoking past a middle-aged guy in a Prius. The cart straightened onto the road.

"Clinic is one mile ahead on your right!" Billy yelled. "Almost there!"

Flashing blue and red appeared behind us. We didn't

have time to stop for a cop. I jammed the gas pedal to the floor. The engine burst into flames and the cart rolled to a stop. The officer jumped out of his car and caught up to us on foot, his flashlight blazing into our faces.

"Sofia?"

I looked up and squinted. "Officer Lopez?"

"Sofia, there's a bottle of Betadine next to the table," Dr. Hamby said. "Grab it and pour it wherever I tell you, okay? It's the dark orange stuff."

"I know what it looks like," I said.

Dr. Hamby had already grilled us about the dog's injuries. We were in the operating room of his clinic now. Officer Lopez stood to the side, busy on his radio. All the other officers were at the school, but everything was calming down there. My story about the animal had everyone panicked, but no one had seen anything. Officer Grant, the one injured at the school, had regained consciousness on the way to the hospital. He didn't remember anything except his dog growling, and a flash of pain when something hit him on the head.

Dr. Hamby poured Betadine over the dog's leg before he started an IV. I watched the needle go in, and she lifted her head, licking Dr. Hamby on his hand. Tears sprang up in my eyes, hot and stinging. I hated needles.

I tried to hide my face from Billy, who was standing on the opposite side of the table, covered in blood and dog hair. He walked over and put his arm around me. He didn't have to say anything.

Dr. Hamby inspected the dog's scalp and head and seemed to find nothing serious. Then he peeled back the skin on either side of an obvious chest wound. I could see the white of the bone. Billy left my side and wheeled a big metal box over and positioned it above her.

"Wait!" Dr. Hamby told Billy. Then he looked at me. "No chance you're pregnant, right?"

"No." It was the most awkwardly spoken single word ever.

Dr. Hamby nodded and Billy flipped the switch. A low buzz told us the X-ray machine had snapped the picture. They turned to a computer screen on a table behind them. Blurry black-and-white images came to life. Billy exhaled hard.

"What?" I asked, my voice rising.

"No broken ribs. Lungs look good too. It's a bad cut. That's all," his dad said.

Mom burst through the clinic's front doors, yelling my name. Alexis was with her.

Dr. Hamby didn't wait for introductions. He plunged a syringe into the IV and depressed it, sending a light pink medicine into the line. The dog's body relaxed immediately, her breathing becoming more even.

"Your mom was freaking out when she got to the school," Alexis whispered to me. "She called Officer Lopez. He told her where you were."

"Billy, suture kit," Dr. Hamby said.

"Your daughter did a brave thing," Officer Lopez said. "She found an injured police dog and got help."

Dr. Hamby agreed. "And thankfully, Officer Lopez got the dog here in time."

I exchanged glances with Billy.

I reached out toward the sleeping dog and stroked her fur. The monitor registered a change immediately as the dog's heart rate finally pushed back into the normal range. Everyone watched, fascinated.

"She just needs to know that she's not alone," I said. "I think they feel more than we know."

Billy excused himself and walked out.

I found him sitting outside on the curb.

A yellow streetlight beamed down like a low moon hanging in the dark sky.

I managed to sit beside him rather gracefully. Alexis started to come out the door, but I held a finger up to stop her. She stepped back inside, nodding like she understood.

"What'll you tell your dad about the golf cart?" I asked.

"As little as possible," he replied. "I wasn't supposed to be at the dance."

"Or with me," I said.

"You're the only reason I showed up," he said. "I had to see what kind of dress was worth the pain of being friends with Candy."

I looked down at the dress. The fabric hadn't held up

very well in all the excitement; the side seams were splitting and tiny threads poked out of them. It was cheaper than it looked.

"Well, it did look a little better on the hanger," I admitted.

Then Mom came outside and cleared her throat. I nodded in her direction. Alexis stood in the doorway behind her.

Billy grabbed my hand before I could stand up. "My dad won't let us date. So we can't be boyfriend and girlfriend. And we can't be best friends, because you already have one."

"Is everything always so black-and-white with you?" I asked.

"I'm willing to create a new category. I still want to hang out. I'm just not sure what we would call that."

"It's called being friends," I said.

"No, it's something more," he said.

"Okay," I said. "You're my Something More."

Mom cleared her throat, this time really loudly.

"Why did you really show up tonight?" I asked.

"I decided that there's only one thing worse than feeling pain, and that's feeling nothing at all."

He leaned over and kissed me on the cheek. I glanced at my mom to make sure she wasn't watching.

This time, she blushed.

"I better go," I said.

The soft smile on his lips made my stomach flutter.

Mom and Alexis were waiting. I glanced down at my shadow and saw the strange outline of spiky hair and mismatched legs, then forced myself to look back up at the dark blue horizon. The full moon was bright silver, and the stars around it burned gold. I never realized how much color hid in the darkness. Wind rustled the leaves of a nearby tree, and something flew from its branches into the night.

Now I knew that a book really could save you, if it was the right book. And if I had to carry this secret alone, it didn't mean I had to be lonely. It meant I had to burn brightly, like the stars. I had to reclaim what was lost in the darkness.

I am an outpost, a lighthouse, a planet silently gliding past yours. Gravity has set us all in motion and chosen our path. Maybe we don't feel or taste or even believe the same things, and maybe that's not the answer. We have to stop fighting what we see, especially what we see in the mirror, because it is the unseen that truly matters, and I've made my decision.

I will hold my course.

The world around us is full of monsters and freaks and mysteries.

And me?

I am the Guardian who will watch over them all.

ACKNOWLEDGMENTS

I'm grateful to so many people for getting this book into your hands. First, my beloved husband, Mitch, urged me to take the time I needed to write the book I needed to write. He even took over the laundry. My kids, James, Elise, and Lauren, tried very hard to let me write in peace, even when a tree crashed in our yard, blocking the road and unleashing a nest of angry hornets. ("Don't worry, Mom, we have knives!" will always be a memorable line from you guys.)

My own mom and dad contributed a lot to this book, starting a few decades ago, when they brought me to my first horror movie. And while I still hate seeing people's heads explode, I did develop a passion for monsters. Thank you for letting me host my tea parties late at night in case Dracula and the Wolf Man could come. And thanks to my brother, Steve, for taking me on my first Sasquatch hunt. We'll find him next time.

My dear friend Dr. Ana Adams, DVM, gave me advice about the Beast's medical predicament. Dr. Adams is a well-respected vet, and I am grateful my monster had such good care. If you need to treat a giant wolf of your own, please don't rely on this book but consult a qualified cryptozoologist.

My literary agent, Melissa Jeglinski, is a gem. Melissa, you thought this book had heart, and you certainly have mine for all you've done. (Thank you, Cecil Murphy, for introducing us, and thanks to the wonderful Julie Garmon for cheering us all on while we ate gluten-free French food together.) My film agent, Andy Cohen, asked to represent the book and gave me a vote of confidence that meant the world to me. I do love writing, but the people I meet are the real gifts.

And my critique group, the Y-Nots: Johnna Stein, Sharon Pegram, and Sandra Havriluk. I am so indebted to each of you for your encouragement and feedback, but most of all for your friendship, which means so much to me. Please say something extra nice about me in your acknowledgments. I also owe a debt to my favorite nemesis, Jim Reinoehl, and his wonderful wife, Louise. I love you both!

And finally, the team at Delacorte Press, especially Krista Vitola. Thank you for believing in the book and then showing me how we could make it even stronger. You truly have an alchemist's gifts, and it was my honor to work with you. I hope our work impacts a lot of readers.

Designer Sarah Hokanson and illustrator Dinara Mirtalipova, I'm thrilled you were chosen to create the "welcome mat" for the readers. You captured the heart of the book with your pencil, which is rare magic indeed.

And, finally, my copy editor, Deb Dwyer. Your attention to detail made this book shine. Although I expressed my gratitude a bazillion times, let me say it once more: thank you!

ABOUT THE AUTHOR

Ginger Garrett graduated from Southern Methodist University in Dallas with a major in theatre arts and a focus on playwriting. Although she applied to the CIA to become an international master of espionage, she had to settle for selling pharmaceuticals for a global corporation. She eventually traveled the world on her own dime and without a fake mustache.

Ginger now lives in Atlanta with her husband, three children, and two rescue dogs. She spends her time baking gluten-free goodness for her friends and family and mentoring middle school students who want to become working writers. Passionate about science, history, and women's studies, Ginger loves exploring new ideas and old secrets. She especially loves good books read late at night.

Ginger is a popular speaker and a frequent guest on radio and television shows. She has been featured in and on media outlets across the country, including Fox News, *USA Today*, *Library Journal*, and 104.7 The Fish Atlanta. You can learn more at gingergarrett.com.